LETHAL LEGEND

Other books by Kathy Lynn Emerson

The Diana Spaulding Mystery Series:
Deadlier than the Pen
Fatal as a Fallen Woman
No Mortal Reason

The Face Down Mystery Series:
Face Down in the Marrow-Bone Pie
Face Down Upon an Herbal
Face Down Among the Winchester Geese
Face Down Beneath the Eleanor Cross
Face Down Under the Wych Elm
Face Down Before Rebel Hooves
Face Down Across the Western Sea
Murders & Other Confusions (short stories)
Face Down Below the Banqueting House
Face Down Beside St. Anne's Well
Face Down O'er the Border

Nonfiction:
How to Write Killer Historical Mysteries : The
Art and Adventure of Sleuthing Through the Past
Wives and Daughters: The Women of Sixteenth-Century
England
Making Headlines: A Biography of Nellie Bly
The Writer's Guide to Everyday Life in Renaissance England

Novels for Ages 8-12:
The Mystery of Hilliard's Castle
Julia's Mending
The Mystery of the Missing Bagpipes

LETHAL LEGEND

⤶⤷

A Diana Spaulding Mystery

KATHY LYNN EMERSON

PEMBERLEY PRESS
CORONA DEL MAR

Published by
P E M B E R L E Y   P R E S S
P O Box 1027
Corona del Mar, CA 92625
www.pemberleypress.com

A member of The Authors Studio
www.theauthorsstudio.org

Cover art by Linda Weatherly
Cover design by Kat & Dog Studios

ISBN13 978-0-9771913-5-2
LCCN 2007030420

Library of Congress Cataloging-in-Publication Data

Emerson, Kathy Lynn.
  Lethal legend : a Diana Spaulding mystery / Kathy Lynn Emerson.
    p. cm. -- (Diana Spaulding mystery series ; 4)
  ISBN 978-0-9771913-5-2 (pbk. : alk. paper) 1. Spaulding, Diana
(Fictitious character)--Fiction. 2. Women journalists--Fiction. 3.
Archaeologists--Crimes against--Fiction. 4. Maine--Fiction. I. Title.
  PS3555.M414L44 2007
  813'.54--dc22
                                        2007030420

For the online communities at
CrimeThruTime,
DorothyL,
and
Buffybuds.
No better way to start the day.

CHAPTER ONE

෨)ල

June 1888

Schooners, steamboats, yachts, and fishing boats navigated the choppy waters of Penobscot Bay, but Ben Northcote was too deeply troubled by what he'd found on Keep Island to appreciate the attractive picture they made. The promontory upon which he stood was the highest point of land on the island and commanded a spectacular view of surrounding landmarks. He had a clear view of Eagle Island with its beacon light. Shifting his gaze just slightly, he could see North Haven, Vinalhaven, and the Gulf of Maine beyond. Still farther out was the Atlantic Ocean, and if one kept going, England.

Slowly, he turned until he could see almost the entire length of Islesborough with the undulating Camden Hills beyond. Rotating further, he found himself looking across a cluster of tiny islands to Cape Rosier and Castine Head, its lighthouse prominent on a rugged cliff on the mainland. As he completed his circle, he remembered another time when he'd stood just here on a clear day and been able to pick out the top of Cadillac Mountain on Mt. Desert Island.

He could not see that far today. Nor could he put off making his report much longer. If he didn't go in, Graham Somener would come looking for him. Keep Island's seventy-five acres was comprised of meadows, cliffs, pebble beaches, rocky outcroppings, a swamp, and a cave. The latter offered the only possible hiding place, but held little appeal to Ben as an adult.

When he'd been a young boy and stayed on Keep Island as a guest, he'd always had hopes that what they'd named "the pirate's cave" would one day yield a buccaneer's treasure. If such a thing had ever existed, he and Graham had never been able to find it.

Keep Island belonged to the Somener family and had for at least three generations. Graham's grandfather, Jedediah Somener, had made his fortune in shipping and built the house. Jedediah's daughter, Graham's Aunt Min, had planted imported shade trees. Grown to respectable size now—black walnut, copper beech, and chestnut—they complimented the island's fragrant native pine and cedar. When Graham had moved back to the island five years earlier, he had made numerous improvements, the addition of indoor plumbing and a gas plant the most obvious.

Overhead a gull screamed in counterpoint to the sound of waves breaking on the rocks below. Ben breathed deeply of the salty air and squared his shoulders. Procrastination solved nothing. Resigned, he headed back down the path that led to the Somener mansion.

He found Graham in his library, seated at the huge partners' desk that dominated the room. He was not alone. Miss Serena Dunbar had arranged herself in a most unladylike fashion in one of the overstuffed chairs, head resting against one arm, lower limbs dangling over the other. Just as well she was present, Ben decided. She needed to hear his conclusions, too.

"Well?" Graham was tall, only a bit shorter than Ben himself. Like Ben he had dark wavy hair, but where Ben's eyes were dark brown, Graham's were the color of agates.

"All three men were poisoned."

Miss Dunbar did not move but her unfashionably sun-browned skin blanched, making her freckles stand out. "You're certain? There couldn't be any possibility of a mistake?"

A frown knit Graham's brow. "Food poisoning, do you mean?"

Interesting, Ben thought. Miss Dunbar assumed and accepted the worst while Graham continued to search for a more benign explanation. He wasn't sure if this change in his old friend's outlook was an improvement or not.

"Unless Miss Dunbar's assistants are habitual opium eaters, it is unlikely they could have ingested that much morphine through error. One man might take an accidental overdose, but all three show the symptoms of narcotic poisoning—sleeplessness and dizziness alternating with bouts of unconsciousness, vomiting, a yellowish tinge to the complexion, rapid pulse, and pupils retracted to the size of pinpoints."

Miss Dunbar righted herself and stood, brushing absently at the wrinkles in her divided skirt. "Will they recover?"

"If they survive another twenty-four hours without respiratory failure, the prognosis is good, but I make no promises."

"Morphine?" Graham couldn't seem to grasp the concept. "Narcotic poisoning? How can that be? Where would anyone get such a thing on my island?"

"Morphine has come into wide use as a painkiller in the last year or so. It would not be particularly difficult to obtain, though it is hardly something one acquires on the spur of the moment."

"Do you mean to say that someone intended to murder my crew?" Miss Dunbar glared at Ben as if that were his fault.

"Possibly, although if so, they made a poor choice of weapon. There are other poisons more readily available that would have done a better job of it. If I had to guess, I'd say someone wanted to make whoever ingested the morphine ill and simply didn't care if one or more people died instead."

"That's horrible!" Miss Dunbar exclaimed.

"Yes, it is." And it made Ben wonder who the real target was. Paul Carstairs and Frank Ennis were new to the area. George Amity was a local man who'd been hired to do the heavy digging at the excavation site when Miss Serena Dunbar had somehow talked Graham into letting her conduct an archaeological excavation on his private island.

Ben took the chair Miss Dunbar had vacated and stretched his legs out in front of him. It had been a long day. He'd been up at dawn—around four at this time of year—and had gone early to his surgery in Bangor. Graham's telegram had arrived just before seven, giving Ben barely enough time to catch the 7:15 train. He'd scarcely had a moment since to draw in a deep breath.

"You're certain it couldn't have been food poisoning?" Graham asked. "They weren't particular what they ate. Meals out of tins half the time. Maybe that—"

"Why did you send for me if you thought the answer was that simple?" Ben interrupted. He did not move, but his sharp tone belied the relaxed posture. "There are other physicians closer to Keep Island. One on Islesborough, another in—"

"None I'd trust to keep silent about this!"

Alert for anything that might indicate a return of the depression and dementia from which Graham had suffered five years earlier, Ben watched his friend intently, albeit through half-closed eyes. The unfortunate and well-publicized collapse of a building Graham had designed had culminated in claims that he had been responsible for the loss of several lives. Deeply affected by the tragedy, hounded by the press, he had retreated from the world to live on Keep Island year round.

"Are you certain you didn't suspect foul play?" Ben asked.

"No! I swear to you, I was sure it was just food poisoning. But rumormongers might easily have turned that into something else."

"What? Plague?"

Ben hoped the sarcastic suggestion would jar Graham back

to reality before he convinced himself that another spate of half-truths and false accusations was imminent. He had a deep-seated fear of attracting attention to himself, and Ben well understood why. Unfounded speculation among his former associates and in the press had driven Graham out of Boston and very nearly driven him mad.

Miss Dunbar's long strides took her back and forth over the diamond trellis design of leaves and flowers on the carpet. She came to an abrupt halt in front of one of the floor-to-ceiling bookshelves and turned to face Ben. "Some people think there is a curse on this island."

Ben's eyes popped all the way open, and he sat up a little straighter, thinking he must have misheard her.

"Don't look at me like that, Dr. Northcote. I did not say that I believe in such nonsense. The notion came from Mr. Somener's housekeeper."

The redoubtable Mrs. Prudence Monroe. Ben remembered her well from his childhood. She was as prickly as a porcupine, but she could turn a bit of dough, a few apples, and a dash of cinnamon into ambrosia.

"Tell me about this curse." Ben was certain he'd never heard of it before.

"What is there to say?" Graham's exasperation had increased to the point where he'd raked agitated fingers through his hair, leaving clumps of it standing on end. "The locals never inhabited this island before my grandfather built here. They seem to have gotten it into their heads that it was a dangerous place. I don't know why. The rocks off shore are no worse than anywhere else in Penobscot Bay. There have been no shipwrecks—"

"That you know of," Miss Dunbar interrupted.

"No matter what happened here in the distant past, Keep Island has not been unlucky for the Someners. For me it has been a blessed refuge."

"I understand your desire for seclusion," Ben said, meeting

Graham's eyes, "but this looks like a case of attempted murder. You can't just ignore it and hope it will go away. You need to contact the sheriff."

"Out of the question. Besides, what good does it do to close the barn door after the horse has escaped?"

"Whoever poisoned those men could try again."

Tossing aside the pen he'd been toying with, Graham huffed out an exasperated breath. "I do not see how some stranger could come to my island and tamper with supplies without anyone noticing. It defies logic."

"Someone already here, then."

At Ben's suggestion, Graham sent a speculative look in Miss Dunbar's direction.

Affronted by the very idea that one of her crew would poison both himself and his associates, she swept across the room to within striking distance of Graham's chair. Hands on hips, lower limbs braced wide apart, she fixed Ben's friend with a fulminating stare.

Graham slowly rose, regaining the high ground. "Perhaps we should ask—"

"The notion is absurd. I have total confidence in my men."

"Well acquainted with each of them, are you?"

"Well enough!"

Ben interrupted before the quarrel could escalate. "My patients are too weak to be interrogated just yet, but I do have a few more questions for the two of you."

They turned on Ben as one, identical glares scorching him. He found that strangely reassuring. Under the circumstances, Graham's display of temper was a normal reaction.

"What do you want to know?" Graham asked.

"This house is huge. Why were those three men obliged to camp out while Miss Dunbar stayed in one of the guest rooms?"

"It was their choice," she informed him in a lofty voice. "They preferred to be close to the excavation. I would have stayed with them had Mr. Somener not insisted I accept his hospitality."

"And meals? Why didn't they join you for those, or eat in the kitchen with the servants?"

This time Graham answered. "They chose not to."

"Two of them are accustomed to living rough when on an expedition," Miss Dunbar elaborated. "Mr. Ennis spent several seasons excavating in Egypt. Mr. Carstairs is just back from studying the Casa Grande ruins in Arizona. I believe Mr. Somener's mansion intimidated them. It certainly awed Mr. Amity. They all felt more comfortable sleeping in tents and cooking their own food."

"Then whoever administered the morphine expected it to be ingested by one or more of those men, but not by one of you," Ben concluded.

Graham and Miss Dunbar exchanged a startled look.

"None of the victims seems likely to have provoked the wrath of anyone who would use morphine as a weapon," Ben continued. "That makes me wonder if the motive was to close down the excavation."

"Deliberately poisoning three innocent men seems an extreme measure if that was his only purpose." Miss Dunbar boosted herself up to sit on the corner of Graham's desk while he subsided into his chair.

"I agree, but if it doesn't turn out to be the result of, say, a quarrel one of the victims had with someone, then you need to ask yourself if you have any enemies who'd resort to such measures."

"I have professional rivals," she admitted, a thoughtful expression adding creases to her brow. "There is one archaeologist in particular who seems to delight in ridiculing my theories. But why would he try to kill my men when he's so certain I'm never going to find anything? Besides, no one knows what I'm doing here. I've been careful to keep it secret."

"People are aware there is an archaeological excavation on

Keep Island. They can see that much from a passing boat."

"But they don't know what it is I'm looking for."

Neither did Ben, but at the moment that seemed irrelevant.

"Consider this rival carefully. Might he simply have meant to disrupt things? Someone who doesn't understand how powerful a drug morphine is could have thought it would stop work by making your men sick." A dangerous mistake, but possible. "Mischief like that could easily have turned into murder."

Ben heaved himself out of the chair. "I need to return to my patients. I'll stay until they're out of danger."

"I appreciate that, Ben." Graham managed a bitter laugh. "I don't need any more deaths on my conscience."

"Then reconsider calling in the sheriff."

As a parting shot, Ben doubted it was effective. Graham guarded his privacy as ferociously as a lioness did her cubs.

Only for an old and dear friend, Ben thought, would he have offered to remain more than the one night he'd initially planned on. He had pressing obligations at home, not the least of which was his own wedding. He was to be married in just eighteen days.

He made one detour on his way back to the former nursery that had been converted into a temporary hospital. He stopped off in his own room to pen a brief letter to his intended bride. The last thing he wanted was to have Diana worry about him . . . or become curious as to why he'd left town so suddenly and mysteriously. He reckoned the letter would go out on the afternoon delivery boat and Diana would have it in hand by the following day.

Three Days Later

"Mother, please!" Exasperation laced Diana Spaulding's voice. She willed her hands to remain folded and motionless in her lap. If she reached for her cup while she was in such an agitated state, she'd spill every drop of tea and likely put a crack the delicate china as well.

Elmira Leeves ignored her daughter. Calmly taking another sip of the beverage in her own cup, to which she'd just added a dollop of whiskey, she aimed her piercing blue-eyed stare at the third individual in the crowded parlor of Ben Northcote's house in Bangor, Maine.

Diana's future mother-in-law, Maggie Northcote, was a study in outrage as she sat enthroned on the rococo sofa. Swathed in purple fabric, from the loose gown flowing around her sturdy form to the turban that covered her graying hair, Maggie's countenance had taken on a shade almost as vivid as her garments. It appeared to Diana that an explosion was imminent . . . or a fit of apoplexy. Although she looked younger—her complexion was smooth as that of a woman half her age—Maggie Northcote was in her fifties, just as Elmira was. Diana feared for her health.

"How dare you suggest such a thing?" Maggie demanded in a strangled voice. "Ben is no coward. Why he—"

"Where is he, then?" Elmira's knowing smirk was almost enough to drive Diana to violence. "That's all I asked." She took another sip of her adulterated tea. "The wedding is only a fortnight from now and the bridegroom seems to have disappeared off the face of the earth. Has he changed his mind and fled? Or is he just off indulging in one last debauch?"

"He was called away on a medical emergency," Maggie said through gritted teeth.

"He's been gone for days and you haven't heard a word from him. You don't even know where he is," Elmira persisted. "Do you?"

Diana's hands ached from clasping them so tightly together. The delicious evening meal she'd consumed not a half hour earlier, before the ladies withdrew for tea and left Elmira's new husband to his post-prandial cigar in the library, churned in her stomach. She drew in a slow, calming breath and tried to dismiss the disloyal thought that Ben might have left town solely to avoid being witness to the inevitable clash between Maggie and Elmira. Their faint hope that two such strong-minded, independent, eccentric women would find common ground and become friends had died a quick death. Barely twenty-four hours after their first meeting, they were at each other's throats.

Worse, Elmira's none-too-subtle hints had fallen on fertile ground. Diana could not help but feel abandoned. Ben hadn't even told her in person that he was leaving town. He'd gone in to his surgery early on Tuesday morning. Diana had barely begun her own day when a note had arrived, delivered by a boy Ben had paid to carry it. The brief and unsatisfying message had contained no explanation and nary a hint of when Ben would return. Neither had it said where he'd gone. He'd left a similarly uninformative note on his surgery door, telling patients to go to Dr. Randolph in an emergency.

Maggie rose from the sofa, compelling Diana's attention. In spite of her stature—she was only of medium height—she had a regal air about her as she looked down her nose at Elmira. "Foolish mortal. You do not realize how great your suffering will be. The gods punish those who offend them. You'll be squashed flat as a bug under a schoolboy's foot."

Elmira's braying laugh made the teacups clatter. "If you're a deity, I'm the Empress of India!"

"I am descended from Gypsies. And from the nobility of Europe. The blood of a countess runs in my veins."

Elmira lifted an eyebrow at this, then downed the last of the liquid in her cup. She stood slowly, brushing crumbs off her dark green skirt and squaring her shoulders. She was a stout woman, two inches taller than her daughter, and should have been able to cow Maggie Northcote by her greater size alone.

"Mother, you are a guest in this house," Diana hissed.

Both women turned on her. Elmira's gaze was acrimonious but the bemused look in Maggie's odd, copper-colored eyes suggested she'd forgotten Diana was there.

With a sniffing sound Diana supposed was meant to indicate that her feelings were hurt by Diana's criticism, Elmira stepped away from the grouping of sofa and loveseat and headed for the grand piano in one corner of the room. In no hurry, she paused in front of a mirror to check her appearance en route.

At fifty-three, Elmira's mahogany colored hair, which Diana had inherited, was liberally streaked with white. In contrast to Maggie's, Elmira's face was scored with deep furrows, and her cheeks got their high color not from raw good health or from the application of cosmetics but from tiny broken capillaries under the skin. She'd had a hard life, Diana reminded herself, but that was no excuse for rude behavior. It wasn't as if Elmira didn't know any better. For years she'd hobnobbed with the cream of Denver society.

Elmira plunked herself down on the piano stool and ran idle fingers over the keys. She winced at the sound this produced. "Don't you ever tune this thing?"

"Why bother?" Maggie answered. "No one in this household plays."

The enormous, long-haired black cat who had been asleep on top of the piano uncurled himself and stretched. With a hiss in passing at Elmira, he hopped down and crossed the room to Maggie, stropping himself enthusiastically against her skirts until she stooped to pick him up.

"Cedric always has had good taste," his mistress murmured, cuddling him close and shooting Elmira a superior smile.

"Cats! Can't abide them. They aren't even good eating."

"Cedric isn't just a cat. He's my familiar."

Another bray of laughter greeted Maggie's claim to be a witch. "Better get busy with your spells, then. Maybe you can locate your lost lamb. Diana tells me the minister insists on talking to them together before their nuptials. A nuisance, I'm sure, but there it is." She hit a series of discordant notes before abandoning the piano to roam the parlor.

Maggie muttered something unintelligible.

"What's that?" Elmira demanded.

"I said I tried that already!" Maggie all but snarled the admission.

"Well, then, it's a good thing I took matters into my own hands."

Diana sprang to her feet in alarm, setting the china rattling. "Mother, what did you do?"

"I searched his room, of course, and when that yielded nothing useful I sent my darling new husband to Ben's office to search there. Ed is better than I am at getting into locked buildings." When the cries of outrage died down, Elmira added, in a tone that set Diana's already strained nerves on edge, "Men are always leaving their possessions lying about."

"Well," Maggie demanded in the lull that followed this statement, "what did you find?"

"A telegram, one sent very early on Tuesday, the same day Dr. Northcote so abruptly left Bangor."

"You're enjoying this," Diana said with considerable asperity, "and enjoying drawing it out."

Elmira shrugged. "Why not? I have so few pleasures in life."

Maggie's snort of disbelief threatened to start another round of snide comments and outright insults. Diana held up a hand to silence them both. "Enough! Where is the telegram now?"

"You never let me have any fun," Elmira complained, producing it from a pocket in her skirt.

Diana had to shake off the eerie conviction that, had she not been staring at her mother, she'd have had difficulty telling which woman had spoken. She'd more than once heard Maggie accuse Ben of the same thing.

Taking the telegram, Diana unfolded the paper and read its contents aloud: "Need medical assistance. Meet noon Belfast. Tell no one. Somener."

"Somener," she repeated, recognizing the name from the list

of wedding guests. "Graham Somener. He's one of Ben's closest friends."

He was also a very wealthy man, one she intended to ask for an interview when they met. Was that why Ben hadn't told her who had asked for his help? Diana bridled at the notion that *tell no one* had applied to her. Just because she refused to resign her position as a reporter for the *Independent Intelligencer* was no reason to shut her out. All Ben had to do was ask her not to write about his friend. She had no desire to pursue reluctant subjects.

As she puzzled over the implications of the telegram, Maggie and Elmira resumed their seats. Maggie poured more tea.

"That perfume doesn't suit you," Elmira remarked to her hostess. "Lily-of-the-valley is all wrong. Almost as bad a match as the gardenia scent my daughter seems to have bathed in."

Since the ornate crystal bottle of *Eau de Gardenia* had been a birthday gift from Ben, given to her only a few days before he'd left. Diana had to bite back a waspish response. Ben said her skin reminded him of gardenia petals. She'd always considered it a very pretty compliment.

Maggie didn't bother with restraint. "Something with nettles would suit you, I think. Or adder's tongue."

Elmira chuckled. "Good one."

Belatedly, it occurred to Diana that the two women were enjoying the exchange of insults. That was the final straw. Out of patience with them both, she left them to their verbal sparring and went out into the garden.

Twilight still lingered, although it would be gone in a matter of minutes. Diana relished the longer days and milder temperatures of June after the violent storms of March and the long, cold weeks of April and May. She needed no shawl as she wandered the paths that surrounded Ben's house, and the illumination spilling out through various windows was sufficient to light her way as the last of sunset's rosy glow was swallowed up by the night sky.

Peaceful quiet engulfed her as she moved away from the house. For a time her thoughts roamed as freely as she did, but she was not altogether surprised when her ramble brought her to the carriage house. Aaron Northcote's studio was on the upper level, and Aaron, for all his peculiarities, was exactly the person she needed to talk to. However strange it might be to seek out Ben's brother as the voice of reason, at this moment that course seemed to make perfect sense.

Diana smelled the distinctive scents of linseed oil and turpentine even before Aaron opened the door to her tentative knock. "If you're working, I can come back another time."

"My muse! Don't you know you're always welcome?"

The studio was a single large room, sparsely furnished. Aaron offered her the one comfortable chair, an overstuffed behemoth that was sinfully soft and yielding. He seized the bentwood chair off the small pedestal, where it usually served to seat artist's models, turned it around, and straddled it, leaning his elbows on the curved back and fixing his intent gaze on her face.

She wondered what he saw in the half light. In contrast to the level below, here only one lamp had been lit and the room was deep in shadow. The finished canvases piled against the walls, many of them face out, created an eerie atmosphere, for the majority portrayed fantastic scenes of mermaids and monsters. A number of the former had Diana's face.

"Be quiet!" Aaron spoke sharply, but not to Diana. His focus had shifted to a point beyond her right shoulder.

She ignored the interruption. She knew no one was there. Ben had warned her it was best to let Aaron deal with his voices as he saw fit, rather than try to convince him that they were imaginary. They were real to him.

After a strained moment or two, Aaron smiled at her as if nothing odd had transpired. "What brings you to my lair? No, let me guess. They've murdered each other and you want my help to dispose of the bodies? Or perhaps you've murdered them both.

Yes, that's more likely."

Shocked and amused at the same time, she found herself returning his engaging grin. Like his mother, Aaron enjoyed saying outrageous things. "They were both alive and well when I retreated from the field of battle," she assured him.

"I like your mother," Aaron said. "She speaks her mind. When I met her earlier in the garden, she asked me straight out if I was the madman in the family."

"Oh, Aaron, I—"

He cut short her apology with a dismissive wave of one hand. "Better she knows all, don't you think? Besides, I had a comeback ready that put her in her place. I said I was *one* of them."

"How can you *joke* about it?"

He shrugged. "How can I not? But that's not why you're here. What is it, Diana? You haven't ventured into my studio alone since Mother locked you in the crypt and I had to rescue you."

She couldn't control a shiver at the memory, but if he was able to speak so calmly of events that had almost led to his death, then she could do no less than answer him honestly. "What do you know about Graham Somener?" she asked.

"Is that where big brother's gone? To Keep Island?"

"So it seems. Not that he bothered to tell me that was his destination. Or let me know he'd reached there safely." She'd believed she and Ben had the best of relationships. That they were friends as well as lovers. But friends didn't keep secrets from each other or fail to send a reassuring note or telegram.

"You could go after him," Aaron suggested. "It's no great distance. Eighteen miles to Bucksport, then another twenty or so across the waters of Penobscot Bay."

"Is there a ferry?" As the expression on his face deteriorated into a smirk, her eyes narrowed. "What?"

"Some might say this is divine retribution," Aaron murmured. "Not me, of course. But it wasn't so long ago that I had to listen to Ben rant and rave because you'd failed to communicate your whereabouts to him. Since he followed you to find out what was going on, I suppose it is only right that you imitate his action."

"It's not the same."

"He was angry at you. Now you're angry at him."

"Annoyed." The same emotion had her on her feet, too het up to sit still. She moved restlessly from chair to window and back. What she felt wasn't so much anger as envy. Ben's disappearance had not only gained him a respite from the hectic wedding preparations, but also from the responsibility of dealing with family members, more of whom were due to arrive any day. Since several of them were at odds with her mother, there would be no diminution in the bickering and backstabbing.

"As I recall, Ben was spitting nails, he was so furious with you."

"I had good reason for what I did."

"I imagine Ben would say the same about the present situation."

"Oh?" Now temper did simmer, setting sarcasm loose. She'd been hurt that Ben had failed to confide in her before he left. That oversight pained her every time she thought of it. "And who, pray, has been murdered on Keep Island?"

The moment the words were out, Diana regretted them. Murder was not a matter to be taken lightly.

"No one . . . that I know of."

"I am very glad to hear it."

"But I haven't visited there in years. Why did Ben? Why now?"

Diana stilled. "There was a telegram. It said 'need medical assistance.' That must mean someone was ill or injured, but the message came three days ago. Even in the midst of treating the sick, Ben would have spared a thought for me. Wouldn't he?"

Aaron's troubled expression offered no reassurance. He didn't try to tease her out of her concern. "Go after him, Diana," he said. "You're right. Ben should have sent word to someone before this."

Diana returned to the house by way of the kitchen door a short time later, still undecided about following Ben. She'd intended to go straight up to her bedroom, but when she heard the faint rumble of a male voice from the direction of the parlor, she changed her mind. It was not Ben, she realized as she drew closer, but by then she was too curious to retreat.

Her footfalls nearly silent on the thick carpet, Diana reached the doorway and paused. There was no sign of her mother. Diana supposed she had retired early, as she had the night before. She felt heat climb into her cheeks, remembering the risqué parting comment Elmira had made the previous evening just before toddling off to bed with her brand new husband.

A stranger now sat on the loveseat Diana and Elmira had been sharing earlier. He had a stocky build and dark brown hair, but Diana could tell little else about him save that his suit was well cut and looked expensive. He had inclined his body in Maggie's direction, his head canted in a way that suggested he was staring at her intently. Maggie gazed back at him, a fatuous smile on her face.

"Ben has gone to Keep Island," she said. "We do not know when he will return."

Diana didn't think she'd made any sound, but the stranger turned in her direction the moment she stepped over the threshold, pinning her with a steely gray-eyed stare. Maggie blinked rapidly several times and looked surprised to find Diana in the room.

The stranger rose, showing himself to be of average height. "Ah," he said. "Mrs. Spaulding, I presume?"

"And you are?"

"This is Justus Palmer, Diana," Maggie said. "I knew his father aeons ago." Now her smile was flirtatious. "You look just like him, Justus. You even have his voice. I could never forget its remarkable resonance. Why, if I didn't know better, I'd say you *were* him."

Mr. Palmer seemed a trifle taken aback by this statement, but he recovered quickly. "I have been told before that I resemble him." He returned his attention to Diana. "Will you join us, Mrs. Spaulding. I am hoping you can help me on a matter of some importance."

Responding to the innate charm of the man, Diana seated herself on the loveseat. He did have a wonderful baritone voice, she thought. Almost as captivating as Ben's. She wondered if he was an actor.

Palmer chose one of several straight-back chairs in the parlor rather than crowd either of the women. Maggie, Diana saw, had poured him a cup of tea, but he didn't seem to have touched it. "May I offer you a stronger libation, Mr. Palmer?" she asked.

"Thank you, no. I do not drink spiritous liquors."

"Your father kissed me once," Maggie announced. When they both turned to stare at her, she shrugged. "Well, he did. But it was before I married Ben's father, so there was no harm in it. He was a very good kisser, as I recall. Quite romantic. Though now that I think about it, I did come away from it with a cut on my lip. My but that man had sharp teeth!"

Diana sent Palmer a sympathetic look. Maggie's outrageous comments must be embarrassing to him, but he managed to keep a polite expression on his face. "How can we help you, Mr. Palmer? I presume it is a matter of great importance indeed to require a visit so late in the evening."

"I do a great deal of work after dark, Mrs. Spaulding," Palmer said. "I am a private detective by profession."

"Pinkerton?"

He winced, as if he'd heard that question one too many times before. "No, I'm not one of the Pinkertons. I have my own detective agency in Boston. Just now I am employed by a client who is concerned about activities on Keep Island."

"Activities?" she echoed, puzzled. "What kind of activities?"

"That's the question, isn't it? Illegal activities, or so my client believes."

Diana felt herself go cold inside and had to struggle to preserve her outward composure. She had reported on crime in New York City and elsewhere for her newspaper. She and Ben had encountered murder more than once in their personal lives. She had no wish to become involved in "illegal activities" again.

"I understand Dr. Northcote is visiting the island at present," Palmer continued.

Since Maggie had already told him that much, Diana saw no harm in confirming it. "He left three days ago in response to a request from an old friend."

"That would be Graham Somener, I presume."

Diana nodded.

"Are you aware of Mr. Somener's past?" His eyes cut briefly to Maggie and, following that path, Diana saw the other woman's face harden.

"All lies," she muttered. "Scandal." She gave Diana a pointed look. "Newspapers made up stories about him that were not true."

Diana said nothing. The accusation might well be justified. Her employer, Horatio Foxe, editor and publisher of the *Independent Intelligencer*, had been known to stretch the truth until it snapped. When it came to a choice between reporting only the boring facts or embellishing a bit to pique his readers' interest, he always chose to print the more colorful version of a story.

"In this case," Palmer said, "there seems to be some basis for the published reports. Mr. Somener was an architect, Mrs. Spaulding. An extremely successful one. Some years back, he was involved in a construction project for a very tall building. He cut corners to save expenses. When the building was finished, and occupied, it collapsed. People died. His callous disregard for safety was directly responsible for those deaths."

"It was a terrible accident," Maggie protested.

"It is true that no criminal charges were ever brought." Palmer leaned closer to Diana, capturing her gaze and holding it. "Immediately following, however, Mr. Somener retreated to his island. He's been there for five years now and if he's left it more than a half-dozen times I'd be surprised to hear it. That could mean the man is riddled with guilt. It could also be that he is a coward. And if he was, and is, a ruthless businessman, then he'd not be averse to increasing his fortune by other underhanded means."

"Of what, exactly, are you accusing him, Mr. Palmer?" Diana asked.

"Crimes, Mrs. Spaulding."

A flash of memory made Diana frown. She'd recently told Ben, in no uncertain terms, that she did not want to become involved with crimes or criminals ever again—not to write about, not to read about, and definitely not to encounter in person. She'd meant it at the time, but now found her reporter's instincts roused by Palmer's hints. Besides, she thought, if Ben's oldest and dearest friend stood accused of being involved in criminal activity, how could she not pursue the matter? To exonerate Graham Somener, of course.

Palmer leaned closer and spoke in a low, compelling voice. "You must tell me anything you know, Mrs. Spaulding. Everything. All you know about recent criminal activity on Keep Island."

Diana found the man's steady regard unnerving. It almost seemed as if he were trying to mesmerize her with that concentrated stare. His voice, too, was hypnotic. She blinked several times before she answered him.

"I know nothing about Keep Island or Graham Somener."

"Now if it were Jedediah," Maggie mused aloud, "I'd believe it. He was an old reprobate if there ever was one!"

"Jedediah?" Diana repeated, confused.

"Graham Somener's grandfather. He's the one who bought

Keep Island years ago for a song. Cheated the fellow that sold it to him six ways to Sunday, that's the way I heard it, and the rightful heirs were some put out about it, too. Nothing they could do, naturally, except curse the island for all eternity."

"My information indicates very recent crimes," Palmer said. "It has been no more than a few months, perhaps only a matter of a few weeks, since these illegal activities began."

"What nonsense! Graham Somener is an honest man." Maggie placed one hand over her ample bosom as if this would add sanctity to her conviction.

Diana regarded Justus Palmer with suspicion. "Just what particular crime do you believe Mr. Somener has committed?"

"Oh, yes, do tell," Maggie interrupted. "We're all agog! Has he opened a gambling hell on the island? A brothel? Or is it smuggling he's taken up for fun and profit."

For once, Diana was grateful for Maggie's foolishness. It broke the spell Palmer's unrelenting gaze seemed to be spinning around her.

"You must be specific, Justus."

If Maggie's sarcasm irritated Justus Palmer, he did not let it show. His voice was calm and matter-of-fact. "I fear I am not at liberty to say more, and even if I could betray my client's confidences, I would not wish to distress you ladies by discussing such unsavory matters."

Maggie snorted. "We are more worldly than you think, Mr. Palmer. No delicate sensibilities here."

He accepted that statement with laudable aplomb but would not relent. "My client requires discretion, ladies. I cannot reveal his secrets simply to satisfy your curiosity."

"And we," Diana said, "cannot answer *your* questions simply to satisfy his. Perhaps you should come back after Dr. Northcote returns."

Accepting his dismissal with apparent good grace, Palmer stood. "I believe I will do just that, Mrs. Spaulding. Thank you."

He started for the door.

"I'll see you out." Diana didn't know what to make of the man. He was charming, but there was something . . . odd about him. And he was much too secretive for her peace of mind. She wouldn't put it past him to sneak upstairs and search the house the moment their backs were turned. She went with him to the door, intending to see him safely through it, to be *certain* he left.

He stopped at the coatrack, where he had left a tweed great-coat with a double cape. He shrugged into the heavy garment, in which he would surely be too warm on this mild June night, making Diana wonder if this was a delaying tactic. She certainly hadn't needed a coat to walk in the garden.

"Have you a hat?" she asked, not seeing one.

"Never wear them."

"How very odd." Even Ben, who did not particularly care to cover his head, wore one sometimes, and if Mr. Palmer needed a coat—

The sudden realization that his lips had quirked into a wry smile as he watched her watch him left Diana feeling disconcerted.

"I mean you and yours no harm, Mrs. Spaulding." Palmer stepped outside, but he paused just across the threshold to glance over his shoulder at her. "I don't suppose you'd heed a word of friendly advice?"

"Probably not, but feel free to offer it."

"Keep Island is a dangerous place. By all means do everything you can to convince Dr. Northcote to leave, but under no circumstances go there yourself."

CHAPTER TWO

෪ඏ

"**W**hat do you mean, you can't allow passengers to disembark on Keep Island?" More puzzled than concerned, Diana awaited an answer. She had not journeyed all the way to Bucksport by train to be put off at the first hitch in her plans.

Amos Cobb, captain of the steamboat *Miss Min*, scratched his bulbous nose with the side of this thumb and gave her a gap-toothed grin. "Orders is orders, miss. No visitors allowed unless Mr. Somener himself vouches for them. In advance."

"But you must have taken my fiancé there four days ago. I—"

"Nope. Never did. No one out, no one back, not on my boat. Not for a week, at least, and then it was only that peculiar Miss Dunbar who's digging up the place and her workmen."

"Is the island quarantined?" Diana asked.

"Course not." Cobb looked astonished by the very idea. "Man just wants his privacy, is all."

Privacy for what? Diana wondered. The vague hints Mr. Palmer had dropped suddenly seemed much more ominous. "Dr. Northcote is on Keep Island. I'm sure of it."

"That's as may be, miss, but I've got my orders."

"It is extremely important that I contact my fiancé."

Cobb tugged on one ear, shuffled his feet, and finally allowed that if she'd write a note to Mr. Somener, he could take it to him. "Will that do?" he asked. "If he says you can visit the island, I'll take you there tomorrow."

Given little choice, Diana did as he suggested. With luck, her message would bring Ben to her instead. She hoped so. The problem with the captain's offer was that the *Miss Min* would not be back in Bucksport until evening. According to the schedule posted at the steamship office, he delivered mail, groceries, and sometimes passengers, to ten of the inhabited islands in Penobscot Bay.

At least he made two stops, morning and afternoon, at Graham Somener's island. That would give Ben time between to respond to her note, but she'd have to wait all day long in Bucksport just to find out if she had been given leave to visit him on Keep Island. By then the last train for Bangor, which left at 4:50 in the afternoon, would already have departed. She'd have to stay overnight in Bucksport. Alone, if Ben was unable to accompany Captain Cobb to fetch her.

As she watched the *Miss Min* leave the wharf, Diana stewed over this setback to her plans. Bucksport's steamboat dock was right next to the railroad depot. She could go back to Bangor on the 9:40 train and make the trip to Bucksport all over again at two in the afternoon, but she did not particularly want to return to the city. Still, it was not yet nine o'clock in the morning and she could scarcely wander aimlessly along the riverfront for the rest of the day.

Bucksport was a pretty little town, with its white clapboard houses and brick bank and library rising on a gentle slope. The buildings of what looked like a seminary stood out in stark relief against the sky on the summit of a hill. Thinking to find someplace better to wait, perhaps a respectable hotel, Diana set off on foot to explore. A few minutes' walking revealed a monument of

Scotch granite to the Union dead and at least four churches.

When she encountered a matron wheeling a baby carriage, Diana inquired about hotels and was told that the Robinson House had been operating as an inn for more than sixty-five years.

"Are you alone, miss?" The woman's nose twitched with suspicion.

"I've been . . . delayed in meeting someone."

The woman eyed Diana's gripsack. Disapproval creased an otherwise pleasant countenance into an unappealing expression.

Diana sighed. She'd forgotten how straitlaced small towns could be. "Perhaps I will just wait at the depot." There was still time to catch the train.

The baby's fussing distracted its mother. "Perhaps you'd best," she said, clearly dismissing Diana from her thoughts as she bent to tend to the infant.

She walked back to the dock at a fast clip. By the time she got there, the *Miss Min* was no more than a speck in the distance, indistinguishable from other vessels, and it would not be returning for hours yet.

Waiting, doing nothing more productive than twiddling her thumbs, did not sit well with Diana. "You there," she called, addressing an old man mending a fishing net. "Where can I find a boat to hire?"

Repeated inquiries along the fringe of shoreline, where shipbuilders, carriage makers, stonemasons, and carpenters plied their trades, eventually led her to a fifteen-year-old boy with a sailboat just big enough to hold two people. For a fee—half the money Diana had brought with her—young Caleb Reed agreed to take her to Keep Island. Diana didn't give herself time to change her mind. Somewhat awkwardly, she climbed into the small craft and they were on their way.

"Is it a good day for sailing?" she asked as he headed out into the channel.

"Finest kind."

Diana knew nothing of sailboats, although she thought one steered with something called a "tiller," but she had sense enough to hang on to her hat with one hand and the edge of her seat with the other when Caleb performed a practiced maneuver to avoid running into a buoy. For a terrifying moment the small craft seemed to Diana to be on the verge of flipping over. But then it righted itself.

"Why was that in our way?" she asked when she'd caught her breath. To her mind, the buoy appeared to be more hazard than aid to navigation.

"Marks a sawdust bar." At her blank look, he added, "They build up in the river from all the ships that sail past here loaded with lumber from the saw mills in Bangor."

Diana frowned. "The Penobscot seems too narrow here for much traffic."

Caleb chuckled and jerked his head to indicate that she should look behind her at what she'd assumed was the opposite shore. "That there's an island. See up on that rise?" He pointed to the higher ground beyond and the formidable structure that surmounted it. "That there's Fort Knox. That's where the far side of the river is."

The way widened quickly and soon spilled out into Penobscot Bay. As land on both sides slipped farther and farther away, Diana became increasingly uneasy. "Must we stray so far from land?"

"Can't swim, eh?"

She felt herself pale. "No."

"Me, neither." The cheerful unconcern in his voice was not reassuring.

The open water was dotted with sails, both white and gray, and the smokestacks of steamers great and small. To take her mind off how tiny Caleb's sailboat was, she asked if all the islands were inhabited.

"Some yes, some no. My uncle says there are over 500 of them in Penobscot Bay. Little ones only a half acre in size. One big enough to hold two whole towns."

"And Keep Island?"

"I expect that's one of the littler ones."

At the note of doubt in his voice, Diana's eyes narrowed. "You *do* know where you're going?"

"Don't you worry. I sailed past it once before on the way to Rockport. Uncle Ralph pointed it out as being Mr. Somener's island. Didn't pay it much mind back then, but I reckon I can find it again easy enough."

The wake from a passing steamer set the small sailboat to rocking with a violent motion that had Diana's heart, and the remains of her breakfast, lodging in her throat. Water sloshed into the small craft as it tilted at a precarious angle, soaking her feet and spattering the rest of her with icy droplets.

"Why is the water so cold?" she gasped. "It is June!"

"Come August, it might be warmed up a bit. Not before."

The brisk breeze propelling the sailboat towards its destination cut right through her garments, right through her skin, chilling her to the bone. Wet and miserable, Diana lapsed into silence. Caleb seemed confident. He was a native of these parts. She'd just have to trust he could get her where she was going.

Ten minutes later, to take her mind off her chattering teeth, Diana asked another question: "Do you know anything about the man who owns Keep Island?"

"Rolling in money, they say. Owns the *Miss Min*. Cap'n Cobb says he pays a bonus every time he wants her schedule changed."

That explained Cobb's refusal to go against orders. She supposed she couldn't fault him . . . unless he was in league with the criminals Mr. Palmer had mentioned. Diana tried unsuccessfully to picture the stubbornly polite captain as a smuggler. She thought that if he grew a full beard, he might fit the popular image of a pirate, but that stretched the imagination even further.

"What about the island itself?

Caleb shrugged. "Heard it had a curse on it."

"What kind of curse?" Hadn't Maggie mentioned someone cursing Jedediah Somener?

"Don't know. 'Keep away from Keep Island.' That's all they say."

"You might have mentioned that before we set out."

"Don't put much stock in such foolishness. Besides, you offered to pay."

And the price, Diana thought cynically, might have been even higher if Caleb had remembered this "curse" in time. If Caleb hadn't just invented it for her benefit, then Graham Somener's desire for privacy was probably behind "Keep away from Keep Island." She smiled in spite of her acute discomfort. It sounded more like an advertising slogan than a threat.

Her smile vanished and her thoughts scattered as the tiny craft suddenly dipped and shook. The wind tried to tug Diana's hat right off her head and the waves peppered her with a fine, cold spray.

"Fine day for a sail," Caleb declared.

Diana decided she'd hate to see a poor one.

After what seemed an eternity, they arrived at what Caleb claimed was Keep Island. By then, the hem of Diana's skirt was drenched, most of the pins had been shaken loose from her hair, and the tip of her nose had turned bright pink from exposure to the sun and wind. Although her hat was made of sturdy straw, the brim was not quite wide enough to protect her face from the elements.

On shaky limbs, she clambered out of the sailboat, so grateful to be on solid ground again that she gave Caleb a generous tip.

"You want me to come back for you?"

"No!" One by one she pushed the hairpins back into place, but without a mirror she had no idea whether or not she'd made a neat job of it. "No," she said again in a calmer voice. "There's no need to return." Captain Cobb might not have agreed to bring her to Keep Island, but she was certain he would not object to taking her off.

She watched until the sailboat was well on its way back to Bucksport, then picked up a decidedly damp gripsack and trudged inland along what appeared to be a rough path. Her goal was a flight of wooden steps leading to the top of a low cliff.

Although it gave evidence of being regularly used, the way was uneven. When Diana's foot came down wrong, an ominous popping sound reminded her that she had to be careful of the ankle she'd twisted back in March. She worried that if the surface didn't level out soon, she'd end up in an undignified heap and heartily wished she had left off her corset and worn her rationals instead of packing them. Unless she wanted to hide behind a rock to change her clothes, however, it was far too late to do anything about her attire. She kept going.

Diana stopped at the foot of the steps, shading her eyes against the sun as she looked up. Somewhere above, out of sight of her present location, was Graham Somener's hideaway and, she hoped, her elusive fiancé. Since there did not seem to be any other way to reach him, she would have to make the climb.

Pausing only long enough to shake sand off her hem, she juggled her gripsack so that she could use the same hand to lift her skirt above her ankles. Keeping a tight hold on the railing with the other, she gritted her teeth and began the ascent. She had no head for heights but she told herself she would be all right as long as she did not look down.

Halfway up, when Diana paused to catch her breath, she let her gaze leave the landing at the top of the stairs to scan the height of land. A little gasp escaped her as she caught sight of a man silhouetted above her and to the right. He was looking out at the water, not down at her, and for that Diana was grateful. She could not see him clearly, but she could tell he was a large, muscular fellow . . . and that he carried a rifle.

She remained motionless for several minutes after he disappeared from view, her heart pounding so loudly in her ears that

she was certain the sound must echo off the cliff. That Graham
Somener had at least one armed guard alarmed her. Yes, he was
wealthy. Yes, the rich and famous sometimes needed protection.
But this was an island in rural Maine. What possible danger could
Somener need to be guarded from here? The obvious answer was
that Justus Palmer was right. Keep Island was being used for illegal activities.

All the way to Bucksport on the train, she'd been plagued by
second thoughts. Palmer's warnings had raised grave doubts in
her mind about Ben's host. To be blamed for loss of life, whether
Graham Somener had been responsible or not, must change a
man. Was he the same person Ben had known in his youth? Or
had he altered so completely as to become a villain?

Maggie Northcote, surprisingly, had encouraged Diana to go
to Keep Island and tell Ben everything Palmer had said. She insisted the Someners were good people. "Salt of the earth," she'd
said, predicting this would all turn out to be "a tempest in a teapot." Diana could only hope she was right.

With renewed determination, she resumed her climb. Ben was
up there, on top of the cliff. For all she knew, he was in mortal
danger.

Already short of breath by the time she crested the stairs,
the sight that met her eyes momentarily took what was left of
it away. A spacious mansion sprawled before her, venerable but
well-maintained. The white paint gleamed in the sun and flowers
bloomed in profusion in a series of well-tended beds. Here the
smell of the sea was tempered by their fragrance . . . and with the
faint scent of wild strawberries.

Although a half dozen gardeners could find employment on
grounds like these, Diana saw no sign of life as she made her way
up a flagstone walk and a set of stone steps that ended at a terrace-
sized front porch. She was relieved, she told herself. She did not
want to encounter a guard.

In an automatic gesture, she went to tug her jacket straight and smooth the folds of her skirt. The damp, gritty feel of the fabric had her looking down at herself in dismay. The exertion of the climb and the warmth of the day had plastered the dark red fabric to her bosom. Her skirt, already wet from the ride in a small, open boat, had acquired a layer of salt spray and sand. She lifted a hand to her hair and discovered that her pins had come loose again, allowing damp tendrils to escape what had once been a neat coil at her nape. A shipwreck survivor would probably look more presentable.

Diana made what repairs she could, squared her shoulders, and reached for the ornate lion's-head knocker at the center of the front door. Made of solid brass, it appeared to be growling a warning. Diana had to summon considerable willpower and no small amount of muscle in order to lift the ominous-looking thing. It felt cold to the touch and fell back onto the wood with a resounding thump.

Nothing happened.

She repeated the effort several times, stopping in between to listen for any hint of activity within the house. The thickness of the oak masked any footfalls. She tried turning the knob but the door was locked.

Reluctant to leave cover, she lingered on the porch, but she knew she'd have to venture out of its shelter sooner or later. With extreme caution, alert for any sound that might indicate the presence of armed men, Diana made her way around the side of the house. She kept as close to the wall as she could, given the presence of a variety of flowering bushes.

At first she heard nothing but a gentle breeze ruffling the leaves and the occasional raucous call of a gull, but as she approached the rear of the mansion, she became aware of an odd ringing sound. Metal on metal, she thought, and her imagination called up the image of a hammer and anvil. Puzzled, she stopped at the corner of the house. Uncertain what she would find, Diana first glanced over her shoulder, then edged forward until she could peer beyond the end of the shrubbery.

She gasped at the sight that met her startled gaze. That clashing sound was steel striking steel. Two men armed with rapiers thrust and parried their way across an expanse of green lawn. Blinding sunlight glanced off their blades, making it difficult for her to see exactly what was happening, but the little she could make out filled her with a terrible fear. One of the men was Ben, and as she watched he stumbled and lost his grip on his weapon.

"I've got you now, Northcote!" the other combatant cried. With deadly intent, the gleaming length of steel in his hand descended towards Ben's chest.

"No!" Diana screamed.

Ben's opponent pulled back, whirling around to stare at her.

Diana ran full tilt across the grass, reaching him before he could resume his attack. Without stopping to think of the danger to herself, she swung her gripsack at him, striking him on the shoulder. He swore at her and dropped his weapon. Her second blow caught him on the side of the head, causing him to fall to his knees. She followed up with a kick, wincing in pain when her toe connected with his chest.

"Diana! Enough!" Ben's strong arms caught her about the waist, hauling her away from the other man. "Are you all right, Graham?"

Diana twisted her head around until she could see Ben's face. His eyes gleamed. His mustache trembled and his lips twitched. He was trying very hard not to *laugh*!

With dawning dismay, Diana realized she had misinterpreted what she had seen. Relief battled with chagrin. Ben had been in no danger. And she had just struck down his oldest friend. Embarrassment engulfed her, heating her cheeks, but she forced herself to face Graham Somener.

He'd retrieved his rapier and staggered to his feet. Clutching the side of his head with one hand, he raised the blade with the other, fully prepared to use it to defend himself. A ferocious expression distorted his face. Suddenly terrified, Diana took shelter behind Ben's reassuring bulk. The breath backing up in her throat made speech impossible.

Ben spoke sharply: "Graham, enough!"

The enraged expression vanished, but just to be on the safe side, Ben reached out and confiscated the fencing foil. Only then did Diana realize that she'd never been in any real danger. Nor had he. The point of the weapon was blunted with a leather button.

Even knowing she was safe, Diana's insides quivered like freshly unmolded gelatin. Her hands trembled, too, and in a moment she feared she'd be shaking all over. To avoid that ignominious fate, she focused on the man she'd attacked.

Like Ben, Somener was tall, well-built, and dark haired. Unlike Ben, he wore fencing garb, a salient fact she'd failed to notice in her earlier agitation. He was dressed in low leather shoes, snugly tailored trousers, and a short jacket with a standing collar and buttons down the side. The fabric was pale gray and heavy. Neither man, however, wore a face mask. If they had, Diana thought, she'd have realized at once that they were engaged in a bout with épées and not trying to kill each other.

"This is my fiancée, Diana Spaulding, Graham. I'd consider it a personal favor if you did not skewer her."

Somener had himself under control, but his icy expression was anything but conciliatory. Like Ben, he had a beard and mustache, but where Ben kept his neatly trimmed, Somener had clearly not visited a barber in some time. The result was an unkempt thicket that made him look less than civilized.

"It is a pleasure to meet you, Mr. Somener," Diana said. Her voice came out as a tremulous squeak.

"How did you get to Keep Island?" Somener demanded. "I told Captain Cobb no visitors. And the guard—"

"Didn't see me," Diana interrupted. She swallowed convulsively. This was not how she'd imagined her reunion with Ben

would go, or her first meeting with the wealthy recluse, Graham
Somener. "Your captain did his job." Gradually, her voice steadied. "I found alternate transportation. A boy with a small sailboat.
I'm sorry to invade your privacy by coming here unannounced
and uninvited, but it was imperative that I speak to Ben."

Ben's amusement vanished. "Is everyone all right? Aaron?
My—"

She hastened to reassure him. "No one is hurt or ill." She
glanced at Somener, who was still regarding her with intense dislike and considerable suspicion. "May we speak in private? The
matter is . . . personal."

"This is Graham's house, his island," Ben reminded her.

"Go wherever you want," Somener snarled. "I need to have
a word with my worthless excuse for a watchman." The guard,
looking astonished to see Diana, had just appeared at the edge of
the lawn.

"The parlor is quite pleasant," Ben suggested. "Or the library."
He seemed to notice her dishevelment for the first time. "Or perhaps you would like the opportunity to freshen up?"

"Why are there armed guards?" she hissed at him.

"It's a long story, but I can promise that no one will shoot
you. Come inside, Diana. Put yourself to rights while I change
my shirt and find my jacket. Then we can discuss why you came
here."

A short time later, Ben watched Diana move away from the
porch. From his window he had a bird's eye view of more than
half the island. She was easy to track as she retreated—a bright
spot of red moving without much sense of direction through a
landscape of artfully arranged shrubs and flowers. If she kept going, she'd probably end up on the promontory.

Behind him he heard Graham stomp into the room. "Why is
she here?" he demanded.

"I won't know that until I talk to her."

Graham came up beside him, his glower fading slightly as he stared at the rapidly moving female figure below. "Good-looking woman." He sounded grudging.

"Yes." Beautiful, to Ben's mind, with her wide-spaced blue eyes and her soft skin and that glorious mahogany-colored hair. But he loved her mind as well, and that quick, unpredictable, impetuous streak that so often led her into trouble.

"Can you control her?"

"Yes."

It was simpler to reassure Graham and deal with Diana later, but Ben wished he'd never told his friend that Diana was employed by the *Independent Intelligencer*. The New York City scandal sheet had a bad reputation, well deserved in Ben's opinion. He'd felt he should warn Graham that although Diana had given up reporting on theatrical gossip and on crime, she now intended to focus on interviews.

It was her plan to write about Maine's nationally-known summer residents, calling her column "Profiles of the Rich and Famous." Even though Graham lived on Keep Island year round, Diana meant to make an exception in his case. Ben had seen the gleam in her eyes when he'd put Graham's name on the list of wedding guests and identified him as the architect who had designed several important buildings in Boston. He had not told her why Graham had given up his career.

"Damnation!" Graham swore. "It only needed this!"

"Settle down. She's not going to cause trouble."

Graham's face was a study in conflict. He wanted to believe Ben but he'd learned the hard way not to trust reporters.

At least his self-control was better, Ben thought. That uncertain temper flared quickly, but he had given himself healthy outlets to vent the anger. Swearing aloud, even in the presence of ladies, was one. Fencing was another, although he rarely found an opponent here on the island. A pity Diana had interrupted the bout, but all in all Ben was relieved by the way Graham had reacted. Only for a moment had he been dangerous.

"We'll both leave this afternoon," Ben promised as he finished tying his cravat. "My three patients have recovered well. In fact, they are clamoring to go back to work."

"How much will you tell her?"

"All of it."

"Are you mad?"

Ben shrugged into his jacket. "Would you prefer she investigate on her own? Perhaps draw false conclusions?"

"I want her off my island, and I don't want anyone else coming here, especially reporters."

"I'll handle it," Ben promised.

Ten minutes later, he located Diana just where he'd thought she'd be—on the promontory, staring out at the water. He paused to appreciate the view, but not the same one he'd so often admired. Today he only had eyes for Diana. The brine-scented breeze caught at her glorious red-brown hair, freeing several thick strands from the knot she'd tried to force them into. Wisely, she'd removed her hat before it could blow away. She held it in one hand and shaded her eyes with the other.

"I overreacted," she said when he reached her side.

"You have a gift for understatement."

"I saw a man, a stranger, coming at you with a weapon. I'd just caught a glimpse of another man armed with a gun and clearly on patrol. What was I supposed to think?"

The catch in her voice had him clasping her to him and holding her tight. He spoke to the top of her head, since she seemed fascinated by the middle button on his coat. "Diana, what's wrong? Why did you come here?"

"I was concerned about you. Your mother is too. And my mother—well, never mind what she's been saying."

"You've had to cope with both of them without me. I'm sorry for that."

"And I didn't sleep a wink last night." She made a strangled sound. "What pitiful excuses! You must be thoroughly put out with me. I realize it was unpardonably rude of me to show up here unannounced, but you vanished without a trace, which was even more inconsiderate. Was it too much trouble to write to me once you got here? I've been worried sick. And then I thought he was trying to kill you. I—"

"But I did," he protested. "I wrote to you on Tuesday, after I arrived here and realized my services as a doctor would be needed for several days."

"I received no letter."

"It should have reached you on Wednesday." She looked skeptical but said nothing. "I wrote, Diana. I did. Why would I want to cause you unnecessary worry?" *Or risk you'd come looking for me?*

"And what," she asked in a chilly voice, "was so important that it took you away from your regular patients. It can't have been Graham Somener who was sick. Your friend looks the picture of health."

"It wasn't Graham who was ill."

He hesitated, not because he didn't trust her with his friend's secrets, but because he was wondering what had happened to that letter.

"Well?" Diana prompted. "Who is your patient? What's wrong with him?"

He'd value her opinion, Ben realized. She'd give them a fresh perspective on the situation. "Not him. Them. The letter I sent you didn't give any specifics. I didn't want you involved in this. I didn't think you'd want to be."

"Explain."

"Do you remember what you said to me a little over three weeks ago? About not wanting anything more to do with crime?" She nodded. "I believe there has been a crime committed here, Diana. A particularly insidious one, if I am correct in my assumptions."

She did not look surprised. "Go on."

"There is an archaeological excavation on the island. You can see where they are working from there." He gestured towards the promontory. "Come and have a look."

Diana hesitated, then moved closer to the railing, wincing as she put weight on her right foot.

He could have predicted she'd balk at first. He knew she did not like heights. But the expression of pain was both unexpected and alarming. "What's wrong?" He came up beside her, taking her elbow to guide her to a nearby boulder the right height for sitting.

Even through her jacket and the blouse beneath, he felt her muscles tense when he touched her. As soon as she sat down, she jerked her arm free.

"It's nothing," she insisted.

"Did you fall?"

Her color deepened. Huffing out a breath, avoiding his eyes, she mumbled her answer. "When I kicked your friend, I bruised my toe."

Fighting a smile, he risked sitting beside her. He resisted the urge to lift her injured foot onto his lap and massage it for her. He contented himself with inhaling *Eau de Gardenia*.

Her gaze drifted back to the promontory. "Tell me about the excavation and how it is connected to crime. What are they looking for? Indian relics?"

"An archaeologist friend of Graham's is searching for evidence of an early settlement and a long-ago shipwreck."

The water looked deceptively peaceful, a pretty picture. But Ben had seen it during a fierce gale. On this side of the island there were hidden ledges everywhere.

"Only days after the work began, several of the archaeologists began to complain of dizziness and nausea. All of them were lethargic. One suffered bouts of unconsciousness. Another couldn't stop vomiting."

"That's why Graham sent for you."

Ben nodded, even though it was not a question.

"What illness afflicted them?" She sat very still, but tension radiated from her as she waited for his answer.

"Graham assumed it was bad meat or shellfish. Or tinned food that had gone off. He asked me to come in secret because he shies away from publicity." Ben didn't mention the curse on the island. It was too preposterous and he knew the real reason Graham was so leery of wild rumors.

"And was it something they had eaten?"

"In a way. They'd been systematically dosed with morphine, most likely added to their food. They were poisoned, Diana. If Graham hadn't sent for me when he did, they might all be dead by now."

CHAPTER THREE

જીભ

Ben's announcement left Diana uncharacteristically speechless. She tried to think how this might fit in with what Mr. Palmer had told her, but she could make no sense of it.

While she'd brushed her clothes, washed her hands and face, and repinned her hair, she'd debated whether or not to tell Ben what the detective had said. She hadn't yet decided what to do when she'd ventured back outside. She'd been hoping a dose of fresh air would clear her head . . . and she'd wanted to avoid running into Graham Somener again.

She'd been certain Ben would find her wherever she wandered, as he had. Now, however, she had to wonder if she had been wise to leave the safety of the house.

"Are you saying that someone attempted to murder those men?"

"I believe that is the case, yes. I am completely certain of my diagnosis," he added in a tired voice, "but over the last few days Graham has convinced himself that I must be mistaken. He didn't want to believe me to begin with, since we could discover no reason why anyone would want to kill those men, and since nothing else has happened . . . ."

"And yet he posted guards."

"A compromise. I wanted him to send for the sheriff. He agreed to ban visitors from the island and to assign two of the groundskeepers he employs as watchmen." He sent a wry grimace in her direction. "Apparently more stringent measures are needed. If you managed to land on Keep Island unseen, making no effort to hide your presence, then any number of strangers could have arrived in secret before you did and even now be lurking in the bushes."

She placed one hand on his arm and waited until he met her questioning gaze. "Perhaps the poisoning had more to do with Mr. Somener than with the victims."

"Meaning?"

"A few years ago, your friend was responsible for the loss of innocent lives." Diana watched his face carefully for a reaction, but Ben merely looked sad.

"That was a great tragedy, but not Graham's fault. There were no charges brought. Ever since, he has lived very quietly here and avoided calling attention to himself, which is precisely why he asked for my assistance. He didn't want any foolish rumors to get started."

"Too late for that."

"What have you heard?"

Diana hesitated, but she saw no alternative to telling him about the visit from Justus Palmer. As briefly as possible, leaving out Maggie's comments and her own strange feeling that there was something not quite right about the man, she repeated what Palmer had said.

"Illegal activities?" Ben's look of astonishment was almost comical. "Absurd."

"You're certain? You haven't seen him in some time, and he does seem to have a penchant for secrecy."

"Only because he was hounded by the press over that building collapse. And because he doesn't want wild rumors about the archaeological excavation to attract treasure hunters."

"Is there a chance of treasure?" Her interest piqued, Diana shifted on the boulder that served them as a bench until she could see Ben's face more clearly.

"Doubtful. The archaeologists are seeking evidence of an early settlement on the island. But perhaps you should hear about that from the horse's mouth."

She sent him a searching look. "I'd like that. Especially since I gather the archaeologist is a woman."

"How did you—ah, you talked to the captain of the *Miss Min*."

She nodded.

"Miss Serena Dunbar. A most unusual woman. You'll no doubt find her fascinating. You'll meet her shortly. Graham likes to dine promptly at one."

"I'm not sure—"

"He won't bite," Ben promised, "and we can't leave here until the *Miss Min* returns at around four. You'll be half starved if you don't eat before then."

"I'm half starved now." It was just past noon and she hadn't eaten since early morning.

"Then Graham will have to feed you. First, though, I need to check on my patients one last time. I set up a temporary infirmary in the old nursery on the top floor of the house. Would you like to accompany me?"

Diana felt as if a great weight had been lifted off her heart. He'd said *they* could leave. He was coming with her. Even better, he hadn't balked at answering her questions. Without hesitation this time, she went with him into Graham Somener's mansion.

"You're certain none of these men has an enemy who'd try to kill him?" she asked, as they stepped into the foyer. Fresh flowers of a variety she did not recognize filled vases in the corners and on a small table, suffusing the space with a sweet, pungent scent.

"I've questioned them thoroughly. They had no information

to offer. They saw no strangers, noticed no one tampering with their provisions, have no enemies they know of. They just fell ill."

"I am surprised they're willing to go back to work after what happened." She followed him into a long hallway hung with portraits and lined with curio cabinets.

"They'll be eating in the house from now on, and sleeping indoors, too. They should be safe enough."

"Unless the cook is the one who poisoned them."

He chuckled at that and abruptly changed course. Instead of heading upstairs, he led her towards the back of the house. "I think you should meet Mrs. Monroe," he told her. "She's both housekeeper and cook here and has been for years. She's devoted to the Somener family."

Prudence Monroe was a beanpole of a woman somewhere in her middle years. She was clearly accustomed to being in charge in the kitchen and looked with disfavor upon intruders. "What do you want, Mr. Ben? I've got work to do."

"Don't let us stop you, Mrs. Monroe. I simply wanted you to meet the lady I'm about to marry."

Mrs. Monroe gave a sniff and continued rolling out the dough for a pie. "About time you got married. Mr. Graham, too, though I can't say I like the way the wind blows in that quarter."

The entire kitchen smelled of cinnamon and apples and of the freshly baked rolls cooling on a rack. Predictably, Diana's stomach growled.

Ben chuckled. "If you're very polite to Mrs. Monroe, Diana, I am sure she will offer you a ham sandwich from the leftovers of last night's meal."

"You know where the fixings are, Mr. Ben," Mrs. Monroe told him. "I'm in the middle of making dessert, and you know how fussy Mr. Graham is if his dinner's late."

While Ben set about slicing bread and ham, Diana seized the opportunity to talk to the cook. "Do you know anything about what happened to those archaeologists?"

"Young Ben here says it was morphine. I ask you, what's the world coming to? In my day, no one had even heard of such a thing." She slammed the rolling pin down on the counter and seized the crust, slapping it into a tin pan. With strong, expert fingers, she pressed the dough into shape.

"Are you concerned for your own safety?" Diana asked.

"Why should I be? No one wants to hurt me." She dumped a bowl full of apple slices, already sugared and dotted with cinnamon, into the pie pan and picked up the rolling pin to prepare the top crust.

Ben handed Diana two slices of bread with a slab of ham between them. She bit hungrily into the sandwich while continuing to contemplate Mrs. Monroe. The woman had a dangerous gleam in her eyes, and Diana didn't like the look of that rolling pin. It was heavy—not wood but marble—and would pack quite a wallop. As she took another bite, she put a little more distance between herself and the cook. Then she posed another question.

"Do you know something unfavorable about Miss Dunbar, Mrs. Monroe? I get the feeling you don't approve of her being here."

"Not my place to say."

Ben slanted a warning glance at Diana that prompted her to keep silent and wait. After a moment, Mrs. Monroe started talking.

"She used to come here when she was a little girl. Worse than the boys, she was. Always the little troublemaker."

"Were her parents friends of Graham's parents?" Ben asked.

"Her mother was friends with Miss Min. It was when Miss Min lived here, after old Mr. Jedediah died, that Serena Dunbar used to come visit."

"Miss Min?" Diana asked.

"Minnie Somener, Graham's aunt," Ben supplied. "And yes, the mailboat was named in her honor."

"She was christened Minerva," Mrs. Monroe informed them. "Fancy name. She never did like it much. Often said she wished she'd been named after her mother." She chuckled. "Born too late for that. Some years before Miss Min was more than a gleam in old Jed Somener's eye, his wife stood godmother to *my* mother. Mama ended up being christened Susan and Miss Min, she got stuck with Minerva."

Diana didn't quite understand why more than one baby couldn't have been given the same name, but if Susan Somener had chosen Minerva for her own child, she had probably had a reason. Perhaps she'd had an interest in mythology. "Minerva is another name for Athena," she said aloud, "the goddess said to embody wisdom, reason, and purity."

Ben looked thoughtful. "I only met Min Somener a few times. I can't say if she embodied those virtues or not."

Slapping the top crust onto her pie, Mrs. Monroe picked up a knife. "Sometimes yes. Sometimes no. She did like to read them old books. Died about ten years back." She made a series of decorative cuts. "Don't you have patients to tend to?"

Taking the hint, and what was left of Diana's sandwich, they left the kitchen. The back stairs were close by, but so narrow that they had to climb single file. "Had you met Miss Dunbar before?" she asked his ascending back.

Ben took his time about replying. "Till now she was never here at the same time I was."

"Did you come here often?" With two steep flights of stairs behind them, Diana paused on the landing to catch her breath.

"A fair amount. Graham's mother and mine were distant cousins, and he and I are close in age." He reached the top floor and waited for her, then indicated a closed door. "I'm about to give these men a clean bill of health. They've been chomping at the bit to get back to work."

Before he could knock, the sound of raised voices reached Diana from the other side. "You're making a mistake!" a man shouted.

"I know what I'm doing!" The second voice was softer but sounded just as angry.

Ben opened the door to reveal two men engaged in a game of cards on one side of the room and a pair of combatants in the opposite corner. At first Diana thought they were also male. Then she realized that one was a woman wearing masculine attire.

Diana was accustomed to seeing females dressed in a variety of split skirts. The popularity of rational dress had grown enormously in the last few years. But this woman—Miss Dunbar, Diana presumed—wore men's trousers, high boots, and a loose shirt. The first garment clearly defined her lower limbs, stretching the bounds of propriety by emphasizing a lush feminine figure.

The woman turned to glare at them, revealing an arresting face surrounded by thick, sun-streaked brown hair braided and wound in a style that was as flattering as it was unusual. She appeared to be about Diana's age.

"May I present Miss Serena Dunbar," Ben said.

Tension radiating off her like heat from a fire, Miss Dunbar ignored him. She flounced off to the other end of the long room to stare out a window.

With a shrug, as if her rude behavior did not surprise him, Ben turned his attention to the card players. "George Amity," he said.

Grizzled and gnome-like, the signs of arthritis already plain in his fingers, Amity nodded in a friendly fashion.

"Paul Carstairs."

Carstairs set down a bottle of Moxie Nerve Food he'd been sipping from and regarded Diana with suspicion. He wasn't much older than she was, but to judge by the loose folds of skin in his face and neck and the excess material in the trousers held up by braces, he'd recently lost a good deal of weight.

"And this is Frank Ennis." Ben indicated the man who'd been arguing with Miss Dunbar. "Gentlemen and Miss Dunbar, may I present my fiancée, Mrs. Diana Spaulding."

"Charmed," Ennis said, bending over Diana's hand. His pallor was the only thing left to indicate that he had been deathly ill. He was a man in his prime, without an ounce of excess fat on his sinewy frame. Yet for all his appearance of familiarity with manual labor, he had the dreamy, inward-looking eyes of a scholar . . . or a poet.

In better control of herself for her stint at the window, Miss Dunbar advanced on Ben. "Are my men fit to resume their duties?"

"I'd prefer that they rest for one more day."

A chorus of protests drowned out the last word. Frank Ennis's voice was loudest. "I'm ready to make that dive. More than ready."

"Dive?" Interest piqued, Diana looked to Ennis for clarification.

"We were preparing to explore underwater the day we fell ill. It is perfect weather today. I want to get on with it."

Diana studied each face in turn. George Amity seemed ambivalent, but the others wore remarkably similar expressions of stubborn determination.

Ben reached for his stethoscope. "No one is going to do anything until I have examined each of you men one more time. Ladies, will you wait in the hall?"

∞

"Where is Miss Dunbar?" Graham Somener glared at the empty place at table. "She rarely misses a meal, and she is partial to corn chowder."

From the look on Diana's face as she tasted a spoonful, Ben concluded that she was also partial to the dish. He trusted she'd do justice to the entire meal, in spite of the ham sandwich she'd eaten earlier. His Diana had a healthy appetite.

Leaving his own food untasted, Ben answered Graham's question. "Miss Dunbar is preparing for Mr. Ennis's dive."

She hadn't waited to hear his verdict. Abandoning Diana in the upstairs hallway without a word, she'd gone to the shed where the diving equipment was stored and begun to ready her equipment. Ben had tracked her there to confirm that Frank Ennis was healthy enough to go back to work.

"That confounded shipwreck." Graham slathered butter on a roll with a heavy hand.

"Do a great many ships come to grief along this coast?" Diana asked.

With obvious effort, Graham forced himself to be sociable. "Not so many since the lighthouses were built, although the *City of Portland* sank off Monroe's Island just four years back. And there was a very famous shipwreck south of here during colonial times, the *Angel Gabriel*."

Inevitably, Graham's love of history overcame his aversion to talking to a journalist. "An ancestor of mine was aboard the *Angel Gabriel*," he told Diana. "Fortunately the ship was close to shore when a hurricane hit. Most of the passengers survived, although they lost all their worldly goods. In 1635, that was."

"What is it Miss Dunbar is looking for?" Diana asked.

"Do you know much about early explorations in this part of the world?"

"Not a great deal, no."

"Fishing boats have been coming to these shores for centuries," Graham said. "They kept the best grounds secret, of course, so the competition wouldn't know where to find them. Other ships came, too. Explorers. Settlers. It is Miss Dunbar's belief that one of these ships was wrecked on the rocks off Keep Island during a long-ago storm. That's what she's looking for—proof that there were survivors and that they settled here. She hopes to find remains of their buildings, perhaps even artifacts from the ship itself."

"Would there be anything left of a vessel that sank more than a few decades ago? Surely any wooden parts that weren't dashed to bits against the rocks would have been dispersed by the tide or would have disintegrated over the years from sheer age."

"The water here is deep and cold. Those are preservative properties. If the ship sank in mud or sand, protecting it from being washed out to sea, then it is possible there are remnants left. Enough to identify. More likely, of course, is that she will find some trace left on land by the survivors of the shipwreck. That is why the present excavation centers on a small cove below the promontory. Since they have diving equipment, however, it only makes sense to take advantage of good weather to explore underwater."

"How frustrating it must have been to have to postpone the dive."

"I doubt that a few days delay did any harm. Miss Dunbar's ship has already been down there for four hundred and eighty seven years."

Ben smiled as Diana blinked in surprise. She'd assumed, as he had at first, that Miss Dunbar was looking for a colonial settlement, which would have meant a place established some *two* hundred and fifty years ago.

"Four hun—"

Graham Somener chuckled at her amazement. "Yes, Mrs. Spaulding. You heard correctly. The ship Miss Dunbar is looking for went down in the year of our Lord 1401—almost a hundred years before Columbus 'discovered' America."

"And you think something could have survived?"

"Miss Dunbar does." He shrugged. "Enough to be recognizable as part of a ship. There might even be bits of the cargo left. As I understand it, if the ship hit one of the ledges that surrounds this island and sank, it would have settled either on the ledge, in which case the remains were quickly broken up and swept out into deeper waters, or to the bottom. If it came to rest in sand, there's a chance some of it has been preserved. It would have been covered up all this time, you see, and thus protected."

Diana's brow wrinkled in thought. "If only tiny bits of a ship-wreck are left, how will anyone be able to recognize them for what they are?"

"Ah, that is the purpose of Mr. Ennis and his diving suit."

As the meal progressed and Graham expanded upon his ex-planation, it occurred to Ben that his old friend had taken more than a passing interest in Miss Dunbar's quest. He was not only remarkably well informed about the shipwreck, but about deep sea divers and their gear, as well. Well, why not? Graham had likely been the one who'd paid for it all.

"Everything is sealed," Graham assured Diana, "so there is no risk of the suit filling up with water. In addition, these suits have a double security system. Air comes in by way of a hose that is close to the right ear and has a manually adjustable valve. A second hose goes straight to the mouth. Air escapes from a non-return valve on the helmet. That is necessary, you see, to get rid of stale or excess air."

"I think I will need to examine an actual helmet to understand what you mean," Diana admitted. "It sounds very complicated."

"Much less so than earlier models. In the old days, helmet divers were hindered by lines and hoses and could move only with difficulty. To make things worse, their passage would stir up a cloud of muddy water, limiting visibility. In the best of condi-tions, if a diver wanted to take a closer look at something, he'd only dare lower his face glass for a moment. There was great dan-ger otherwise of accidentally inflating his suit, which would blow him to the surface and likely kill him."

"A dangerous business, then."

"Indeed, and that wasn't the only risk. If the anchor dragged on the tender carrying the air pump, the diver was as good as dead."

"Fascinating." Diana shifted eager eyes to Ben. "Will we have time before we leave to watch the start of the dive?"

He glanced at the ormolu clock on the sideboard. "We should be able to see a bit of the action, but then we'll need to head back to the wharf to watch for the *Miss Min.*"

Graham put down his fork with a clatter. "You *did* make her promise not to speak of any of this, or write about it?"

The surprised look on Diana's face answered him before Ben could explain himself. "Ben?" she whispered, seeing the flash of temper in Graham's eyes.

"Settle down, both of you. Diana's not here to expose any secrets."

"But if Miss Dunbar finds what she's looking for, it will cause a sensation. Surely she'll want credit for her discoveries. I—"

Graham rose to his feet so abruptly that his chair toppled over backwards. "You'll not write one word. I forbid it."

"If it concerns the excavation, it will not be up to you." Cheeks flaming, Diana stood, too. She clutched her napkin so tightly that her knuckles shone whiter than the linen.

"Calm down!" Ben shouted.

Both parties jumped at the crack of his voice.

Graham drew in a deep, steadying breath. "I'm afraid you won't be able to watch the dive, after all. There won't be room in the rowing boats to take you around to the cove."

"We can get there by way of the promontory path," Ben countered, annoyed by the sudden renewal of his old friend's mistrust of Diana. "She's not going to betray any confidences, Graham. You have my word on it."

Diana said nothing.

Graham took several deep breaths, calmed down and, finally, nodded assent. "That's a difficult descent for a lady, but if you don't mind the climb, I suppose it will be alright for you to watch."

Only Ben noticed the tight compression of Diana's lips before she accepted Graham's grudging invitation. "I've had quite enough of small boats for one day," she told him. "I will be glad of a brisk walk."

Courageous or foolhardy? Ben was never quite sure which word best described his fiancée. What he did know was that Diana Spaulding had enough determination to keep her fear of heights at bay. Because she'd said she would, she'd climb down the steep, narrow path that led from cliff top to beach and utter not a single complaint along the way.

"Difficult" did not begin to describe their descent, Diana thought. Safe at the foot of the promontory at the seaward end of the island, she looked back the way they had come and shuddered. A rock-strewn goat path twisted and bumped its way upward. If she had not had Ben's arm to hang on to, she was certain she'd never have kept her feet. Worse, she'd had to keep her eyes open the whole way. Twice she'd been unable to repress the urge to look down. Both times the dizzying, stomach-wrenching aftermath had stopped her in her tracks for several long minutes while she'd fought to regain her courage and continue.

Now she made a production of straightening the divided skirt of sturdy blue serge that she'd changed into before they'd set out. The action did little to hide her trembling hands but Ben, gentleman that he was, pretended not to notice.

"The boats are just arriving," he remarked. "We've plenty of time before they are ready for the dive."

She pasted a bright smile on her face and once more took his arm. "Onward then."

"A moment first. I need your promise, Diana. No word of Miss Dunbar's explorations must leak to the press. Nor can you publish anything about Graham."

"I will write nothing without their permission," she temporized.

Ben considered her answer carefully, searching her face, before he nodded his assent and started walking towards the landing site.

She was not on ground that was either level or solid, since the sand shifted with every step and was littered with rocks besides, but it was easier going than on that wretched path. As they picked their way along she studied her surroundings, paying particular attention to details that might interest her readers. She was convinced that she'd eventually write about Serena Dunbar's archaeological expedition. To create a sense of being on the scene, she'd have to report sounds and smells and textures as well as a factual description of what she saw.

"What is that?" she asked Ben, pointing to a bird she did not recognize.

"Osprey. There is a colony of them on the island. Also gulls, cormorants, herons, ducks, and loons."

"I'm well aware there are gulls." Their plaintive, annoying cries were as constant a part of the background on Keep Island as the sound of waves lapping against the shore. An even more unpleasant racket reached her ears as they advanced upon the tents set up in the cove.

"Pigeon hawk," Ben answered, before she could ask. "Nasty birds. They deplete the songbird population."

Underfoot, the way continued to be rough and rocky—no white sand beaches on this part of the coast. In fact, the ragged shoreline was littered with large, irregularly shaped rocks, worn down by water and wind but far from smooth.

She sniffed cautiously. Brine. Seaweed. And the distinctive odor of mud flats. She could not tell if the tide was coming in or going out but to judge by the high-water line, they were in no danger of being cut off and drowned.

"Look there." Ben stopped suddenly to indicate a point of land that curved back upon itself like a sheltering arm to create the small cove.

"What am I supposed to see?" Nothing about the rather bleak bit of beach and the low, jagged cliff above seemed unusual to her.

"See that dark, irregular circle? That's the entrance to the cave Graham and I played pirate in as boys."

The opening was all but invisible until Diana stared directly at it. Even after she located the spot, she could see no way to reach it. "Wasn't that a dangerous place for young boys? How on earth did you get up there?"

He directed her gaze to a large boulder at the base of the cliff. "The path begins just behind that rock and winds out towards the point and up. At high tide, of course, it is entirely submerged."

"Does the inside of the cave flood?"

"We speculated that the back portion stayed dry, but we were never foolish enough to allow ourselves to be trapped inside in order to find out." He grinned at her. "Those were good days. Carefree days. Graham's Aunt Min kept to herself and let us do as we wished. She said we couldn't get lost, this being an island and all, and that we'd turn up when we got hungry."

"In her place I'd have been afraid you'd drown, or fall off a cliff."

"Sheer luck we didn't, I imagine. I'm a good swimmer, though. So is Graham."

Diana shivered. "I never learned how." A very good reason, she thought, to stay out of sea caves.

Continuing on towards the excavation, Ben assisted Diana over the uneven terrain by keeping a reassuring grip on her arm. As they drew closer, she could see that two large rowing boats had been pulled up onto the shore. Quite a number of people stood clustered around them. Graham Somener and Miss Dunbar were there, and Ennis, Carstairs, and Amity, but so were Mrs. Monroe and two men Diana did not recognize, although she thought one of them might be the guard she'd seen earlier.

"Who are they?" she whispered to Ben.

"The groundskeepers Graham temporarily reassigned as watchmen. The fellow with the fiery red mustache is MacDougall. The other is named Landrigan."

The latter *was* the guard from the cliff. He was younger than Diana had thought, his face clean-shaven. He kept a wary distance from his employer and further betrayed his uneasiness by repeatedly adjusting the fit of his checked cap. The second time he shifted position she saw that he still had his rifle with him.

By the time Diana and Ben came abreast of the group, Miss Dunbar and Mr. Ennis had moved a little apart from the rest. They were speaking in low voices, but from his rigid stance and her flushed face, Diana could tell that the exchange of words was heated. As she watched, Ennis put his hand on the lady archaeologist's upper arm. Miss Dunbar froze, her eyes locked with his and the tension between them was suddenly so palpable, and so charged with frustration, that Diana felt her own face warm.

In the moment before Miss Dunbar pulled free and stalked off, Diana was certain Frank Ennis was about to haul his employer into his arms and kiss her. She shook off the fancy when Miss Dunbar reached Graham Somener's side and tucked her arm through his in a familiar manner.

"Would you care to see our camp, Mrs. Spaulding?"

Diana jumped.

It was Frank Ennis who had spoken. He'd come up close beside her while she'd been staring at Miss Dunbar. He offered her his arm, pointedly ignoring his employer. She pretended to take no notice of him, either.

Diana cleared her throat. "If you have time, I would very much enjoy a tour."

"There's not a great deal to see. We hadn't been here long before we fell ill."

"Lead on then," Diana invited, and she and Ben followed the archaeologist up an incline into a more sheltered area well above the high tide line.

Even in bright sunlight, the place was chill and damp. Diana could not imagine why anyone would prefer camping out to living in the mansion. As for the excavation itself, there was indeed very little evidence of archaeological activity.

"Sand and bedrock," Ben said in a low voice. "Not much to dig in."

But the area had been marked off with posts and criss-crossed with cord, and off to one side Diana could see what looked like a giant sifter made of wood and wire mesh.

"This is our work area," Ennis said, ushering them into one of the tents. It had been furnished with tables and shelves but at present seemed to be in use only to store equipment—trowels, brushes, and other implements Diana could not identify.

The second tent provided living quarters and contained three cots and case upon case of food. Two crates, one open and one still nailed shut, were marked with the distinctive brand name "Moxie Nerve Food."

"Those belong to Paul Carstairs," Ennis said, seeing the direction of her gaze, "although he's talked me into drinking a bottle once or twice. Claims it's good for digestion, fatigue, insomnia, and whatever else ails you." He grimaced at the memory. "To tell you the truth, when we first got sick, I was sure it was the Moxie that had poisoned us!"

Diana grinned back at him. She'd once tried a sip of the carbonated beverage herself. That had been more than enough of the horrible stuff. It had a bitter taste appropriate to the medicine it claimed to be.

"Why does he have so much of it?" she asked.

"Says it affords him more relief than anything the doctors gave him after the accident." At her questioning look, he added, "He took a bad fall on his last expedition."

"Frank!" Miss Dunbar's voice, sharp and impatient, reached them from the other side of the tent flap. "If you're going to dive, let's do it now."

Ennis grinned. "She's like a broody mother hen about this excavation. Wants to keep it all safely tucked under her feathers so nobody can get at it."

He was already pulling off his outer garments as he left the tent. Beneath, he wore heavy woolen underwear. Diana managed not to blush, but she had an uncomfortable moment wondering just how much more he intended to strip away.

Apparently, the long johns would stay on. Over them, with Mr. Carstairs's help, Ennis donned a waterproof suit made of rubber. Next came a curved metal plate that covered his upper chest and back and had studs protruding from it.

Diana moved closer to get a better look.

"The opening for the head and neck is surrounded by a waterproof gasket," Mr. Carstairs said, seeing her interest.

He drew the upper edges of the suit up and over the breastplate, matching each hole in the suit to a stud. Then he placed metal straps over the studs and made them tight with wingnuts, sandwiching the suit between the breastplate and the straps, to create a waterproof joint. Lastly, he dropped a huge brass helmet into the opening of the breastplate and locked it in place with a one-eighth turn.

Two flexible hoses rose out of the helmet. Remembering what Mr. Somener had told them earlier, Diana studied them with considerable curiosity. One went in close to the right ear. The other was aimed directly at the mouth. She could see that the first hose was connected to the pump. The second, however, was not. It appeared to be a speaking tube of some sort.

"Safe as houses," Carstairs proclaimed, giving Ennis's helmet a smack. "Everything is sealed tight, so there's no risk of filling up with water. And as you can see, air comes in through a hose, supplied by a force pump, to circulate freely through both the helmet and the suit."

"How does the pump work?"

"It's hand operated, designed for use in warm, shallow water. It supplies air from the surface. Amity and I will man it from the tender while Ennis drops over the side of the boat and walks along the bottom, looking for any odd formations. Something shaped like the hull of a ship would be nice." He grinned, and a gold tooth glinted in the sun.

"I wouldn't call the water off this coast particularly warm," Ben remarked. "Or all that shallow, either."

Carstairs shrugged. "It's mid-June. The water temperature is no longer frigid. And soundings indicate it's no deeper than about forty feet out there where the ledge drops off."

Carstairs's confidence and the care she'd witnessed him take to outfit Ennis convinced Diana she should not worry overmuch about Mr. Ennis's safety. Carstairs seemed to know what he was doing, and she was frankly fascinated by the idea that they might find something underwater after all this time.

When the men were in the boat and on their way out to the spot where Mr. Ennis would go overboard, she turned to Miss Dunbar. "I am surprised you aren't in the tender with the others."

The archaeologist responded with an unfriendly glare, but Graham Somener seemed to have recovered from his fit of temper and become mellow once more. "There isn't room enough," he told her, "and since it is a two-man pump, it only made sense to leave the physical labor to Amity and Carstairs."

Diana didn't bother to ask about the underwater work. Just imagining it caused a delicate shudder to pass through her. How closed in it must feel in that suit. In Mr. Ennis's place, she knew it would be all she could do not to scream at the sound of the bolts fastening the helmet in place. No, she did not believe she would care to spend any time deep under water. She enjoyed new experiences but there was a line between adventurous and foolhardy.

"How does Mr. Ennis get back to the boat?" she asked Mr. Somener.

"He wears weights to take him down to the bottom and keep him there. When he's ready to surface, he removes them and floats up. The weights are secured by a separate line so they can be pulled up afterward."

"And he is looking for an unusual formation or shape on the bottom?"

"An anomaly of some sort, yes," Miss Dunbar interrupted, the desire to lecture on her area of expertise evidently overcoming her aversion to talking to a journalist. "Assuming anything *did* survive the shipwreck, that is the most likely place to find it. You see the way that bit juts out?" She indicated the curve of land that contained Ben's cave. "If the ship sank—during a storm perhaps—while anchored in that spot . . ."

Her voice trailed off. Frowning, she shaded her eyes, trying to get a better look at what her men were doing.

Ennis went over the side with a barely audible splash.

"Four hundred and eighty-seven years is a long time for anything to survive," Diana said.

Miss Dunbar shot an accusing glance in Mr. Somener's direction. "You *told* her?"

"If I hadn't, Ben would have."

"Was it a fishing vessel, Miss Dunbar? I suppose shipwrecked fishermen would have had to settle where they were wrecked, but would they have stayed on Keep Island long? Surely they'd have been able to build some sort of water craft, a raft at least, and reach the mainland."

"They were *not* fishermen. They came to these shores intending to stay. To colonize."

"So early?" If Diana remembered her lessons, the first settlers in America had been at Jamestown, and then at Plymouth in Massachusetts. She was fairly certain those settlements dated from the seventeenth century, not the fifteenth.

"If Europeans sailed this far in medieval times, they discovered not only rich fishing grounds but also unlimited forests. In the Old World, supplies of timber had been badly depleted by the fifteenth century. It only makes sense that some early entrepreneur would think of establishing a colony to harvest and export wood."

"You're saying they meant to found a trading center?"

"I believe so, yes. And I believe that the colonists who came here to Keep Island originally set out from Scotland. They wanted timber for shipbuilding, in particular for masts. No doubt they also wanted the advantage this would give them over their traditional enemy. That was England," Miss Dunbar added, sounding a bit condescending.

"How do you know all this? "

"Years of research." Miss Dunbar's brusque tone would have discouraged further questions from anyone less determined.

"Even if Mr. Ennis finds remnants of a ship, how can you possibly prove—?" Diana broke off when Miss Dunbar caught her forearm.

"There's a second boat out there."

"There are dozens of boats plying the waters of Penobscot Bay," Diana said.

"There!" She pointed. "At anchor. Carrying two men."

She was right. There was a small vessel a short distance from the tender, in an excellent position to observe the dive. Archaeological rivals? Reporters? Or simply curious passers-by?

Miss Dunbar swore under her breath.

"Looks like a dory," Graham Somener said. "Most likely fishermen from one of the neighboring islands." He did not sound unduly concerned about its presence.

"Whoever they are, they've no business here," Miss Dunbar complained.

"Shall I have MacDougall fire a warning shot?"

"Your sarcasm in not appreciated, Graham!" In her irritation, Miss Dunbar so far forgot formality as to use her host's given name. The slip, and the similar one Somener had made earlier, confirmed Diana's suspicions about the nature of their relationship.

Somener peered at the distant craft. "One of them has binoculars. I can see the sun reflecting off the glass. Damnation! There's no such thing as privacy anymore."

"We have a bigger problem," Ben said in a strained voice. "Something's wrong on the tender."

Diana shifted her gaze to the other boat. Carstairs and Amity had abandoned the pump. They were leaning over the side, tugging at the cables and hoses that led beneath the surface to Frank Ennis.

"Dear Lord!" Miss Dunbar whispered in a tone that made Diana's chest go tight with sudden fear.

Ben was already moving, stripping off his coat and shedding his shoes as he ran towards the shore. Graham Somener hesitated only a moment before following suit.

"Ben! No!"

Ignoring Diana, Ben plunged into the water and struck out for the tender. He was a good swimmer. He'd told her so himself. But that knowledge was not enough to keep Diana's heart out of her throat.

"It's already too late." Miss Dunbar's voice was thready and Diana had never seen such a ghastly color in a living face. "If the pump failed, they'll never get him back to the surface in time. He's already run out of air. Frank is already dead."

CHAPTER FOUR

෨ාcෟ

Heartsick, Diana could not take her eyes off the tender. She wanted to look away but couldn't. Her stomach clenched, and she gulped in air, imagining what it must be like to be trapped underwater, struggling to breathe. As she watched, beset by a terrible sense of helplessness, the swimmers finally reached the boat.

With what seemed to be excruciating slowness, Frank Ennis's limp body was hoisted aboard. Although the men worked frantically to get him out of the diving suit and Ben was clearly doing all he could to revive him, nothing had any effect. Well before they began their slow journey back to shore, it was obvious to Diana that Miss Dunbar had been right. Frank Ennis was dead.

"How could the pump fail as long as your men kept working it?"

"I don't know."

Miss Dunbar's voice was so flat that Diana turned to look at her. Her expression was equally devoid of emotion. She stood with her arms tightly pressed against her sides, her hands fisted, stiff and silent as a statue. Only the tracks of tears on her cheeks betrayed the depth of her feelings for the dead man.

Belatedly, Diana remembered that they were not the only

women on the beach. She glanced at Mrs. Monroe and found on her face all the shock and grief she'd expected to see on Miss Dunbar's. Diana hadn't thought Mrs. Monroe knew the archaeologists except in passing. They'd been camping out, doing their own cooking, until . . . until they'd been poisoned.

Diana frowned. Was it possible? Could this, somehow, be connected to the earlier attempt on the lives of Ennis, Carstairs, and Amity?

When Somener's two watchmen had pulled the tender up on shore, Diana picked her way towards it, careful to avoid sharp rocks, clumps of wet seaweed, and barnacles. Miss Dunbar pushed ahead of her. By the time Diana caught up, the other woman stood beside the boat, staring without visible emotion into the lifeless face of Frank Ennis.

"He's dead," Ben said. "Murdered."

The bald announcement did not surprise Diana. It only confirmed her worst fear. On almost everyone else, however, it had the effect of a firecracker in a church.

Miss Dunbar took a quick step back, hands raised as if to ward off a blow. Mrs. Monroe gasped. MacDougall went stiff as a poker, except for the quivering of his mustache. Landrigan started, then looked wildly about, as if he expected an ax-wielding madman to leap from behind the nearest boulder.

Only the men in the tender failed to react. Diana presumed that was because they'd already heard Ben's opinion on the cause of death.

Miss Dunbar recovered first. "What are you talking about?" Irritation brought bright spots of color into her cheeks. "He can't have been murdered. It was an accident. A tragic accident." Her voice broke on the last word.

It was not that Miss Dunbar did not have softer emotions, Diana decided. She was simply adept at hiding them.

"See for yourself." Ben indicated a section of the hose attached to Ennis's helmet.

Diana's eyes widened when she observed its condition. The once-smooth surface was now horribly corroded, pitted and broken to the point where water had been able to get in.

"I admit I'm no expert," Ben said, "but I don't need to be to see that this hose has been treated with a chemical—an acid of some sort that reacted to the salt water—causing it to eat into the hose. My best guess is that all seemed well until after Ennis reached bottom. Then the hose failed too quickly for him to do anything to save himself."

"Horrible," Mrs. Monroe whispered, turning away. Diana hadn't even realized she'd followed them down to the tender.

It *was* horrible, she thought. It was also part and parcel of the strange happenings on Keep Island. Graham Somener's request to his old friend had placed Ben smack in the middle of Somener's troubles.

"Did he say anything?" Diana asked Paul Carstairs. "Shout for help? Indicate he needed to be hauled up?"

"Nothing," Carstairs said.

George Amity confirmed it. "Not a peep."

"It was only when I asked Frank a question through the speaking tube and didn't get an answer that I realized something was wrong. From our end, the pump looked to be going great guns. The air must have been venting straight into the bay." The hand Carstairs scraped over his pale face trembled.

"Shouldn't there have been bubbles?" Diana asked. "If the hose failed, shouldn't you have seen bubbles rising to the surface?"

"Didn't notice," Amity admitted.

"Wouldn't matter," Carstairs said quickly. "As long as Frank's diving weights were still in place, we wouldn't have been able to haul him out quickly enough to save him."

Miss Dunbar had been examining the diving suit and helmet they'd taken off the body. "There was nothing wrong with this equipment earlier today. Frank inspected it himself. He was always careful."

"If it was acid applied to the hose," Ben said, "it might not have been visible."

He'd retrieved his coat and shoes but did not put them back on. He was dripping wet and shivering, as was Graham Somener. Miss Dunbar didn't seem to notice.

"Wouldn't it smell? Feel odd to the touch? I tell you he checked *every*thing."

"I don't know what might have been used." Ben's teeth had started to chatter, and Diana was relieved to see that Mrs. Monroe had gone to the tents to fetch blankets off the cots. "I can only say this looks like the kind of damage acid would cause."

"Could someone have tampered with the hose between the time Mr. Ennis last checked it and the time he went into the water?" Diana took a blanket from the housekeeper and wrapped it around Ben's shoulders. His shirt was icy to the touch. Who would have supposed that the water in the bay would be so cold in the middle of June?

Miss Dunbar's breath hissed in through her teeth. Diana had the feeling she was silently cursing. She didn't answer at first. When she did, disgust was rife in her voice. "Frank—Mr. Ennis—and Mr. Carstairs loaded all the gear into the tender. Then they went to the kitchen for something to eat. Anyone on the island could have gotten at that hose."

"Why didn't they row around to this cove and make the dive as soon as they'd checked the equipment?" Diana asked.

"Graham wanted to be present. He said he had some business to take care of first." Miss Dunbar was careful not to meet Graham Somerer's eyes. Somener himself kept mum, busying himself with drying his hair and beard with a corner of his blanket.

An ugly suspicion crossed Diana's mind. Where had Graham Somener gone after the midday meal? She was all but certain there had been a romantic relationship between Miss Dunbar and Mr. Ennis. Had Somener been jealous? Had he—

"You'll have to send for the sheriff," Ben said, interrupting her chain of thought. "It's up to him and the county coroner to decide whether Ennis's death was accidental or not."

"Damnation, Ben! An investigation into a suspicious death is the last thing I need." A mulish expression on his face, Somener looked ready to argue against it till doomsday, but Ben was not about to change his mind about reporting a crime.

"If there is even the slightest chance he was murdered, you have no choice but to report his death to the law."

"It can't have been deliberate," Somener insisted. "If it was, that would make one of us a cold-blooded killer."

"Precisely." Leaning on Diana, Ben removed his wet, sand-caked stockings and shoved his bare feet into his congress boots.

"Your friend Mrs. Spaulding managed to creep ashore without being noticed," Somener said. "Someone else may have, too."

"If so, then the authorities will find signs of it." Handing the blanket to Diana, Ben shrugged back into his coat.

Diana studied each of the company in turn: Ben's old friend Graham, Miss Dunbar, Mr. Carstairs, George Amity, Mrs. Monroe, MacDougall, and Landrigan. Their faces were singularly unrevealing and no one obliged her by blurting out a confession.

"I don't like the idea of police tramping all over my island."

"You don't have to like it, Graham. Neither do you have any choice. You aren't a sovereign nation. Keep Island is part of Hancock County. When the *Miss Min* arrives, tell the captain to go for the sheriff. He'll call in the county attorney and the coroner. I expect they'll want to come here to view the body and they'll bring with them at least six local men in order to make up a coroner's jury."

"That's unacceptable. And unnecessary. Just ship the body and the diving gear to the mainland and let them look into things there."

"It doesn't work that way, Graham. The law—"

"If you want the law involved so badly, Ben, go and fetch the sheriff yourself! Captain Cobb's got his own schedule to keep."

"None of us, myself included, should leave here until the coroner has been and gone."

"The sheriff's in Ellsworth. My steamboat is berthed in Bucksport."

"For God's sake, Graham! A man has been murdered!" Mutually disgusted, the two men strode off in opposite directions. Somener's blanket, wrapped around him like a cape, flapped as he went.

"Why is Mr. Somener being so stubborn about this?" Diana murmured, addressing no one in particular. He had been more forthcoming than Miss Dunbar, but only in spurts. That hair-trigger temper of his alarmed her, and he seemed unduly concerned about keeping people away from his island.

They'd all gravitated to one spot, as if to draw comfort from one another in the aftermath of tragedy, and had ended up standing in a cluster halfway between the body and the two quarreling men. In spite of their proximity, Diana was surprised when Prudence Monroe answered her question.

"He values his privacy," the housekeeper said.

Or he has something to hide, Diana thought.

"A true friend would understand Graham's reluctance to have strangers come here," said Serena Dunbar.

"I am sure Ben understands perfectly," Diana shot back, "but there are principles at stake. Ben believes in abiding by the law. He's sworn to uphold it in Bangor." He took his duties as one of that city's coroners very seriously.

"Not gonna let it go," George Amity opined, nodding his shaggy head in Ben's direction. Ben had turned around to pursue Graham Somener. He caught up with him just out of earshot. "Yep. Seen his sort afore. Most times it's a good thing."

Moments later, when the two men rejoined the rest of the group, it was clear that Ben had taken charge. "MacDougall will row the tender to the landing," he announced. "It will be easier to carry the body and diving gear up those stairs than to take them by way of the path," he explained to the others. "I'll go with Mac-Dougall. The rest of you—"

"Leave the other boat, if you please," Miss Dunbar interrupted. Her face was still pale but Diana could now detect not the slightest sign of grief or distress. The lady archaeologist was all business. "We need to clear out the sleeping tent and secure the equipment in the other." She directed a pointed look at the blanket Graham Somener still had wrapped around his shoulders. "You look ridiculous, Graham. Frank's clothing should fit both you and Dr. Northcote. Go borrow his spare trousers and shirts. He certainly has no need of them!"

The others waited in awkward silence until the two men returned in dry clothing. Graham Somener glowered while Ben finished sorting everyone out, but he did not object to the arrangements. Landrigan would stay with Miss Dunbar for protection. Somener, Mrs. Monroe, and Diana would return to the house the way Diana had come.

"I'll meet you at the steamboat landing," Ben called to Graham Somener from the tender as Paul Carstairs gave the boat a shove to send it back into the water. "We'll wait for the *Miss Min* together."

As Diana watched MacDougall row away, she belatedly remembered the other boat, the dory that might or might not have been spying on them. She scanned the water but there was no sign of it now.

Pointedly ignoring everyone else, Graham Somener strode off in the direction of the path to the promontory. Diana let Mrs. Monroe set their pace, one much slower than Somener's, but her mind raced ahead.

Murder. Terrible as it was to contemplate, still more appalling was the possibility that Graham Somener had committed the crime. Diana sent Mrs. Monroe a sidelong glance as they picked their careful way over the uneven shore. The woman looked harmless enough, but old family retainers tended to be loyal to the death.

"I did not understand about the *Miss Min*," Diana ventured, thinking this topic might provide a way to ease into questions about Graham Somener's motive. "Is there some particular reason for Mr. Somener to object to his captain fetching the sheriff?"

"Steamboat leaves here, she's supposed to go back to Bucksport. The water route to Ellsworth—that's the county seat, where the sheriff is—that's in the opposite direction. Ellsworth's a ways inland, too, up the Union River from the coast. Makes no sense to send Captain Cobb so far out of his way. Prob'ly take him eight or nine hours to get there." She picked her way around a boulder, holding her skirts away from the barnacles.

So much for the idea that Graham Somener had deliberately been trying to delay the arrival of the law. "Captain Cobb said he didn't bring Ben here on the *Miss Min*. Was he telling me the truth?"

"Honest as the day is long, is Amos Cobb. When those men got sick, Mr. Graham took his own boat over to the mainland to send a telegram to Bangor." She paused in the climb to catch her breath. Her face was flushed, indicating that she was unaccustomed to so much exertion. "Waited for him in Belfast and brought him back himself," she added after a moment.

"I didn't realize Mr. Somener had a boat. In fact, I had the impression he never left the island."

"Where'd you get a fool notion like that?" Mrs. Monroe chuckled. "He just *prefers* to stay here most of the time is all."

"You've known him a long while."

"Long enough."

"Would you say he's an honest man?"

"Why would you think he isn't?"

"Well, given the evidence, I'd have thought he'd suggest sending for the police himself."

Frowning, Mrs. Monroe paused again to catch her breath.

"'Spect he was upset by what happened. Not thinking clearly."
Her brow creased in a frown. "Don't know why else he'd think
he'd have to send the *Miss Min* way over to Ellsworth when he'd
know the captain could send a telegram from Bucksport."

Or perhaps Graham Somener had been thinking *very* clearly
and had been trying to give himself time to hide evidence. "Seems
to me Mr. Somener still hopes to convince people that Mr. Ennis's death was an accident."

With a shrug, the older woman resumed walking. "Mr. Ben
could just sign the death certificate, if he was of a mind to. Save us
all a lot of fuss."

"You don't know Ben very well if you think he'd ever do that.
It would be the same as condoning murder. If there's a killer loose
on Keep Island, don't you want him to be caught?"

"Ain't no madman running wild here! Someone musta come
in from away. Or else it *was* just an accident. Makes no sense otherwise."

"Unless someone had it in for Frank Ennis."

Ignoring the comment, Mrs. Monroe surged ahead. For the
next few minutes, both women needed all their breath for the
ascent. Conversation ceased.

Diana emerged at the top of the promontory just in time to
spot the *Miss Min* steaming past the cove. She'd have to circle the
island to reach the wharf on the north side, but Diana made no
attempt to get there ahead of her. If the sheriff could not arrive
on Keep Island any sooner than the next morning, then it seemed
certain that she and Ben would not be leaving today.

"I expect I'll have to spend the night here," she said to the
housekeeper, who had waited for her at the top.

If Mrs. Monroe bore any resentment towards Diana because
of her earlier critical comments about Graham Somener, it didn't
show. "I'll put you in the blue room," she said, "right next to Miss
Dunbar."

ဆာၛ

Ben went aboard the *Miss Min* as soon as she docked, still wearing Frank Ennis's trousers and shirt with his own coat and still chilled from his dip in the bay. He quickly apprised Captain Cobb of the situation.

Cobb seemed to take the news, as well as Ben's odd appearance, in stride. "I'll send the telegram to Sheriff Fields as soon as I get back to Bucksport," he promised. "And I'll go to Mr. Fellows's house myself."

Oscar Fellows, Ben recalled, was the county attorney. He'd met him once or twice on social occasions. "I don't know Fields," he said to Captain Cobb.

"Dorephus L. Fields. Prob'ly forty-five or so. Ordinary lookin' fella. Lives in Ellsworth and has done for years. Was a deputy afore he was elected sheriff." Cobb shrugged. "That's pretty much all I know 'bout the fella."

Ben was about to disembark when he remembered that he had another question for Cobb. "Did you pick up any mail here on Tuesday afternoon?"

"Hasn't been any outgoing mail in over a week."

Ben wondered what had happened to his letter to Diana. Obviously someone on the island that day had been responsible for its disappearance. The custom on Keep Island was to leave letters or packages for the mainland in a box at the landing. If Cobb had opened it and found it empty, that meant the letter had been removed between the time Ben had placed it there and the arrival of the *Miss Min*. But who? What difference could it possibly make to anyone here if a visiting physician wrote to his fiancée?

That same fiancée was waiting on Graham Somener's veranda when Ben returned from the dock. Ben led her around to a side door, and after a quick glance to be sure it was unoccupied, escorted her into the room Graham had outfitted with exercise equipment.

A punching bag hung at the center, showing evidence of hard use. Graham's fencing foils were housed in a special cabinet on the far wall. He'd been delighted to have the chance to practice, especially with Ben, who had learned the sport from the same teacher.

"We'll have to stay here overnight," he said.

"I know." Diana's eyes widened as she took in the room's furnishings. Ben did not suppose she had ever been in a gymnasium before. Such places were the exclusive province of men. She tentatively hefted a five-pound weight and quickly replaced it. "Mrs. Monroe has given me a lovely room."

"Do you have everything you need?"

"I brought a gripsack. I suppose I should have thought to pack for you, too."

He looked down at himself and grimaced. "I keep a change of clothing and some toiletries at my surgery, in case I have to stay with a patient overnight. I brought those things with me, and Graham generously lent me everything else I required." He waited. There was something on Diana's mind, and he doubted it was concern over whether or not he had fresh linen.

"Serena Dunbar and Frank Ennis quarreled twice that I am aware of, once in the infirmary and once on the beach."

"Professional differences?" he suggested.

"Perhaps. But it appeared to me to be personal. Miss Dunbar called him by his first name."

Ben had the uneasy feeling he knew where this conversation was headed. "She is an . . . unconventional female. I believe she is on a first-name basis with all her crew."

"She is an *attractive* female. I have no difficulty at all imagining her with more than one suitor. Your friend Graham seems quite taken with her."

"I did notice that," he admitted.

"Are his intentions honorable?"

He smiled at the sarcasm in her voice. "They might be." He

took an experimental jab at the punching bag. It had been years since he'd boxed. "I did not ask." He hit the bag again.

"Then he might have regarded Frank Ennis as a rival."

"Are you saying you think *Graham* killed Ennis?"

"Jealousy is a powerful motive."

Giving the bag one last poke, Ben turned to face Diana. "It seems to me that you've made a better argument for Serena Dunbar to have killed Ennis. She might have been afraid he would interfere in her plans. Marriage to a rich man is a tempting prospect for any woman."

She punched *him* on the shoulder. Hard. "All right, Ben. Let them *both* be suspects. But you must admit that Mr. Somener exhibits contradictory behavior."

"He's a troubled man, Diana. His life was ripped apart five years ago." Ben drew her over to a window, where they could look out on a peaceful vista of green lawn and rose-covered arbors. "The building collapse affected his mind, making him moody and unpredictable, quick to lose his temper, and easily convinced that anyone from the press is out to get him. He's been better lately. His interest in Serena Dunbar's project, and in Serena, has been good for him."

"What if Graham Somener wanted you here because he thought that, as an old friend, you could be persuaded to sign a death certificate without asking too many questions?"

"What are you saying?"

"What if the original plan was for Ennis to die of poison? The fact that he was the target would have been disguised by the fact that two other men also fell ill. Someone killed Frank Ennis, Ben, and that may not have been the first attempt on his life. Your friend Graham—"

"Enough!" Ben sucked in a deep breath and held it. When he was certain he wouldn't snap at her, that his voice would be calm, he resumed speaking. "I don't like this situation any better than you do, Diana, but I know Graham Somener. He's not a cold-blooded killer."

"But—"

He cut her off with a slashing motion. "No. No discussion. The subject is closed. Let the sheriff handle this."

"But—"

"No."

Exasperated, she stood with her hands on her hips, glaring at him.

"I don't want to quarrel with you, Diana."

"Nor I, you."

"Good. Then we'd best change the subject. Tell me what has been going on at home while I've been stuck here. Tell me—" He broke off with a self-deprecating smile. "I can't believe I'm asking this! Tell me about your mother."

Diana, Ben, Miss Dunbar, and Mr. Carstairs joined Graham Somener for a late supper. As soon as the meal was on the table, and Mrs. Monroe had left the dining room, Somener addressed Ben. "I need your help, my friend."

"I'm not going to sign a death certificate that says Ennis died of natural causes."

"I didn't intend to ask you to."

Diana, seated opposite her host, had an excellent view of his face in the candlelight, but she couldn't tell if he was lying or not. The hand holding his wine glass clenched, then relaxed.

Ben glanced up from his plate to give the other man a stare that would have turned a less stalwart fellow to jelly. "I am not involved in the investigation, Graham. Nor do I wish to be."

"Perhaps not, but will you or won't you, you can expect to be badgered by the press. They're vultures, Ben. Once word of this leaks out—and I assure you that it will—the Boston papers will come looking for a story. If they can't find a connection to that business five years ago, they'll invent one. Am I not correct, Mrs. Spaulding?"

Diana wished she could deny it, but he spoke nothing less than the truth. "Even the most reputable newspapers will skewer you if they can. People dearly love to read about the trials and tribulations of their betters. The elite have so much more to lose when they fall from grace."

"Begging your pardon, Mrs. Spaulding," Paul Carstairs interrupted, "but how do you know so much about newspapers?"

"I work for the *Independent Intelligencer*," Diana admitted.

"One of the worst examples of its kind. A scandal-mongering rag if there ever was one." Somener looked as if a thundercloud had settled in over his head.

"That's enough, Graham," Ben said. "We take your point. Neither Diana nor I will talk to reporters."

Diana kept her head down as she ate, but she couldn't resist peeping out from beneath her lashes. Somener bit viciously into a piece of meat and chewed with such force that Diana feared he'd do damage to his teeth. She shifted her gaze to Serena Dunbar. Everything about the woman belied her first name. She was so tense that Diana could swear she saw the air around her vibrate. The other archaeologist, Paul Carstairs, was less affected by the undercurrents in the room, but he clearly wished he were somewhere else. A faint flush of color showed beneath skin the color of whey as he toyed with his food.

Diana continued to eat, but not with her usual hearty appetite. She scarcely tasted the well-prepared roast of beef that Mrs. Monroe had set before them. If Ben was right and Graham Somener was innocent of any crime, then he deserved to know what else scandal-seeking reporters might hear about him.

"There's something I need to tell you before the sheriff gets here, Mr. Somener. Someone has hired a private detective to investigate you. The fellow claims you are using Keep Island as a base for illegal operations of some sort." In terse sentences she recounted the details of Justus Palmer's visit to Ben's house in Bangor.

Somener swore and took a long swallow from his wine glass. The two bright spots of color highlighting his cheekbones suggested barely leashed rage. "There's no basis in truth for such a rumor, but a story like that, especially at this time, is a confounded nuisance." He glared at Diana, as if he blamed her for Palmer's suspicions.

"It will do you no good to kill the messenger." Diana did not believe she was in any physical danger, but Graham Somener's temper was simmering again, threatening to boil over. Serena Dunbar had twisted her napkin into a tight ball and held it crushed in a white-knuckled grip—a powder keg ready to explode. As Diana watched, she flung it away with an anguished cry and reached for the wine decanter to refill her empty glass.

"You should be able to avoid reporters' questions, and Justus Palmer, too," Ben said to Graham Somener, "but we'll all have to talk to the sheriff. What do you plan to tell him?"

"As little as possible." With the caution of a man afraid he might break something, Somener lifted his wineglass and took a single sip before gently placing it back on the table, then delicately ate a small bite of the beef. Narrow-eyed, he glanced at Ben.

"I'd advise you to tell the truth," Ben said. "All of it."

"The truth is that Frank Ennis is dead." Surliness had replaced Somener's anger. "If his equipment was tampered with, and I'm not convinced it was, then I have no idea who did it or when. There's nothing else I can tell the authorities."

"Miss Dunbar?"

Unprepared for Ben's attention to shift to her, she spilled her wine.

"You hired Frank Ennis. You knew him before he came here. Do you have any idea who might have wanted him dead?"

"Of course not!" She collected herself almost at once, although she ignored the stain spreading across the tablecloth. "He was a capable archaeologist. He'd worked on a number of excavations. There is no reason I can think of for anyone to wish him ill."

"Was he the only one who would have used that diving suit?" She answered him with a reluctant nod.

"That's right." Paul Carstairs spoke for the first time, his voice low but easily audible. "It's too big for either Amity or me."

"What about that other boat?" Graham Somener interrupted. "The dory. Who were those men and what did the one with the binoculars see?"

"Nothing!" Miss Dunbar's voice was sharp. "They saw nothing. Frank died underwater, out of sight." Righting her empty glass, she refilled it and gulped down half the contents.

"What if that private detective was one of the men in the boat?" Somener had caught hold of a new idea, and he clung to it with the tenacity of a terrier.

Diana closed her eyes, trying to call up an image of what she had seen, but the dory had been too far away. "I didn't recognize anyone, but I suppose it's possible."

"I don't like this," Somener muttered. "I don't like it at all. I want to know who hired that detective. Can you find out for me?"

"I can try," Ben said.

Miss Dunbar abruptly rose to her feet. Taking her wine glass with her, she bolted from the room.

"Serena!" Somener started to follow her.

Diana was faster. "I'll make certain she's all right," she promised, sprinting after the other woman.

Behind her she heard Ben speak in his most soothing tone of voice. "It has been a stressful day, Graham. Most likely she needs a little time alone."

More likely, Diana thought, she has a guilty conscience.

Close on the heels of her quarry, Diana sped up the stairs. Miss Dunbar ran straight into her bedroom and attempted to slam the door in her pursuer's face. Diana caught it with her shoulder, which hurt quite a lot. Wincing, she pushed harder, preventing Miss Dunbar from closing and locking the portal. The aggressive action seemed to catch the other woman off guard. That was fortunate, since she was not only more physically fit than Diana, but two inches taller and a number of pounds heavier.

Surprised but pleased by her success at getting into Miss Dunbar's room, Diana ignored the archaeologist's repeated demands that she leave. Instead, she settled herself in a comfortable chair upholstered in dark green plush.

Glaring at Diana all the while, Miss Dunbar defiantly drained her wine glass. Diana rearranged the skirt of her traveling suit. Mrs. Monroe had brushed and freshened it and, at least by gaslight, the salt water stains no longer showed.

Miss Dunbar stalked to the window. Pushing aside the sheer draperies, she stared at the night sky. She had a spectacular view, Diana observed. The stars seemed much closer here than they did in Bangor. In New York City, where the buildings crowded close together and arc lights illuminated the nearest open space at Union Square Park, it was rare she saw them at all.

Reminding herself that she had not followed Miss Dunbar to study the constellations, she addressed the other woman. "What is it that upsets you—one lover's death or the possibility that the other may have killed him?"

Diana's blunt question was intended to surprise the other woman into an honest answer. The result was not quite what she expected. The empty glass Miss Dunbar still held shattered in her hand. Shards fell to the exquisitely patterned carpet along with a drop of blood.

Diana was on her feet in an instant, catching hold of Miss Dunbar's arm to prevent her from putting her cut finger directly in her mouth. "Stop that. It needs proper disinfecting and you can't be sure all the glass is out."

Miss Dunbar scowled. "There's brandy in the bottom drawer of the bedside table."

Diana led her first to the washstand. Mrs. Monroe had filled the pitcher in preparation for the next morning's ablutions. Diana poured water into the basin and instructed Miss Dunbar to soak her hand while she located the brandy bottle. She removed the glass stopple and poured a liberal amount of the clear red-brown liquid over the slashed finger. It was only a small cut, but deep.

"Wasteful," Miss Dunbar muttered. "That was imported. And aged. It came to me from Min Somener, and she's been gone for a decade."

Diana ignored the grumbling and tended to the wound. The bottle was still half full.

Miss Dunbar murmured a grudging thank you once her hand had been neatly bandaged.

"You're welcome. I did not mean to startle you."

"Yes, you did. I wonder why?"

"You were exceedingly nervous throughout dinner. You behaved . . . oddly after Mr. Ennis died. So did Mr. Somener. What is it you are afraid the sheriff will discover?"

"He will find nothing because there is nothing for him to find. No one had any reason to kill Frank, and there is no reason to think that anything Graham has done is in the least suspicious. He is a man who values his privacy, that is all. And I am justifiably concerned about the security of my excavation."

"Yes. Your excavation," Diana murmured. "Is it not curious that your expedition should be to this place, where I am told you spent considerable time during your childhood. What makes you think there was a settlement here on Keep Island?"

"Research." The reply was quick and curt.

"What sort of research?"

"The study of documents. Old documents."

Diana had the feeling Miss Dunbar was being deliberately vague, and that she was hiding something. Miss Dunbar's mother, Diana recalled, had been friends with Graham's aunt, but that did not mean Serena Dunbar herself was either honest or trustworthy. And Graham Somener was a very wealthy man.

Early settlers before Columbus? A shipwreck? Now that Diana thought about it, such notions seemed preposterous.

They sounded like fodder for a confidence game.

Did Miss Dunbar intend to salt her excavation with artifacts from somewhere else, one genuine but most clever forgeries? Diana had heard of such things. The promise of treasure would lure investors in, at which point she could make off with their money.

One thought led to another. What if Serena Dunbar was not an archaeologist at all? She might well have created that role for herself in order to gain access to Keep Island, Graham Somener, and the Somener fortune. The old family connection would have been enough to give her access to the first two. Once Somener was properly smitten, he wouldn't trouble to ask intrusive questions.

"Where did you study archaeology?" Diana asked.

Miss Dunbar did not answer at once. She had just taken a healthy swallow of brandy directly from the decanter. An odd expression on her face, she wandered to the bed and crawled up onto the foot.

"Miss Dunbar?"

"Harvard. Under dear Dr. Putnam. Dr. Frederick Ward Putnam. He thought I was brilliant before . . . ." She sighed and took another swig.

"Before what?"

"Nothing. Never mind. I don't want to talk to you any more. I'm tired."

She was also inebriated, or pretending to be. If the latter, it was a ploy to allow her to evade Diana's questions. Highly suspicious behavior!

Over the last few months, Diana had gained considerable experience dealing with confidence women. It was not such an outrageous possibility that Serena could be one of their number. Diana could readily believe that Serena Dunbar had come to Keep Island intending to perpetrate a fraud.

"Plans ruined." The words were muffled. Miss Dunbar, lying on her stomach, had pulled a pillow over her head.

"What plans?" Diana stalked to Miss Dunbar's side to lift the edge of the pillow.

The other woman was not a pretty sight. Eyes glassy, mouth open far enough to drool, she clutched the brandy bottle to her bosom. Diana recoiled as the fumes reached her nose.

Miss Dunbar blinked and managed, for a moment, to focus on Diana. "People keep trying to ruin my plans," she whined. "Not fair."

"Perhaps you should change your plans," Diana suggested.

She might *not* go through with her confidence game, Diana realized. Why should she? The confidence woman could retire and let the fortune hunter take over, assuming it hadn't been her intention from the first to snare Graham Somener. She appeared to have succeeded, though to what degree it was difficult to tell. Certainly there was something between them . . . just as there had been something between Serena and Frank Ennis.

Diana thought again of what Justus Palmer had told her. There were reports of criminal activity on Keep Island—recent criminal activity. That sounded to her as if the rumors had sprung up at just about the same time the so-called archaeologists had arrived on Keep Island.

A third possibility occurred to her. Perhaps Miss Serena Dunbar herself was the leader of a band of smugglers. Not a confidence game at all, or fortune hunting, but an elaborate cover for more nefarious activities. And if there had been a falling out among thieves, if Frank Ennis had become a threat, she'd—

The soft thud of a brandy bottle hitting the carpet interrupted Diana's theorizing. The next sound she heard was a soft snore.

Miss Dunbar would not answer any more questions tonight. Sprawled fully dressed across the foot of her bed, she was out like the proverbial light.

CHAPTER FIVE

ജ‍ൽ

It was late morning before the sheriff, county attorney, and coroner arrived. Just as well, Ben decided. He had stayed up late the previous night, drinking brandy and smoking Graham's very fine imported cigars. The two of them had avoided the subject of murder, reminiscing instead about their shared boyhood. Diana had briefly reappeared to say that Miss Dunbar had retired for the night and then had gone off to bed herself.

Ben had not risen until ten and had not yet had a private word today with his fiancée. He was pleased to see she looked well rested and alert. Miss Dunbar decidedly did not. Her eyes were bloodshot, as if she had been crying, and the area beneath them had the hollow, bruised look he usually associated with lingering illness.

They gathered in Graham's parlor, where Mrs. Monroe had set out pots of coffee and of tea, together with an assortment of pastries. The sheriff greeted the sight of these with delight.

"Missed my morning meal," Dorephus Fields explained. "Had to start out some early to travel the eighteen miles between Ellsworth and Bucksport on horseback." The others had waited for him there and the entire party had set out as soon as he'd arrived.

This being Sunday, the *Miss Min* did not make her regular delivery run, but the county attorney, Oscar Fellows, had commandeered her for their journey.

Fellows, a tall, thin man with a neatly trimmed, if somewhat sparse, beard, edged closer to Ben's side as Ben poured himself a cup of coffee. "Dr. Northcote."

"Mr. Fellows."

"You were only recently involved in another sensational case, as I recall."

Which one? Ben wondered. But of course Fellows would only know about the murderer captured in Bangor back at the beginning of April. Ben and Diana had expected to be called to testify at the trial, but in the end there had been no need. Instead of languishing in prison, the villain was now being cared for in the Maine Insane Hospital in Augusta. To Ben's mind that fate was far worse than simple incarceration.

Aloud he said only, "My duties as city coroner frequently bring me in contact with murder."

"And the lady?"

"My fiancée, do you mean?"

"Ah. Congratulations are in order, then. She is a charming creature."

Ben presented Fellows to Diana and the others, and they made small talk until the coroner finished viewing the body and joined them. Frank Ennis's remains had been stored in the ice house, together with his diving suit.

Ben had purposely stayed away, to avoid any suggestion he might be trying to influence the coroner's observations. With the coroner were his clerk and six stalwart citizens of Bucksport, Captain Cobb among them, who had been duly sworn in and instructed to declare whether the victim had died by felony, mischance, or accident.

That part of the proceedings did not take long. When the eight men had assembled in the parlor, Graham Somener urged them to help themselves to refreshments. He was not happy about the invasion of his island, but he'd resolved to make the best of it.

The coroner refused food or coffee, impatient to begin. He was a young man, fresh out of medical school and cocky with it, but he seemed to know his job. He announced that everyone who had been present on the beach at the time of the death would be called upon to give a statement, which would be written down by the clerk. Familiar with the drill, Ben offered to go first.

"Do you solemnly swear that the evidence which you shall give to the inquest, concerning the death of the person here lying dead, shall be the truth, the whole truth, and nothing but the truth, so help you God?"

"I do."

"State your name, place of residence, and profession."

"Benjamin Northcote, Bangor, physician."

The coroner's sharp look told Ben the other man had heard of him, but in what context Ben could not guess. When asked what he'd observed, Ben gave a full account of the previous afternoon's events, concluding with his discovery that the air hose had been tampered with.

With each word, Graham Somener's expression grew darker. He could not contradict what Ben said, but he did not like having it become part of the official record. When Ben volunteered the story of the earlier incident of morphine poisoning, Graham's hands curled into fists at his sides. It all sounded much worse when couched as testimony.

Once Ben had finished, the others were called up one by one. Paul Carstairs, looking distraught, described how the diving equipment worked and explained that he and Amity had been unaware of Ennis's difficulties until it was too late to save him. Amity said much the same thing.

When it was Serena Dunbar's turn, she came forward reluctantly and it was clear she was not only in an emotional state but suffering physically, as well. Headache, Ben diagnosed. Perhaps a migraine, since she appeared to be sensitive to light.

For once she'd dressed conservatively, in a plain, reddish-brown dress with a small bustle. She spoke in a quiet—almost inaudible—voice.

"I know this must be trying for you, Miss Dunbar." The brusque manner the coroner had used to question the men vanished and he all but patted her hand in an effort to reassure her of his kindly intentions. "I'll be brief. You have heard what the others said. Does that agree with your memory of events?"

"Yes, sir, it does, except for one thing."

"And what is that, Miss Dunbar?"

She took a moment to collect herself. "I do not believe anyone deliberately murdered Mr. Ennis. Some chemical must have been spilled on the air hose by accident. We have photographic supplies, strong cleansers . . . with our equipment. I—" She broke off, apparently overcome.

"Take your time, Miss Dunbar."

"Yes. Thank you." Then she leaned forward, sincerity radiating from every pore. "It is a terrible thing to speak ill of the dead, but Mr. Ennis, although a brilliant archaeologist, was sometimes careless. And a bit of a daredevil. He wanted to make that dive very badly, to prove he'd recovered from the . . . food poisoning. I fear he may not have been as thorough as he should have been about examining his equipment."

With that she lowered her face into her handkerchief—very prettily—and her shoulders heaved just enough to suggest silent tears. Skeptical, Ben caught Diana's eyes and saw there a reflection of his own doubts.

Graham, who echoed Miss Dunbar's opinion that both the morphine poisoning and the damaged air hose might have been no more than terrible accidents, Mrs. Monroe, and the two watchmen were deposed in short order. After their testimony, the coroner's jury acted with dispatch, declaring that Frank Ennis "died of drowning on the 16th of June, A.D. 1888, by means as yet unknown."

Miss Dunbar's testimony had planted seeds of doubt, as she'd intended. With no evidence to indicate what person had killed Frank Ennis, or even if he had been murdered, the coroner was unable to order Sheriff Fields to arrest anyone. He ordered his clerk to write out the official verdict and adjourned the inquest.

Ben caught Graham's arm and hauled him out of earshot of the others. "What was that all about? I thought we agreed to tell the truth."

"How do you know that *wasn't* the truth? Accidents happen."

"This was no accident!"

"Let it go, Ben. Let the law decide."

Unfortunately, Ben did not have a great deal of confidence in the law just now, not when the young coroner seemed inclined to believe anything Serena Dunbar told him. "At least be careful. If someone *did* murder Ennis—"

"We may all end up dead? This isn't one of Damon Bathory's tales of terror, but I will take precautions. And I still want to know more about this Palmer fellow who questioned Mrs. Spaulding."

Swallowing everything else he wanted to say, Ben again promised to see what he could find out. What else could he do? Graham was still his friend.

"Ready to go?" Diana called from a short distance away. While Ben had confronted Graham, she had collected his carpet bag and doctor's satchel as well as her gripsack.

"Be careful," Ben warned again. He had more than potential murderers in mind. He had serious reservations about leaving Graham to the tender mercies of Miss Serena Dunbar.

He'd done all he could, he told himself as he joined Diana and they headed for the steamboat wharf. At least there was one bright spot in the day. The *Miss Min* was not bound by her regular schedule. They would be back in Bucksport in time to catch the afternoon train to Bangor.

A short time later, as they chugged away from Keep Island,

Fellows joined Ben and Diana at the rail. "Have you known Somener long, Dr. Northcote?" he asked.

"Most of my life."

"Good man?"

"He's not a likely murder suspect." Ben firmly believed that, although he knew that Diana was not so certain.

"I didn't say he was, but his name has come up in connection with another matter. Have you ever heard of a fellow named Justus Palmer? Seems he paid a visit to the sheriff last evening to inquire about your friend."

Ben felt Diana tense at his side and reached down to give her gloved hand a squeeze where it rested on the railing. He listened without comment as Fellows detailed Palmer's claims—the same insubstantial charges he'd voiced to Diana.

"I think I'd like to hear a first-hand account," Ben said when Fellows had finished.

"I believe the sheriff has gone to fetch that picnic basket Mrs. Monroe sent along." Graham had not invited any of them to stay for Sunday dinner.

Over cold chicken and hard-boiled eggs, Ben set about discovering what Dorephus Fields knew of Justus Palmer.

"Came by the house," Fields said. "About eight o'clock, it was. Said he was a detective working on a case."

"And you took his word for that?"

Fields balanced a chicken leg on a napkin on his knee and fished in his vest pocket for a piece of pasteboard. "He gave me this."

Engraved on the card were the words "Justus Palmer, Private Inquiry Agent" and Palmer's business address in Boston. In the corner, in smaller letters, it read, "Discretion Guaranteed."

"I asked him if he was a Pinkerton man," Fields said, "and he said he was more akin to James R. Wood."

"I don't know that name," Diana interjected.

"James R. Wood? He's a Boston policeman who started his

own detective agency in that city. I met him once. He's often called in on cases in Maine and New Hampshire. Hard to miss him. Bushy eyebrows. Oversize mustache. Dapper dresser. And he's one smart fella. The way he solved that constable's murder down to Bath four or five years back was some impressive."

"Matchsticks, wasn't it, that led him to the killer?" Ben remembered reading about the case.

Fields nodded. "As clever a piece of detecting as I've ever heard."

The sheriff seemed to have a far more vivid recollection of Wood's appearance than Palmer's and was likewise vague about what he'd told the Boston detective.

"Did he question you about Keep Island?" Ben asked.

"Now that you mention it . . . ." Fields's vacant stare was not encouraging, but after a moment he added, "Said something about criminal activity." He reached for another hard-boiled egg. "I told him I never heard nothing about anything illegal going on there in the whole five years Somener's been wintering on the island. Then he said it was likely a recent development and that he'd send someone to investigate except that visitors aren't welcome on Mr. Somener's private island. Said I could go, since I've got jurisdiction over all of Hancock County." Fields snorted. "Can't just go barging in for no reason. Told him that."

"But by eight o'clock last night, you must already have known you'd be visiting the island today," Diana interrupted. "Why didn't you tell him you'd check into the matter at the same time you investigated Frank Ennis's death?"

The look of bewilderment on the sheriff's face troubled Ben. It was almost as if he couldn't remember parts of his visit from Justus Palmer. "I must have been some tired," Fields muttered, more to himself than to them. "I shouldn't have said anything about that."

"So you *did* tell him someone might have been murdered?" Diana's fingers twitched, as if she could barely contain the impulse to make notes.

The sheriff scratched his head and the frown lines around his mouth deepened. "Must have, because I remember inviting him to come along this morning. Shouldn't have done that. Good thing he turned me down."

Ben exchanged a puzzled look with Diana. "He had a chance to visit Keep Island and he didn't take it?"

"Nope." Fields relaxed and helped himself to more chicken. "Seems he's got a tendency towards seasickness."

"A feeble excuse." Diana had polished off almost as much of the picnic lunch as Fields had. She paused in the act of wiping her fingers on a napkin. "I wonder, though. Do you suppose he was trying to manipulate me into making the trip by telling me I shouldn't go?"

No better way to assure that she did, Ben thought. He didn't care for the possibility that Palmer might plan to question Diana a second time in order to discover what she had learned on Keep Island.

Fields was frowning again, trying to call up Palmer's exact words. "Said travel over water didn't agree with him." Satisfied, he went back to eating. "Poor fella. Doesn't know what he's missing. Nothing better than spending the day on a boat. I served in both the army and the navy during the war and let me tell you, the navy's better."

Ben could not share the sheriff's enjoyment at being aboard the *Miss Min*. With twelve passengers sharing limited space, he could hardly turn around without bumping into one of the jurors. Further discussion of what Justus Palmer might be up to, and speculation about the reasons for Serena Dunbar's testimony, would have to wait until he could be alone with Diana.

That took longer than he'd anticipated. Fellows waited with them for the train to arrive and once on board the crush of passengers left them without sufficient privacy for a discussion of murder. Ben did not want to chance being overheard. Before he knew it, a remark he or Diana made would show up in the news-paper. That was the last thing Graham needed right now.

It seemed to take forever before they were clattering through the familiar covered bridge that spanned the Penobscot River be-tween Brewer and Bangor. They arrived at the depot in Bangor right on time—6:05. Since Ben had sent a telegram ahead from Bucksport, his "doctor's wagon"—a four-wheeled buggy painted black with green trim and silver markings, and fitted with a spe-cial storage area at the back to hold medical supplies—was wait-ing at the station. That gave him the length of the drive to the house to discuss matters with Diana.

"I don't know what to make of Palmer's claims," Ben confessed as he gathered up the reins and urged the horse out into traffic. The streets around the depot were crowded with folks heading home for supper.

"Nor do I, but I do think it odd that the charge he made against Mr. Somener is so vague. Is he supposed to be involved in smuggling, or some other nefarious crime? Then, too, while it's clear your childhood friend has an enemy, since someone is spreading rumors about him, it is possible that this business with Palmer has no connection whatsoever to Frank Ennis's death."

Ben nodded thoughtfully, leaning forward a bit to compensate for the steepness of the hill. "Why kill Ennis? That's the most important question. It can't have been a mistake. Graham would never have been the one wearing that diving suit. Still, I suppose it could have been Palmer, or his employer, who came onto Keep Island by stealth and tampered with the diving equipment."

"You promised to locate Justus Palmer," Diana reminded him. "How do you mean to go about finding him?"

"I could travel to Boston. That's where his office is." Ben had kept the card Palmer had given to Sheriff Fields. "But it's likely he's still in Maine."

Ben slowed the horse as they passed the Entwhistle mansion. In a few more minutes they would be home, their opportunity for private conversation at an end. "If he's in Bangor, it shouldn't be too difficult to track him down and talk to him. There are only so many hotels in the city and I know them all."

"How can I help?" Diana asked.

"By staying out of it. Let me deal with Palmer."

"I have no real desire to encounter Mr. Palmer again," Diana admitted. "I must confess he made me a trifle uneasy. He has a rather . . . dominating personality. But I am not prepared to forget that there has been murder done. It did not appear to me that much investigation took place on Keep Island. Mr. Fellows and the sheriff seemed content to take statements and view the body."

"They took away the diving suit."

"But were they convinced the air hose had been tampered with?"

Ben hesitated. "I don't know. And there may not be much they can do to prove it even if they did believe me."

"Can do or *will* do?" Diana asked. "Are police here like those in New York City? Few murders are investigated there without the promise of a monetary reward."

Ben stiffened, offended. "We are not so corrupt here." But he could not claim high moral ground for long. "It is usually public outcry that drives an investigation, and even then, local authorities generally admit they are not qualified to investigate murders. Sometimes, if there is money to pay one, a private detective is called in, as was the case in Bath with James R. Wood."

"I don't suppose Mr. Somener will—"

"I don't suppose he will. The truth is, Diana, we've no business getting involved in this investigation."

"That's never stopped us before."

"I'll see if I can find out who hired Palmer and pass that information on to Graham, but once that's done, our part in the matter will be over." He pulled in beneath the porte cochere and glanced sideways at Diana. Consternation puckered her face.

"What?"

"I'm sorry, Ben, but I don't see how we can simply let the matter drop." She sent an apologetic smile his way. "Distasteful as it is, we're caught right in the middle. Graham Somener put us there by sending for you when those men were poisoned."

"What do you want to do, then? And I warn you, if you say you plan to track down a killer on your own, especially if you still think Graham is the guilty party, I'll lock you in the attic until the wedding." He was not entirely joking.

"I'll do nothing that will put me in harm's way. I promise. But I want to investigate Serena Dunbar."

"Serena?" He couldn't say he was surprised, especially given her testimony at the inquest.

"You were right in what you said yesterday. She's as likely a suspect as Graham Somener. More likely. She may well be the reason Palmer was hired. The claims of illegal activities on Keep Island coincide with her arrival there. I doubt that is a coincidence. Perhaps Frank Ennis caught on to what she was doing. She may have had to kill him to protect herself from arrest."

"Or it could be that Ennis was the smuggler," Ben suggested. "Serena may have killed him to protect her archaeological expedition."

"If she really *is* an archaeologist. What if she is a confidence woman planning to salt the site?"

"Either way, why would she poison her entire crew, or kill Ennis when he was the only one who could make that dive for her?"

Diana waved away his objections as if they were trifles. "She's hiding something. I'm certain of it. And she has designs on your oldest friend. Don't you think he should be warned if she's up to no good?"

Using the island as a base for smuggling? Running a confidence game? Scheming to marry a rich man? None were possibilities he liked to contemplate. Diana was right. If Serena Dunbar wasn't what she claimed, then he owed it to Graham to find out.

"Where will you start?"

"The library, I think, to discover if there are any legitimate archaeologists living in the area."

"Excellent plan." Book research. And likely she'd send a telegram to her editor, Horatio Foxe, who seemed to have limitless resources to find answers to questions. Both sounded like perfectly safe endeavors, but Ben knew Diana well. "Just promise me you'll be careful."

"I will."

One danger averted, Ben thought. Now all he had to do was survive the other—an evening meal, now imminent, shared with Maggie Northcote and Elmira Leeves.

"Ben?" Diana placed one hand on his arm as he was about to hop out of the buggy.

"Yes, my dear?"

"I vow I won't keep any more secrets from you. Not even little, unimportant ones. Everything I learn, I will share with you as soon as is humanly possible."

Her voice throbbed with such sincerity that he couldn't help but respond in the same vein. "You have my promise, too, Diana. I will confide everything I discover about Justus Palmer."

Her face alight with a brilliant smile, she allowed him to hand her out of the buggy. As he'd hoped, she had not noticed how carefully he had chosen his words. She did not guess that there were other secrets he was not yet willing to share with her.

∞∞

It felt good to wake up in her own bedroom in Ben's house in Bangor. Diana stretched languidly in the massive four-poster bed, a smile on her face as she looked up at the canopy. It was Monday, the eighteenth day of June in the year 1888, and in just twelve more days she would be Mrs. Benjamin Northcote.

Her pleasure at the thought popped like a balloon when the door flew open to admit her mother. Elmira Leeves didn't bother with greetings. She cut straight to the point. "How could you, Diana? You know I cannot bear to be in the same room with the man."

"What man, Mother?"

"My brother Myron. Who else? After the way he treated me—"

"Good lord, Mother, that was decades ago. You don't have to talk to him. Just restrain any impulse to physically attack him." She wondered how Elmira had learned Myron Grant was on the guest list. Diana certainly hadn't shown it to her. She'd planned to tell her mother who was coming, but not until the last minute.

"I will not tolerate—"

"You will, or you'll leave before they get here." Diana slid out of bed and reached for her dressing sacque, pulling it on over the comfortable old mother hubbard gown she'd slept in. "I invited Uncle Myron, Uncle Howd, Uncle Howd's fiancée, and his daughter to the wedding. Uncle Myron isn't happy about the prospect of seeing you again, either. In his version, you abandoned him."

"I eloped." Elmira sniffed, but Diana did not think the sound was a prelude to tears. Her mother was made of stronger stuff than that.

"Precisely."

At the oak commode Diana poured water into the wash basin before splashing a healthy portion onto her face. Dealing with her mother required a degree of alertness impossible when one had been blissfully asleep only a short time ago. The water, at room temperature, was not cold enough to do much good. Diana reached for one of the soft cloths hanging on a built-in towel rack while studying her bemused expression in the mirror affixed to the high back of the commode. She needed coffee, and lots of it.

As if on cue, a gentle scratching sounded at the door. Diana opened it for Annie, the maid. Smile bright as a new penny, black dress covered with a freshly starched white apron, the Irish girl had brought a breakfast tray. "Mornin' mum. Here's your coffee."

"Bless you, Annie."

Annie set the tray, which also held a covered dish containing toast, on an oak table next to a chair. "Will you be needin' any help with your dressin' this mornin'?"

"Thank you, no, Annie." If she did, her mother, who had retreated to the window seat, could assist with the buttons.

Diana poured herself a cup of coffee and took several sips of the strong, fragrant brew. As soon as the door closed behind Annie, she addressed her formidable mother. "You may as well know. I have also invited the surviving Torrences—my grandfather and my Aunt Janette—to the wedding. Did you conveniently forget they existed when you finally told me about your own family?"

For years, Diana had believed she had no one in the world but her parents. It had been a shock to discover that both her mother and her father had siblings living and that her father's father was also still alive.

"I did not forget, though I did assume the old man was long dead." Elmira shrugged and leaned back against the window sill, a position from which she could keep an eye on both the scene outside and her daughter. "I chose not to mention them. Never liked Janette. Too stuck up by half."

Diana bit into a piece of toast to keep herself from making any comment.

The silence grew heavy between them. Abruptly, Elmira left the window seat to wander around the bedchamber, idly examining anything that took her fancy. She picked up the mother-of-pearl backed mirror on the dresser and studied herself in it, poking at strands of hair already perfectly coiffed, before replacing it next to the matching brush and hair receiver.

Diana's eyes narrowed. Her mother was fully dressed and wide awake. Likely she'd been up for hours. Snooping, no doubt, while everyone else in the house was still asleep.

"A little bird tells me you passed yourself off as already married when you visited my brothers."

Diana's hand jerked as she set the coffee cup down. How on earth had her mother discovered that tidbit? Not that it mattered. Now that she knew, she'd have to be dealt with. "We had good reasons for the deception at the time."

With a snigger, Elmira replaced the spill jar on the mantel-piece and turned to grin at her. "I just bet you did. And I can't say as I blame you. He's a well set-up fellow, your Ben. If I were thirty years younger, I'd have a go at him myself."

"You're a newlywed, Mother. Or had you forgotten?"

"Not for a moment, and I'm pleased enough with my bargain, though I warn you, daughter, once a man gets his ring on your finger he stops being quite so gallant."

Diana frowned. Ed Leeves was a perfect gentleman . . . when he wasn't issuing threats. Now that he was her stepfather, she was determined to ignore his connection to Denver's criminal under-world.

"But my marital state is neither here nor there," Elmira contin-ued, dismissing it with a careless wave of the hand. "My point is that your newfound relations will be most upset with you if they find out that you lied to them. *They* think this wedding is a re-affirmation of vows already taken before a justice of the peace."

"What do you want in return for your silence, Mother? If I tell Uncle Myron not to come, he'll want to know why, and then the whole story will come out anyway."

"The last thing I want is to make trouble for you, my dear girl."

Diana braced herself.

"It's Maggie Northcote. I cannot abide the woman."

"I can hardly throw her out of her own house just to please you."

"But you can stop her meddling in your wedding plans. The minister came to call while you were away. She told him you wouldn't be needing his services after all. Said you were going to jump the broom instead. I think that was it. Some Scottish custom she read about. A hand-fast marriage. Something about a year and a day and then either one of you could change your minds. What nonsense!"

Diana lifted her eyes heavenward in a silent plea for patience. "I'll deal with Maggie, and the minister. But why in the world did you feel you needed to threaten me to ensure my cooperation? Surely you didn't believe I'd really go along with one of Ben's mother's lunatic notions?"

"How should I know what you'd do? I hadn't seen you in years when you turned up on my doorstep in Denver, determined to rush to the rescue even though no one had invited you to interfere."

Diana felt her whole body go rigid. Her hands curled into fists. She'd risked life and limb, health and happiness for her mother's sake. "Enough! You had better leave now, Mother. Maggie isn't the only one whose meddling is unwelcome."

Elmira studied her with undisguised curiosity. After a moment, she apparently decided she had pushed her daughter as far as she could and, with a shrug and a roll of the eyes, abandoned the field.

Diana closed the door after her, sagging against it in relief. She rested her forehead on the smooth wooden surface and took deep, calming breaths. What a way to start the morning! She only hoped the rest of the day would be an improvement.

∞

Ben waited at the bottom of the elaborate cherrywood staircase as Diana came down. She paused, one hand on the ornately carved griffin on the newel post, and smiled at him, instantly lifting his sagging spirits.

"Did you sleep well?" she asked.

"Better than I have for some time," he lied. "Have you eaten?"

"Annie brought me coffee and toast."

"You need more than that to sustain you. We've got a full day ahead of us." He took her arm and escorted her along the length of the main hallway towards the dining room at its end, their footfalls nearly soundless on the thick Oriental carpets that partially covered the highly polished cherrywood floor.

"Why so formal?" Diana asked as she passed between the two enormous gargoyles positioned on either side of a cherrywood arch. "I'd have thought you'd prefer the breakfast room."

"My mother is in there, along with your mother and her new husband."

Diana made a face. "Say no more." She lifted the lid off a serving dish on the sideboard and helped herself to a tender slice of ham. Cora Belle, Ben's cook, had set out a selection of foodstuffs in both the breakfast room and the dining room. She'd been with the Northcotes for a long time and if she did not precisely understand their eccentricities, she did know how to take them into account. Ben wondered if Cora Belle would consider coming with him to the new house.

"I had an early morning visit from my mother," Diana said. "She couldn't wait to tell me about your mother's recent . . . conversation with the minister."

"I already know about that. Don't worry. We'll straighten it out. That's our first stop this morning."

"Don't you have to go to your office? You must have people waiting who are anxious to consult you. You've been gone for several days."

Ben frowned. He was going to have to tell Diana sometime. He wasn't sure why he delayed. Perhaps because he felt so uncertain himself.

At first, he'd wondered that he hadn't felt more guilty for abandoning his patients. On the surface, he appeared to have neglected them shamefully, even though no one had gone untreated because of his absences. Other things had come first: his family; his fiancée; an old friend. But even before this latest crisis, he'd reached the conclusion that his skills were not being put to their best use in a general practice.

"I will stop in to make sure there are no frantic messages waiting," he said to Diana, "but there are other matters I need to deal with today."

"Our pursuit of Mr. Palmer and of Serena Dunbar's past?"

Ben nodded. *And at least one other thing*, he added silently. *My surprise for you.*

"Did you ask your mother about Mr. Palmer?"

"For all the good it did." At her questioning look, he shrugged and slathered marmalade on a piece of toast. "She doesn't know where he's staying. She only met him once before and that was years ago. But she did inform me, in that oh-so-casual way of hers, that Justus Palmer is a vampire."

That surprised a chuckle out of Diana. "She's been studying old legends again, I presume."

Ben couldn't help but be relieved that she didn't take the outrageous statement any more seriously than he did. "Or old novels," he suggested. "I believe we have a first edition of *Varney the Vampire or the Feast of Blood* in the library."

CHAPTER SIX

෨ᅇ

At the Hammond Street Congregational Church, the minister invited Ben and Diana into his study, but he regarded them with wary eyes until Ben managed to convince him that they did, indeed, still plan to have him marry them.

"No pagan rituals will be performed before, after, or instead of the official ceremony," Diana promised.

"I'm glad to hear it." The pastor was a genial man, but he took his responsibilities seriously. He did not allow them to leave until he had delivered a homily on the subject of matrimony and assured himself that they intended to attend church on a regular basis in the future. He made it clear that he did not consider Ben's duties as a physician adequate excuse for absence. He even went so far as to point out that it was against the law in Maine to work on Sunday, save in cases of dire emergency.

"Apparently preaching to a captive congregation counts as an emergency," Ben muttered when they finally made their escape from the church.

Diana barely reached the buggy before giving in to a fit of laughter. "Oh, Ben!" she chided him. "That is really too bad of you. But what a pompous man!"

Ben handed her into the buggy. "He means well enough, I suppose. Though I'd think the fact that you are a widow should have persuaded him to tone down his rhetoric."

"Perhaps he meant his words for you." Her eyes sparkled with amusement. "Naturally, as a *single* gentleman, you'll have had no dealings with women before marriage."

"It is not too late to jump the broom," Ben told her, clucking to the horse. "Or to select another pastor. We could be married at the First Methodist Church or the First Baptist or even at St. John's Episcopal."

"Let us not make matters any more complicated than they already are!"

Ben drove the short distance along Hammond Street to turn onto Harlow and a few minutes later made the right turn for Spring Street. The neighborhood was one of small, single-family dwellings interspersed with boarding houses, stores, and restaurants. His doctor's office occupied the ground floor of a plain wooden house. The place had a deserted look to it. There weren't even any messages slipped beneath the door.

Diana accompanied him as he crossed the simply furnished waiting room and entered the adjoining surgery. There *was* a note there, from the doctor he'd asked to cover for him. "Nothing pressing," he announced when he'd skimmed the contents. In fact it seemed he had a dearth of patients. They'd gotten tired of waiting for him to treat them and found other doctors.

He glanced up from the page to find Diana staring thoughtfully at the ceiling. "You mentioned once that we might consider living in the rooms over the office. The idea has begun to appeal to me."

"Don't worry. We won't be living with my mother and brother after we're married."

He'd never have a better opening, Ben decided, and hustled her out of the office and into the buggy. They set off at a fast clip, back across Kenduskeag Stream and then north along the road that followed its course. Ben reined in at what was clearly a construction site.

"I own this land, Diana," he blurted. He was as nervous as a lad at his first dance. He gestured at the skeletal framework of the building, stark against the trees and sky. "This is going to be our house."

Reaching behind the seat, Ben produced a set of architect's drawings that included a sketch of the finished structure. As he handed them over, it occurred to him that perhaps he should have sought Diana's opinion earlier, before construction began. His chest tightened uncomfortably. What if she hated the floorplan? What if she regarded keeping this secret as deceitful? Not everyone liked surprises.

The moment she unrolled the renderings, however, he breathed easier. Her face alight, Diana touched one gloved finger to the tower that dominated the sketch of the river elevation. "It's beautiful."

Ben grinned at her. "It is a 'country villa,' designed to be built between a street and a river. Because of that, the river elevation is as striking as the front of the house, complete with a veranda and a balcony." He flipped the page to show her the floor plan. "The entrance is by a porch divided from the front veranda by a gothic arch."

She leaned forward, eagerly studying the plans. "Dining room. Parlor. But a butler's pantry? Are we to have a flock of servants, then?"

"Only if you want them. Look here—under the principal flight of stairs is the stair to the kitchen, which is situated under the dining room. Under the butler's pantry is a kitchen pantry with a dumbwaiter. The rest of the basement is devoted to general cellarage."

She turned to the plan for the second floor.

"Three spacious rooms and one smaller one, all with those newfangled built-in closets. And a bath. And in the attic there is more storage space, plus room for more bedrooms."

She gazed at him in mock horror. "Just how large do you think our family is going to be?"

"That, my dear, is entirely up to you."

"A wise answer." Taking the floor plans with her, she hopped down from the buggy and went to stand by the foundation.

"The floors will be laid with one inch pine flooring, if that suits you. And the stairs will be built of black walnut on the newel, rail, and balusters."

"No gargoyles or griffins?"

"None," he promised. "The kitchen will have a pump and sink, with a drain to connect with the drain from the bath. There will even be speaking-tubes from the second floor hall and from the dining room to the kitchen, with porcelain mouthpieces and whistles attached."

A line of worry appeared to mar the perfection of her brow. "Can we afford this?"

"You are not marrying a poor man, Diana." He didn't resent the question. He knew enough of her history to understand why she would be concerned that they might run out of money.

"How much?"

He debated only a moment before telling her. "Five thousand dollars."

When her jaw dropped, he caught her under the chin with gentle fingers and lifted until her mouth closed. Leaning close, he kissed her, then whispered, "I am not as wealthy as Graham Somener, Diana, but I can afford to build this house for the woman I love."

Diana's mind was still full of plans for their new home when Ben escorted her into a handsome building of Frankfort granite and pressed brick with a Mansard roof and awnings over the ground floor windows.

"The library is housed on the second and third floors," Ben

said.

Access to the upper stories was by way of a door midway along the businesses occupying the Kenduskeag Block. Diana's feet clanged on the solid iron plate set into the floor in the recess at the foot of the flight of stairs. It was a handsome staircase, six feet wide and finished in natural woods. The walls on the sides were wainscoted with hard pine. The rails, posts and newels—just like those in the house Ben was building for her—were of black walnut. Diana smiled to herself. She was still having difficulty believing that they would soon have a house of their own. A *beautiful* house.

On the second floor, they entered a room bigger than the dining hall at the Bangor House, where they'd just had their noon meal. Although the place was scrupulously clean, the shelves dusted, the tables and chairs gleaming with furniture polish, the distinctive smell of book permeated every corner and alcove.

High four-light windows provided illumination, revealing a multitude of bookcases arranged in a semi-circular pattern around the librarian's desk. It was to this central position that Diana repaired once Ben left to pursue his own inquiries. She introduced herself to the librarian and asked if non-residents were permitted to use the facility.

"Certainly," the librarian said, "but they must pay three dollars a year for the privilege." At Diana's start of surprise, her thin lips twitched. "But you are about to become a resident, are you not? I saw the notice of your engagement to Dr. Northcote in the newspaper. Since you are to marry a local boy, you may browse our collection—24,397 volumes at present—without charge. If you wish to check out a book, however—and we only permit one to go out to each patron at a time—you must pay an annual fee of one dollar for a library card."

"I do not believe I will need one today, but I will certainly patronize the library in the future."

Diana's first cursory glance at the stacks told her that the library was in dire need of more space. A closer examination of its contents revealed that the collection would probably not be much help to her in investigating Serena Dunbar.

"Archaeology?" The librarian looked doubtful when Diana asked for her assistance. "Most of our books came to us from the library of the Bangor Mechanic Association, an organization which enables carpenters, machinists, iron workers, and ship-builders to get an education. I do not believe they had a great deal of interest in archaeology. But perhaps Professor Winthrop can help you."

"Who is he?"

"He taught at Harvard until his retirement last year."

Harvard? Diana's interest sharpened. That was where Miss Dunbar *claimed* to have been a student.

"Professor Lucien Winthrop was associated with the Peabody Museum. That institution has been a leader in the field of archae-ology since its foundation. The professor lives in Belfast now and spends his time looking into local legends. I heard him lecture a few months ago, about how almost all the Indians had left the state of Maine by the time of the Revolutionary War. Just a few solitary holdouts remained. Well, we all know about Molly Mo-lasses here in Bangor. She was over a hundred years old when she died twenty years ago. She left a daughter, but now she's gone, too. And in the last century there were Pierpole and his family down to Franklin County along the Sandy River—"

"Would the professor be willing to talk to me, do you think?"

"I'm sure he would. He seemed to be a very friendly fellow."

When Diana had the information she'd need to contact Win-throp, she asked to see that morning's edition of the *Daily Whig and Courier*, Bangor's leading newspaper. A report on Frank En-nis's death had been printed, but the editor had relegated it to one paragraph in the "State News" column. There was no hint in this brief account that Ennis might have been murdered. All it said was that he'd drowned while diving in Penobscot Bay. Keep

Island was not mentioned, nor was Graham Somener.

Had Somener used his influence to keep the murder quiet? Diana had to wonder. Any journalist worth the title should have pursued the story. Mysterious death. Private island owned by rich and famous recluse. And then there was all the secrecy about what Serena Dunbar claimed she was searching for—proof that the history books were wrong.

On the other hand, the *Whig and Courier* was not the most adventurous newspaper she'd ever seen. The other items in "State News," which took up a significant portion of the front page, ranged from a fire in a stable in Augusta (caused by rats gnawing on matches) to the escape to Nova Scotia of an alleged bigamist, and the ordination services for a new minister at the Unitarian Church in Presque Isle.

With a sigh, Diana reminded herself that she was no longer in New York City. If a killer was caught and brought to trial, perhaps then the story would be covered in more detail by the Bangor press, but right now no one particularly cared that Frank Ennis was dead.

She skimmed the remaining pages of the newspaper. The Republicans were about to convene their national convention in Chicago. Maine's own James G. Blaine was being touted as a candidate for President of the United States, even though he had lost to Grover Cleveland four years earlier. There was no mention of the Democratic Party's convention in St. Louis two weeks earlier, at which President Cleveland had been the unanimous choice, or of the Equal Rights Party ticket. Washington D.C. lawyer Belva Ann Lockwood was their candidate for President even though, as a woman, Mrs. Lockwood herself could not vote in the election.

"Did you find what you were looking for?" the librarian asked when Diana turned in the *Whig and Courier*.

"Alas, no. Have you any other local newspapers?"

"Only the *Kennebec Journal* weekly edition." She produced a newspaper dated five days earlier. "I do enjoy their woman's column."

Curious, Diana accepted the paper and spent a few minutes looking through it. A woman, she noted, was the editor of the woman's page. Always glad to find a fellow female journalist, she made a note of the name.

In this same 13 June *Kennebec Journal*, there was an account of a murder. This one had occurred on the ninth of June. A mail clerk had been found stabbed to death in a U. S. Mail car, "on bags of mail in a pool of blood," according to the reports of eye witnesses. Curiously, the article did not say in what town the discovery had been made or give any names save those of the doctors who examined the body and the undertaker called in to deal with it, but the report did include the information that the authorities had already solved the case. The man's death had occurred during a fight with another—also unnamed—postal worker. Whether the killer had been apprehended or not remained unclear.

Both the *Whig and Courier* and the *Kennebec Journal* were in need of an experienced crime reporter, Diana thought. Why, one person might even take on the job for every paper in the state, for surely there weren't all that many murders in any given year in Maine. Someone could make a specialty of covering them.

But not you, she reminded herself. She had sworn off investigating criminal activity. Criminals were too likely to take exception to being caught. They tended to strike out at anyone they perceived as a threat to their continued freedom. Diana had decided that she had too much to live for to risk her life for the sake of a byline.

"You're certain you don't want a library card?" the librarian asked when Diana returned the newspaper.

"Not today, thank you." She felt her cheeks grow warm. Ben might be wealthy, but she still had to watch her pennies. She did not have the requisite dollar with her. Her bag contained only one of the small notebooks she always carried, a pencil, an essence bottle, a handkerchief, and seventy-five cents.

"The money is not carelessly spent, I assure you."

"I didn't think it was."

"At one time there were several reading rooms throughout the city. Now all the volumes are here in one place. There is great danger of losing them in a fire. The city of Bangor badly needs a library building, Mrs. Spaulding." She leaned across the expanse of walnut, her voice vibrating with the intensity of her feelings on the subject. "Your support and that of Dr. Northcote could help us achieve our goal."

"I will certainly speak to him," Diana promised.

It occurred to her that as the wife of a prominent physician she would be expected to take an interest in the community. Espousing the library's cause would suit her very well. It would be pleasant, too, not to have to worry about money. She could almost sympathize with those women who wed for financial security alone, but she was very glad she was marrying Ben for love.

Upon leaving the library, Diana walked to the Western Union office. Their facilities were open twenty-four hours a day, seven days a week. The press operator remembered her from several visits a few months earlier and greeted her like an old friend.

"Sending a story to New York, are you?" he asked, sticking his head up above the sound-deadening glass-and-wood partition that separated his cubicle from others like it.

She hesitated. If she asked Horatio Foxe's help in getting information on Serena Dunbar, she risked arousing his interest in Frank Ennis's murder. Worse, she might place herself in a difficult position with Ben. She knew how he'd react when she admitted she'd been in touch with her editor at the *Independent Intelligencer*. And yet, if she didn't tell Ben, in light of her recent vow not to keep secrets from him, she'd have committed a worse betrayal. A quandary indeed!

"Mrs. Spaulding?" The operator looked perplexed, making her realize she hadn't answered him.

"I apologize. My mind wandered."

"Distracting place," he allowed. The clatter of quadruplex repeaters, typewriters, and other equipment created a cacophony of sound. No wonder they needed the noise-deadening glass!

"Yes, I do wish to send a telegram," Diana said. Ben would accept that it had been necessary to use *all* her resources.

ﻼﻼ

In between taking Diana to visit the building site and escorting her to the library, Ben had treated his fiancée to luncheon at the Bangor House. They'd agreed to return there and meet in the lobby at four. It was just past that hour when he arrived to find her deep in conversation with Mrs. Zenobia Entwhistle, wife of the president of a Bangor bank. Trust Diana to meet one of Bangor's most prominent citizens on her own! Ben just hoped she wasn't badgering the woman for an interview.

"Any luck?" Diana asked when pleasantries had been exchanged and Mrs. Entwhistle had gone on her way. She closed the little notebook she'd been writing in and tucked it into the pocket of her skirt. Seeing Ben's look of alarm, she chuckled. "Telephone number. She has one in her home."

"And I do not." Nor did he wish to acquire one of the contraptions. More trouble than they were worth, that was his opinion. "As for my luck, it was all bad. No one named Justus Palmer is registered at any of the hotels I've been to, nor was anyone by that name a guest last week."

"He might be using an assumed name."

"Or he might be staying at a boarding house, or with friends. Or even across the river in Brewer. And we know he was in Ellsworth the evening before last—"

"So he could be anywhere. Rather like looking for a needle in a haystack."

"I'm afraid so. Worse, I cannot discover how Mr. Palmer reached Ellsworth. It was not by stage coach."

If the sheriff had been correct in reporting that Palmer would not travel by water, then the only other ways for him to have reached the shiretown of Hancock County from Bangor would have been to hire a horse for the twenty-six mile journey or to go by train. Ben had also been to every livery stable in town. No one answering Palmer's description had so much as inquired about transportation.

When Diana was once more settled beside him in the doctor's wagon, Ben resumed his account. "I went to the passenger depot and questioned the station agent and other railroad employees, but no one remembers seeing a man of Palmer's description. I begin to think we should not put much stock in anything he told Sheriff Fields. If he lied about criminal activity on Keep Island, then that business about an aversion to travel by water may also have been a lie."

"Why would he make a claim like that it if isn't true?"

"A handy excuse to avoid going to Keep Island?"

"But shouldn't he have *wanted* to go there, to investigate for himself?"

"So one would think, but if he did not travel from Boston to Bangor by train, then he could have come by steamboat, and reached Ellsworth the same way—by boat. I did not have time to stop by the steamship office, but I can do so tomorrow."

"We have something else to do tomorrow. Have you ever heard the name Lucien Winthrop?"

"No."

"He is a retired professor. I believe he can assist us in our investigation of Serena Dunbar. I sent him a telegram, asking to interview him as an expert on archaeology, tomorrow if that is convenient for him. I hope to have his reply this evening."

"And where does this Professor Winthrop live?"

"Belfast? Is that far?"

"To go there and back will take all day, whether we travel by train or by steamer. I am surprised I did not run into you at the Western Union office," he added, steering the horse and buggy through the gates and up the long winding driveway to the Northcote mansion. "I sent a telegram of my own earlier today."

"Did you? To whom?"

"I asked an acquaintance of mine in Boston to pay a visit to Justus Palmer's office. Whoa, girl."

The slight jolt as the buggy came to a stop made Diana's next words sound a trifle breathless. "I sent a second telegram—to Horatio Foxe."

Ben fought a grimace and tried to make his voice sound hearty with approval. "A wise decision. If anyone can unearth dirt on Justus Palmer, Foxe is the man to do it."

"I did not think to mention Palmer. I asked about Serena Dunbar and Graham Somener."

Ben froze, every muscle tensing. "You promised Graham—"

"I couched my questions very carefully." Diana sent him a bright but tremulous smile. "Trust me, Ben. I can keep Horatio Foxe in line."

"Foxe scents scandal the way a . . . fox sniffs out chickens." He winced at the uninspired comparison.

"If Winthrop cannot answer my questions, I am certain Foxe will." She flashed a quick, mischievous grin. "You know what they say—never put all your eggs in one basket."

Ben groaned, but somehow the foolish wordplay relieved his mind. In spite of a few differences of opinion, all was well between them.

෯෬

Maggie Northcote cared not a whit how other folks managed their meals, but she sat down to sup at half past six every evening. As she'd announced earlier to everyone in the household, today she had something "special" planned.

According to the hand-lettered menus she'd set out at each

place, the dishes were all "delicacies from the Orient." Politeness, or perhaps shock, kept everyone silent for the few seconds it took to read down the list.

Certain there was a sickly green cast to her face, Diana tried not to contemplate what sheep's eyeballs or duck feet would look like. Fermented cabbage didn't sound much more appetizing, especially served with "baby mouse wine." There were to be candied grasshoppers for dessert.

She glanced at her mother, who was seated opposite her and next to Ed Leeves. A broad grin spread across Elmira's weathered face. "Can't be worse than rattlesnake," she whispered loudly to her husband, "or Rocky Mountain oysters."

Ben sat at the head of the table, with Elmira on one side and Diana on the other. Although he glared down the length of it at Maggie, she paid him no mind. The last member of the party, seated next to Diana and across from Ed, was Aaron Northcote. Alone of them all, he was visibly upset. His gaze darted from person to person, corner to corner, and sweat beaded on his forehead and his upper lip. He mopped both with his handkerchief. Diana braced herself when Cora Belle brought in the first platter.

In spite of her uneasiness about Aaron, Diana was unprepared when he suddenly produced a pistol from his breast pocket, cocked it, and pointed it at the cook. "Put that disgusting mess at the other end of the table or I'll add brain and bone to the ingredients."

Cora Belle obeyed, but she slammed the serving dish down so hard that the spoon resting on top of the food bounced a good four inches. Hands on hips, she ignored Aaron to address Ben. "That's it! I've put up with him for years but enough is enough. I won't be threatened. You'll have to beg me on bended knee to come back and work in this house again!" Turning on her heel, she stormed out of the dining room, head held high and starched apron crackling as she untied it and threw it to the floor en route to the door.

"You may bring in the next course any time," Maggie called after her.

With a hearty horse laugh that made her daughter wince and Aaron jump and bobble the gun, Elmira helped herself to a heaping portion of "sheep's eyeballs." Popping one into her mouth, she chewed with every indication of enjoyment as she passed the platter to her husband. Ed thrust it at Maggie without taking any. With a fulminating glare for Diana's mother, she followed Elmira's example.

Diana shifted her attention back to the gun. Aaron's gaze had fixed on the entrée. He stared at the platter's contents with a kind of fascinated horror and when his mother whipped a spoonful of the disgusting objects in his direction, he yelped and tipped over backward in his chair. The gun discharged, striking the ceiling and sending a shower of plaster down on everyone at the table.

Ben and Diana dove for the weapon at the same moment, colliding with each other and tumbling down on top of Aaron. By the time they'd disentangled themselves, Aaron was swearing a blue streak, and most creatively, too. Diana fought a blush as she helped him to his feet, but he didn't seem to notice. In fact, he was not aware of any of them. He was berating someone only he could see for not warning him of this evening's fiasco.

"They aren't really sheep's eyes," Maggie muttered. "Honestly, such a fuss. No one ever lets me have any fun anymore."

With the gun safely unloaded and stored in his own jacket pocket, Ben led his brother from the dining room. Diana followed, scooping up the fallen apron on her way out. As she'd anticipated, the servants were clustered just outside the door.

"Find something decent to serve," Ben told Cora Belle. When she started to protest, he silenced her by doubling her salary on the spot.

"Give me that," Cora Belle muttered, snatching the apron out of Diana's hands. "But this is the last time I come back, you mark my words."

No one paid any attention to her, least of all Diana. With the help of Aaron's manservant, she and Ben got Aaron back to his carriage house and settled in for the night with a sedative.

"He hasn't been this bad in a long time," Ben said when they came back out into the garden. "I had hoped . . . ."

"You'll find a cure." The confidence in her voice concealed her doubts. No one really understood why a person suddenly ran mad, not even Ben, who had studied the subject for many years and visited countless institutions for the treatment of the insane.

"I doubt there is only one cure. Not when symptoms manifest themselves in so many different ways. The treatment that helps Graham control his irrational outbursts of temper has no effect at all on Aaron."

Lost in his own gloomy thoughts, Ben did not seem to hear the small, startled sound Diana made. Was Graham Somener really that much like Aaron? Had they both avoided being committed to an asylum by a hair's breadth?

She considered the notion, remembering how unstable Somener's emotions had been. He had run away to his island, shunning society. Had guilt driven him to the brink of madness? Or had it been the constant badgering of newspaper reporters? She found the latter idea all too plausible. Some of her colleagues were relentless in their pursuit of scandal.

They came to a halt beside a rosebush. Ben visibly shook off his dark mood and plucked one of the pale pink buds. After he'd carefully removed all the thorns, he tucked it behind Diana's ear.

"Are you hungry?" he asked. "Cora Belle can—"

"No. For once, I am not at all peckish." Nor did she have any desire to spend more time with Maggie right now. Her own mother was nearly as bad. Diana fingered the soft rose petals, inhaling their delicate scent. "Do you know what Rocky Mountain oysters are?"

He laughed, then winced. "Yes. Poor bulls."

"Cowboys consider them a delicacy."

"Some people will eat anything."

They walked awhile, talking of inconsequential things, and Diana was in much better humor by the time they returned to the house. She brightened even more when she saw that a Western Union delivery boy had just arrived.

"Reply from Winthrop?" Ben asked when he'd given the lad a generous tip and sent him on his way.

"I hope one of them is." She held two telegrams and for some reason felt reluctant to open either.

She was not given to premonitions. Surely it was just a gust of wind responsible for the sudden chill snaking up her spine.

It was true that telegrams had brought her bad news before. Devastating news. But that was no reason to think these were anything but mundane replies to the messages she'd sent earlier. One had doubtless been sent by Professor Winthrop. The other would be from Horatio Foxe.

Silently chastising herself for indulging in foolish, unfounded fears, Diana opened the first telegram, read it, and passed it on to Ben. It was indeed a reply from Lucien Winthrop. He'd agreed to talk to her and her "associate" the next day.

"Associate?" Ben quirked a brow at her.

"You, of course. Telegrams do not give one much room for explanations. *Another* argument for installing a telephone."

"Telegrams," he pointed out, "can be sent anywhere. To speak to someone on the telephone, both parties have to be on the same exchange. At last report, I believe there were only some 250 telephones in Bangor . . . and you are not acquainted with any of the people who have them."

"Except Mrs Entwhistle," she reminded him.

"And why," Ben asked, "would you wish to further your acquaintance with her?"

"Perhaps I do not, but I cannot decide until I know her better. Surely you want me to have friends. And she was kind enough to invite me to come to the next meeting of the Chautauquan Literary and Scientific Circle. They meet, she tells me, at the Baptist Church."

Diana was prepared to go on at length, teasing him about the benefits of joining this group, although she had difficulty imagining herself enjoying a series of *assigned* readings. He stopped the game by reminding her that she had not yet opened the second telegram. She did so, still smiling, but her good humor vanished the moment she absorbed its contents.

"Gracious," she whispered. "A cryptic warning."

She passed the slip of paper to Ben when he reached out to steady her.

"Stop meddling?" His tone mingled disbelief with budding anger.

"Succinct and to the point, don't you think?"

"This is a threat."

"So I gathered." Diana's heart raced and her knees had gone wobbly. This manifestation of physical weakness annoyed her and prompted her to square her shoulders and feign a bravado she was far from feeling. "Which one of them do you think sent it, Justus Palmer or Serena Dunbar?"

"The telegram came to you."

"Serena, then. But how did she know I was planning to look into her background?"

"More to the point, how did she manage to dispatch a telegram? She'd have had to travel to Belfast to send this."

"Why Belfast?"

"That's the nearest place to Keep Island with a telegraph office. If you recall, that's where Graham went to send for me." Ben pulled her close, so that her head was nestled against his shoulder. "I'm not sure it's such a good idea for you to travel there tomorrow."

Diana pulled away from him. "On the contrary. This gives me all the more reason to go! We can stop at the Western Union office while we're there and find out who sent this telegram. Surely someone will remember, especially if it was Miss Dunbar."

"I don't—"

"If someone wants us to cease and desist, that means there's something incriminating to be found. We can't stop looking now."

Ben gave her a long, hard look before relenting. "It is a good thing you arranged for your 'associate' to accompany you to Belfast," he grumbled, extending a hand in her direction, "because as long as there is any possibility that you are in danger, I do not intend to let you out of my sight."

"That sounds promising," she replied in a throaty purr, and went willingly into his arms.

CHAPTER SEVEN

ଚ୬ୠ

After four and a half hours aboard a steamer, it was a relief to Ben to stretch his legs. The city of Belfast was the shire town of Waldo County but had only a quarter of the population of Bangor. It was an easy walk to the Western Union office and not at all difficult to ascertain that Diana's threatening telegram had indeed originated there. Unfortunately, the operator could not tell them who had sent it. The message, together with money enough to pay to dispatch it, had been stuffed under the door. She'd seen nothing but a vague silhouette through the window glass.

"No help here," Diana lamented as they turned their steps towards Lucien Winthrop's house.

The street ran uphill from Belfast Bay, as uneven as it was steep. Diana's cheeks were pink with exertion and even Ben was a trifle winded by the time they reached their destination. It was a large, white clapboard house surrounded by trees. The nearest neighbors were some distance away.

A factory whistle sounded just as they stepped onto Winthrop's porch, signaling that it was noon. Ben glanced at his watch, unsurprised to find it read only 11:30. The previous year, when the Legislature had ordered all towns to change to railroad time and adjust their municipal clocks to that standard, a great many individual citizens, including owners of manufactories, had dug in their heels and stubbornly stayed on "sun time."

"You must be Mr. Spaulding," said the elderly gentleman who answered the door. Sunlight glinted on the thick lenses of his small, round spectacles, preventing Ben from seeing his eyes. Ignoring Diana, he extended his right hand to Ben. His left retained a firm grip on the head of an ornately carved cane.

"I am the one with whom you corresponded," Diana corrected him, stepping in front of Ben to grasp the proffered hand, give a quick, firm shake, and release it. "*Mrs.* Spaulding. This is Dr. Northcote."

Winthrop's face froze, his expression caught between bemusement and disbelief. "*You're* D. Spaulding?"

"I am."

Ben fought a smile. He doubted it had even occurred to Diana that Winthrop would assume she was a man.

Winthrop's body shifted, as if to block entry into his home.

Drawing herself up straighter, Diana refused to back down. "I intended no deceit, Professor Winthrop. I simply want to interview you."

"All women are deceivers." Winthrop showed no sign of moving, either.

"Be that as it may, I *am* a reporter for the *New York Independent Intelligencer*, as I said in my telegram. I wish to interview you because I am writing a series of profiles of outstanding citizens of this fair state—the rich, the famous, the notorious—"

"Which am I?" Winthrop interrupted.

Caught off guard by the abrupt question, Diana stumbled over her answer. "F-f-famous."

"May we come in?" Ben interjected. "Perhaps beg a drink of water? It was a thirsty climb from the steamboat wharf."

Lucien Winthrop did not seem inclined to take pity on them, but the request successfully redirected his attention to Ben. "You're the 'associate' she spoke of in her telegram?"

"I am. In addition, Mrs. Spaulding is my fiancée."

"Northcote, eh? Doctor, she said. Of what?"

"Medicine."

"Know anything about archaeology?"

"A bit. As a lad I spent many summers searching for Indian artifacts along the coast." He added a few details, enough to convince Winthrop that although he was an amateur, he had at least made the effort to learn the names of early Maine tribes. He did not mention that his companion on these "expeditions" had been Graham Somener.

Shuffling as he walked and using the cane to maintain his balance, Winthrop at last stepped back and allowed them to enter. "Thirsty are you?" he muttered. "I suppose you expect to be fed, as well."

He herded them along the hallway and into a parlor, tugging on a convenient bell pull as he passed it. A moment later, an elderly woman, clearly the housekeeper, appeared in the doorway.

"Bring tea," Winthrop barked at her, "and whatever you have prepared for luncheon."

Diana smiled politely and thanked him for his consideration. Ben was happy to let her take control of the conversation. He enjoyed watching her work.

"You made quite an impression on the members of your audience when you lectured on Indians in Bangor," Diana ventured after she settled herself in one of Winthrop's well-worn but comfortable chairs. "I understand you are an expert on local legends and have a particular interest in the ancient peoples of Maine."

"Did you attend my little talk?"

"Alas, no. But I have recently spoken to someone who did and she encouraged me to contact you." Diana explained about her visit to the public library and her failure to unearth much information about local archaeologists. She did not mention why she'd been looking. "As soon as the librarian told me about your lecture, I knew I had found the ideal subject for my column.'"

Winthrop didn't bother to hide his skepticism, but before he could comment his housekeeper returned with food and drink, rolling in a cart containing a teapot, cups, saucers, a platter of sandwiches, and three small plates. Either Winthrop did not have a proper dining room or he was disinclined to use it. After pouring in a rather haphazard manner and passing around the cups, the housekeeper left.

A pleasant expression fixed on her face like a mask, Diana postponed her interview long enough to eat a sandwich. Ben took one for himself, leaned back in his chair, and propped one ankle on the opposite knee, quietly content.

"Do you know anything about a woman archaeologist working near here?" Diana asked.

The sugar Winthrop was about to add to his tea missed the cup and landed in the saucer. Very carefully, he set both down on the small table beside his chair and fixed Diana with a hard look. "A woman archaeologist, you say?" He waited a beat. "And who might that be?"

"A Miss Dunbar. Serena Dunbar. She has begun to excavate on one of the islands in Penobscot Bay."

"Ah."

"So you do recognize the name?" Ben noticed the disappointment in Diana's voice. She'd been hoping Winthrop had never heard of Miss Dunbar, which would support the theory that she was a confidence woman.

"I may be wrong," Winthrop said, "but I believe that's the young woman who caused such a ruckus at the Peabody Museum a few years back. I never met her myself. I was working in Nova Scotia at the time. But the name . . . yes, I am quite certain it was Dunbar."

"What did she do?"

"Attempted to gain admission as a private student. Kicked up a fuss when the graduate school rejected her. Well, what do you expect? No woman has the educational background to qualify."

"She claims to have been a student at Harvard."

Diana inclined her body forward in order to better see Winthrop's face when she made this announcement. Ben already had a clear view. The professor's eyes narrowed to slits.

"Presumptuous baggage!"

Serena? Ben wondered. Or Diana?

Bitterness underscored the old man's words, and he glared at Diana throughout his diatribe. "The Peabody Museum is part of Harvard, but if Miss Dunbar was ever admitted to either, it was not for long. She bamboozled the director with some wild theory she'd dreamed up. He lauded her ideas at first, *and* her. Fortunately others less distracted by her person persuaded him that he was in error. She was nothing but trouble." A flush darkened Winthrop's lined, leathery skin, and behind the glasses his eyes glittered with hatred.

"You seem extraordinarily agitated, sir." Ben, mulling over the idea of Serena Dunbar as a seducer of well-respected archaeology professors, wondered if she'd also tried to work her wiles on Lucien Winthrop. Ben had no trouble at all imagining that she'd granted intimate favors to Graham Somener in order to win his permission to dig up Keep Island.

"I dislike charlatans!" Winthrop snapped. "I am certain you would be somewhat short tempered yourself, Dr. Northcote, if you were asked about the practices of some quack."

"What about Paul Carstairs?" Diana asked.

Winthrop didn't bother to look her way. "Never heard of him." He reached for his cup and took a reviving swig of hot tea.

"Frank Ennis?"

"No." He took off his glasses, cleaned them with his handkerchief, and replaced them on the bridge of a thin, slightly hooked nose. "Who are they?"

"Miss Dunbar's associates."

"Then it is likely they are amateurs with no proper training whatsoever. Such people take up archaeology as a hobby, a treasure hunt. They do more harm than good. They are careless when they dig, destroying as much as they discover, and have a tendency to go haring off after unsubstantiated rumors."

Ben—polishing off a second sandwich filled with thinly sliced chicken and quite tasty—thought that the same things had probably been said about Heinrich Schliemann, before he proved his critics wrong by discovering the ruins of Troy.

"Have you encountered any legends about Keep Island in your studies?" Diana asked.

Winthrop abruptly stopped drumming his fingers on the arm of his chair. "Is that where the Dunnett woman is working?"

"Dunbar," Diana corrected him.

"I am not familiar with the place. I know nothing about it."

Ben found that difficult to believe. As the crow flew, Keep Island was less than fifteen miles from Belfast, and they already knew that the locals had taken an interest. Witness that dory on the day of the dive.

With their modest repast nearly depleted, Diana returned to the subject of Serena's credentials. "Could she have received training elsewhere?"

"I'd have heard of it if she had," Winthrop insisted, "and I would have met her if she'd ever worked on a legitimate excavation anywhere in New England."

"But women *are* sometimes trained as archaeologists, are they not?"

"A few become qualified to *assist*." It seemed to pain Winthrop to admit even that much. "Most do not. They are rank amateurs and unwomanly with it, parading about in men's clothing, as though that alone can make them our equals!"

"Does Harvard ever admit women to—"

"I believe you said you wanted to talk to me about *my* work, Mrs. Spaulding," Winthrop cut in. "Shall we begin?"

Diana did not much like Lucien Winthrop, but at least he proved easy to interview. Asked a single question, he would ramble on at length, so long as it was a topic that interested him. He did not share the common fascination with ancient Egypt or the pre-Columbian cultures of Central and South America, but he proudly showed off the artifacts that decorated the walls of his library and was more than willing to expound on his theories about the everyday life of prehistoric Maine Indians.

"I understand there are ongoing excavations at a place called Casa Grande," Diana said, calling up the name Ben had told her Miss Dunbar had mentioned in connection with Paul Carstairs. "Did you have a hand in that?"

Winthrop scowled. "Why would I? My primary field of study is early New England."

"But you know about that project?"

"Hemenway Southwestern Archaeological Expedition. Yes. It is financed by Mary Hemenway of Boston."

"A woman?" Diana could not quite keep the amusement out of her voice, but Winthrop didn't seem to notice.

"A philanthropist, not an archaeologist. The expedition explored along the Gila River and did some excavating of Hohokam ruins in the Salt River Valley and then visited Casa Grande this past January only to discover that souvenir hunters had vandalized the place. That launched an effort to preserve the ruins. There was a lengthy piece in the *Boston Herald*."

"Did they—"

"Mrs. Spaulding, Casa Grande is an example of a class of structure peculiar to the ancient town-dwellers of the Southwest. While interesting, it has little to do with most Indians, especially those in the Northeast."

"Tell me, sir," Ben interrupted smoothly, "what is your opinion on the existence of the fabled city of Norombega, described by some early explorers as being in the vicinity of present-day Bangor?"

This appeared to be a subject more to Winthrop's liking. Initially Diana found the tale, a local legend, fascinating, but soon the professor had launched into one of his more pedantic lectures. Concluding that it was too technical—and too boring—to keep her attention, Diana decided that the interview was at an end.

Tucking her little notebook with its green cloth cover into her pocket, she considered what more she might learn while they were here. Winthrop's statements about Serena Dunbar had been offhand at first, then more personal. His claim never to have met her had not been convincing, nor had his statement that he'd never heard of Keep Island. He'd been just a little too vehement in his denials. He was hiding something, but what?

One look at Ben and Professor Winthrop assured Diana that they were deeply involved in a lively debate concerning the origins of the earliest settlers along the Maine coast. Ben spoke with surprising authority on the subject, revealing a side of himself Diana had not seen before.

The man was just full of surprises, she thought as she slipped quietly out of the parlor, most of them quite wonderful. A smile on her face, she began to explore the rest of Professor Winthrop's house. If Winthrop even noticed she was gone, he'd assume she'd gone to answer a call of nature.

The professor's library was just down the hall from the parlor. After a furtive glance over her shoulder, Diana ducked inside and closed the door behind her. Let the eccentric old curmudgeon babble on to Ben. She'd see what she could discover on her own.

She found herself in a room lined floor to ceiling with shelves containing books, document boxes, and scholarly periodicals. A roll-top desk held place of honor to the left of the fireplace and it, too, overflowed with thick tomes. Some Winthrop had left lying open. Others bristled with slips of paper marking pages he wanted to look at again. Clearly, in spite of his retirement from Harvard, he was still a working scholar.

Diana slid into the desk chair and began to examine the clutter. One book related to Micmac legends about a hero named Glooscap. Another discussed Abnaki artifacts. There was also a report on the current state of members of the Penobscot and Passamaquoddy tribes. A yellowed and much-thumbed issue of the *Journal of the Royal Geographical Society* from 1835 lay half hidden beneath it.

Since nothing there seemed to have a connection to Serena Dunbar or Keep Island, Diana abandoned the desk to browse among the books on Winthrop's shelves. She was not certain what she expected to find. In fact, after examining several extensive sections of shelving, she began to wonder if she would recognize significant material even if she stumbled upon it.

It was with a sense of pleasure and no little relief that she spotted the annual report of the Peabody Museum at Harvard University for 1886. Diana removed the volume from the shelf and quickly found the list of officers and special assistants. The first name she came to was Frederick Ward Putnam, Peabody Professor of American Archaeology and Ethnology at Harvard University, Curator.

Dear Dr. Putnam, Miss Dunbar had said that evening in her bedroom. *He thought I was brilliant.*

A brilliant confidence woman! And Putnam, no doubt, was the director Winthrop said she'd bamboozled. Miss Dunbar had taken an extraordinary amount of time and trouble with her scheme, whatever it was. She must have picked Putnam's brain to learn how to pass herself off as an archaeologist. Then she'd devised an elaborate plot that required three people and boatloads of equipment to carry out. The only thing she hadn't foreseen was that Professor Winthrop would retire in the vicinity. That was a piece of sheer bad luck for Miss Serena Dunbar.

Diana located Lucien Winthrop's name a few lines below Putnam's. He'd been an "Assistant in the Field." Reading on, Diana realized that almost everyone seemed to be an assistant of some sort. To her surprise, several of them were female.

Qualified to assist, Professor Winthrop had said, making it sound as if women in archaeology were only fit to take notes and wash pots. She read on. One woman was an "Assistant to the Museum," another "Special Assistant in American Ethnology," and still another a "Student Assistant." A fourth held the title "Special Assistant in Mexican Archaeology."

Skipping down to a second list with the heading "Students," Diana found several names identified as being "in the Graduate School" and one was "Class of '87. Private Student." She wondered precisely what that meant, but she did not suppose it mattered. There were no females on this list.

Idly, she skimmed the rest of the report, stopping to read in more detail only when she caught sight of a second reference to one of the special assistants. Professor Putnam had singled a woman out for praise in his curator's report. "She is able to perform thorough and important work," he wrote. "Familiar with the Nahuatl language, having intimate and influential friends among the Mexicans, and with an exceptional talent for linguistics and archaeology, as well as being thoroughly informed in all the early native and Spanish writings relating to Mexico and its people." He called her preparation for her duties "as remarkable as it is exceptional."

Winthrop's contention that women lacked sufficient educational background might be true—the titles "Doctor" or "Professor" did not appear before any female names—but at least one woman had apparently been accepted by the head of the Peabody as an expert in her field.

Diana closed the 1886 annual report and considered what she'd learned. She had a feeling that the addition of this woman to the staff of the Peabody had hastened Winthrop's retirement. It would certainly have done nothing to lessen his obvious dislike of women in a male profession.

Concerning Serena Dunbar, however, Diana was inclined to accept Winthrop's assessment. He had confirmed what she already suspected, that Miss Dunbar was not an archaeologist of any sort. That being the case, she was undoubtedly a confidence woman, an exceedingly clever one who'd taken up with a real archaeologist in order to learn enough about the subject to pass herself off as a professional.

Returning to the parlor with as little fuss as she'd left it, Diana found Ben and Winthrop still discussing colonial days. If either one had noticed her absence, they did not mention it. She settled into the same chair she'd previously occupied and turned her thoughts to what she should do next. A telegram to the Peabody Museum would be in order, she decided, to confirm that Professor Winthrop had told them the truth about Miss Dunbar. A conscientious journalist never relied on only one source.

❧⦿☙

Diana was barely awake the next morning when her bedroom was invaded. Her mother came in first, closely followed by Maggie Northcote and a local dressmaker. The latter, a quiet little woman armed with pins and measuring tapes, listened attentively as Elmira and Maggie gave orders. She paid no attention whatsoever to Diana.

"White corded silk with point lace," Elmira said.

"No. White satin with crystal beads," Maggie countered.

"Satin is too heavy for this time of year."

"June in Maine is not that warm. A bridal suit should be satin. Perhaps brocaded instead of plain? With a full train of the plain, puffed in back, and a pointed waist trimmed with lace."

"Silk," Elmira insisted, "but perhaps Ottoman silk with a pearl front."

Desperate for coffee, Diana was slow to rally. She couldn't understand why they were discussing bridal dresses. She already had the gown she meant to wear at the ceremony, a simple light gray silk dress embroidered in silver. She'd bought it in Denver as part of the trousseau her mother had paid for.

Elmira and Maggie were too busy arguing to notice when Diana slipped out of the bedroom and went downstairs to the dining room. The sideboard was laden with breakfast dishes and—thank God!—a full pot of coffee.

Her mother's husband, Ed Leeves, sat at one end of the table, engrossed in a newspaper. He nodded a good morning to her but left her alone until she'd consumed two cups of strong coffee and a plate of buttered toast.

"Your mother only wants what's best for you," he said mildly.

"My mother is going to drive me to distraction," Diana muttered.

She was awake enough now to comprehend what was going on in her bedroom. Her first impulse was to flee, but even if she had been fully dressed, instead of wearing only her nightclothes, it wouldn't do her any good. She'd have to come back at some point and Elmira would still be here.

"I've found it is easiest to pay lip service to whatever she wants," Leeves said, winking one coal-black eye, "then suit myself."

Diana had no intention of taking advice from a man who controlled half the criminal activities of Denver, but she was grateful for his sympathy. "That is difficult to do when they seem determined to rearrange every aspect of my wedding."

"Is it really so important what dress you wear?"

Diana thought about it. "Yes." Her mother was a formidable woman. So was Maggie Northcote. But it was *Diana's* wedding.

Squaring her shoulders, she marched back upstairs. They had moved on to arguing over the veil—white nun's veiling was Maggie's choice; Elmira opted for point lace.

"I am not wearing a veil," Diana said, stepping into the room. "Only first-time brides wear veils, or white dresses, or carry orange blossoms. Besides, I already have my bridal gown. I'm sorry," she said to the dressmaker, "but I do not need your services today."

"But only look at this one," Elmira wailed, thrusting a fashion print at her. "That's Brussels lace for the trim and the cathedral train is decorated with balayeuse on the inside outer edge."

"I don't even know what balayeuse is," Diana protested.

"Dust ruffle," Maggie supplied, *sotto voce*.

Elmira glared at her. "You could have it made in cream silk faille if white offends you."

Diana waited until the dressmaker had gathered up her paraphernalia and left before she rounded on the other two women. "This is *my* wedding. I have already made all the necessary arrangements and I'll thank you not to interfere with them."

"You can't shut us out," her mother protested. "We have a right—"

"You have the right to attend, nothing more."

Elmira looked sulky. "You might at least share some of the details with us. How else are we to know what you have planned."

"Such as?"

"Who is to give the bride away. Ed would—"

"My grandfather will perform that service." Word had been waiting upon their return from Belfast that Isaac Torrence and his daughter, Diana's Aunt Janette, would be arriving a few days early for the wedding. She was looking forward to seeing them again. Her mother was not.

"He's ninety-two," Elmira objected. "Are you sure he can manage to totter down the aisle?"

"Who is to stand up with you?" Maggie asked. "And with Ben? Is that why he really went to Keep Island? Is Graham—?"

"Ben's brother will serve as his groomsman. I would have liked my old friend Rowena Foxe to attend me, but she is unable to make the long trip from California. I've asked Jerusha Fildale to be my bridesmaid instead."

Maggie brightened. "Oh, I remember her. The actress."

"An *actress!*" Elmira looked horrified at the very idea.

"For heaven's sake, Mother, given what you do for a living, how can you possibly object to acting as a profession?"

Years ago, Diana's parents had disowned her for eloping with an actor, but things had changed since then. Elmira no longer had the high moral ground.

"Shhh! The servants!" Elmira's cheeks flamed, betraying just how deeply annoyed she was.

Diana did not mistake the sudden rush of color for embarrassment. She didn't think it was possible to embarrass either Elmira or Maggie. She did, however, obligingly lower her voice.

"Why are you two suddenly so determined to take control of my nuptials?"

Elmira and Maggie exchanged an enigmatic look before Maggie spoke. "Mrs. Entwhistle called for you while you were away. You didn't tell me you'd met her, Diana."

"We crossed paths in town the other day, but what possible bearing can Zenobia Entwhistle have on my wedding?"

"She's an arbiter of fashion in this town. And she liked you. I must confess I've never cared for the woman myself, and I have no desire to move in her circle, but she's someone to be cultivated if you want to fit into the social life of your new home town."

Did she? Diana sank slowly onto the foot of the bed and thought about that. She couldn't imagine spending all her time playing whist and doing "good works."

"There's time yet to invite the Entwhistles to your wedding," Elmira said.

"No, there is not. The guest list is complete. All the invitations I mean to send have gone out."

"Not even one exception?" Maggie asked, frowning.

Diana sighed. "Who?"

"Justus Palmer."

Diana felt her jaw drop. A moment later she was on her feet and moving in on Maggie. "You know where he is? Tell me."

Caught off guard, Ben's mother took a step back, almost plowing into Elmira. "I don't know where he's staying, no, but I'm sure it's somewhere nearby."

"When did you see him last?"

Two bright spots of color bloomed on Maggie's cheeks. Apparently, Diana thought, she had been wrong about Maggie's capacity for embarrassment. "Well?"

"Around midnight," Maggie mumbled.

"Last night?" Taken aback, Diana's voice came out as a squeak.

Elmira gave a snort of laughter. "What hidden depths you have, Maggie Northcote. The man is at least twenty years your junior."

"Mother, please."

"Looks can be deceiving!" Maggie shot back. She stood a bit taller as she glared at Elmira. "There is nothing wrong with taking a moonlit stroll in a garden. I have nothing to be ashamed of."

"Our garden?" Diana was still struggling to comprehend the ramifications of this new development. The image of Maggie and Palmer together in the garden refused to come into focus.

"I was out gathering herbs," Maggie said. "They're best when picked at midnight, you know, by the light of a full moon. Granted the moon wasn't quite at the full last night. It won't be for three more days. But I wanted to make a particular potion this afternoon, so I decided it was close enough. In any case, I'd just filled my basket and started back inside when, all of a sudden, there he was."

Diana cursed silently. Justus Palmer had been here, right beneath their noses, and they hadn't had an inkling of his presence.

"We walked. We talked. Then he bit my neck. I did tell you he's a vampire, didn't I?"

Elmira burst into laughter. Diana groaned. She should have known better. This was just one of Maggie's outrageous stories.

"No, really! Look, I'll prove it." She undid enough buttons to pull the collar away from her throat. "See!"

There did appear to be two little red marks on the skin, but on closer inspection, Diana concluded that Maggie had made them herself. It looked as if she'd stabbed herself with a two-tined fork.

For once Elmira made no comment. Diana pursed her lips, concern for her future mother-in-law flooding through her. Were the delusions getting worse? Had what Ben insisted on calling "eccentricity" crossed over into insanity?

Diana's troubled thoughts were interrupted when Annie, the maid, scratched at the door. "Beggin' your pardon, mum, but the Western Union boy's come with a telegram."

"Three telegrams," Ben said, entering the room behind her. "Two are for you." He drew her a little apart from their mothers and lowered his voice. "Mine is from the county attorney. Frank Ennis is to be buried tomorrow in Ellsworth. I should attend the funeral. I may need to stay away overnight."

"I'm going with you."

He gestured towards the other telegrams, now crumpled in her hand, "Perhaps you should see what those contain first."

Tearing the first one open, she skimmed the contents. This time it was not a threat, or at least not a threat of the same kind. It came from Horatio Foxe in reply to her request for information. Her heart sank as she read. "Oh, no!"

"What?"

Guilt assailing her, Diana steeled herself to admit that she'd made a mistake. "You were right, Ben. I'm afraid my questions sparked Foxe's interest. He says he's found out something about Graham Somener."

The vein in Ben's neck pulsed once before he exerted tight control over any outward signs of annoyance. "What has he learned?"

"He doesn't say, but he wants me to pursue my 'interview with the reclusive millionaire.'" She gathered her nerve and blurted out the rest: "He says he'll be in Bangor a few days earlier than he originally planned."

"Tell him no. On both counts."

Collapsing into the small boudoir chair across from the bed, Diana sent a fulminating glare his way. He knew better than to believe *that* would work. "He's on the trail of a story, Ben. He'll pursue it with or without my cooperation. You know how he is."

"I do know." Ben paced, looking like a caged lion in the narrow confines of Diana's bedroom. "And since we did invite him to the wedding, he'll be right here on the spot. That's the last thing Graham needs right now."

"I know. I'm sorry. I *was* careful about the way I worded the telegram. I never thought—"

"You don't think," he grumbled. "That's just the trouble!"

She bristled at the criticism but never got a chance to defend herself.

"So that delightful Mr. Foxe is coming early, too?" Maggie sidled up to Ben and put a hand on his sleeve. "How lucky it is that we've room for one more."

"We do not have—"

She talked right over his protest. "The secret of a successful marriage is to share a bed and never climb into it angry. I'll see to it that Diana's things are transferred to your room, shall I, Ben? Then Mr. Foxe can have this one."

"There's no rush," Ben said between clenched teeth.

"That's right," Diana agreed. "Mr. Foxe won't be arriving right away. Even if he left New York today, he wouldn't reach Bangor until sometime tomorrow."

"No time like the present to prepare." Maggie bustled off, doubtless to order Annie to pack up Diana's belongings. Elmira, looking thoughtful, followed her out.

Diana glanced at Ben. His temper had cooled. Now his eyes were filled with regret . . . and with something that looked suspiciously like anticipation.

She felt her blood heat. Sleeping with Ben would be no hardship, even if she did hate being manipulated by his mother.

"Foxe may be a problem," Ben said, pulling her thoughts back out of his bedroom.

"I should never have contacted him. He's worse than a dog worrying a bone when he catches wind of a scandal, and in this case the bone is Graham Somener. I didn't say I suspected either Miss Dunbar or Mr. Somener of murder. I didn't even say there had been a murder. But Foxe could have found out on his own. He has sources everywhere. And once he heard that someone was dead under mysterious circumstances, he'll have leapt to the conclusion that Mr. Somener was involved. With the least bit of evidence, he'll chew your friend up and spit him out, replete with scandalous details he's invented himself."

"I can't let that happen. Graham's been through too much already with that business five years ago. This could push him over the edge."

"There's little you can do to prevent it . . . unless we discover who really did kill Frank Ennis."

"Perhaps we have that answer already." Ben sounded cautiously optimistic. "Is that third telegram from the Peabody Museum?"

Distracted by her concerns about Foxe, Diana had all but forgotten about the last yellow envelope. After their return from Belfast, she had gone through with her plan to query the Peabody Museum, asking the director to verify the facts they'd learned from Professor Winthrop.

She read the reply aloud: "'DUNBAR PRIVATE STUDENT 1885. LEFT WITHOUT COMPLETING STUDIES. NO RECOMMENDATIONS.' Succinct and to the point. That seems to confirm what Professor Winthrop told us."

Ben's lips had compressed into a grim line as he listened to the message. "Graham's likely to attend Frank Ennis's funeral. I should be able to find a moment to take him aside and tell him what we've learned about Serena Dunbar. He won't like hearing it, but the sooner he's warned, the better. At best she's a confidence woman. At worst, she's a cold-blooded killer."

CHAPTER EIGHT

☙☞

Ben was not fond of funerals. He'd attended far too many of them. The service for Frank Ennis was particularly depressing. The dead man had no kin. No close friends were in attendance. The only ones present for services at the Unitarian Church in Ellsworth were his most recent colleagues and a few people who barely knew him. The preacher mouthed the usual platitudes, having never met Ennis in life, and the casket was carted off to be consigned to a lonely grave in the local cemetery under lowering skies that let loose with a light, steady rain as soon as the assembled mourners had tossed their ritual handfuls of dirt onto the coffin.

They adjourned in haste to the Hancock House, the same hotel where Ben had booked two rooms for the night. The only bright spot in this entire affair, Ben thought, was that Diana was with him. She might have her own room at the hotel for propriety's sake, but she would not be sleeping there alone.

Graham had arranged for a private parlor and refreshments. A wake of sorts, Ben supposed, except that nobody was reminiscing about Frank Ennis. Prudence Monroe stood by the window, her back to the rest of them, staring out at Main Street and the Union

River Bridge as she sipped a cup of tea. She was all in black and the hue did not flatter her. It emphasized her bony frame and made her pale, thin face appear gaunt.

Paul Carstairs, who had brought along his own bottle of Moxie Nerve Food, had filled a plate with food and was intent on consuming it. George Amity had not attended the funeral. He had been left behind to guard whatever secret Serena Dunbar was hiding on Keep Island.

Ben and Diana stood on one side of the room, Graham and Serena on the other. They were deep in conversation, oblivious to everyone else.

"I need to talk to him soon," Ben whispered. He'd assumed Graham would stay overnight in Ellsworth, since it was a long trip by water to return to Keep Island. Instead Graham and Miss Dunbar, together with Mrs. Monroe and Paul Carstairs, planned to travel by road to Bucksport after the wake and board the *Miss Min* there in the morning.

"Perhaps one of us should find a moment to speak with Mr. Fellows and Sheriff Fields first," Diana whispered back, "and find out how the murder investigation is progressing."

Oscar Fellows and Dorephus Fields had helped themselves to food but now stood awkwardly, balancing plates and glasses of lemonade. The stranger beside them was attempting, with little apparent success, to engage them in conversation.

Keeping an eye on Graham, lest he miss the chance to take his oldest friend aside, Ben grasped Diana's arm and escorted her to the refreshment table. "Fellows," he greeted the county attorney. "Fields. Any progress on the case?"

"None, nor likely to be any." Fellows had the grace to look a trifle embarrassed by this. His sidelong glance at the stranger was enough to put Ben on alert.

"I don't believe we've met," he said, offering his hand. "I'm Ben Northcote. This is my fiancée, Mrs. Spaulding."

"J. C. Chilcott," said the stranger, who appeared to be in his fifties and had an air of respectability about him. "Editor of the *Ellsworth American*."

"You find Mr. Ennis's death newsworthy, then?" Diana cut in.

"I find the circumstances curious, but I am also a member of this church. I felt it my duty to attend the services."

"I am a journalist myself," Diana told him.

"Diana—" Ben began, catching her forearm, but he was too late to stop her from completing her introduction.

"I am employed by the *New York Independent Intelligencer*."

Chilcott took an involuntary step away from her. An expression of extreme distaste distorted his face. "That scandal sheet!"

Color rose in Diana's cheeks but she stood her ground. "And what, precisely, do you find so objectionable, Mr. Chilcott?"

"A newspaper should have high moral and ethical standards. That one does not."

"My editor is of the opinion that scandal sells newspapers."

"Then how do you explain that the *Ellsworth American* is the most popular weekly newspaper in the state of Maine?"

Ben tightened his grip on her arm. Whatever answer she intended to make died before it reached her lips.

Chilcott tugged on the bottom of his vest, although it was already perfectly straight, and glowered at Diana. "I will not be writing about Mr. Ennis's death," he said stiffly. "There is no place for wild speculation in *my* newspaper."

Ben watched him go with mingled relief and exasperation. "An upstanding citizen," he observed.

"He's a temperance man," said Sheriff Fields, missing Ben's sardonic tone. "Keeps an eye on the hotels to make sure none of them are serving liquor."

"Oh, that's *much* more important than seeing that a murderer is brought to justice," Diana muttered under her breath.

"Not sure it *was* murder," Fields said. "Coroner says what Miss Dunbar suggested makes sense."

"An accident?" Ben couldn't believe what he was hearing. "Sheriff that's—"

Fields held up a hand to stop any objections. "Maybe. Maybe not. But murder's a stretch. Can't see that anyone had a reason to want that fella dead."

Ben had to exert considerable effort to keep his voice level. "What you mean is that you don't expect anyone to make a fuss. No one will care if you pursue the matter nor not, not even the local newspaper."

If the murder had happened in a small town, the local constable would have investigated to the best of his ability. In a city, the police or the city marshals would have handled the case. They might even have asked for outside help because there would have been neighbors who were outraged and town fathers who were pushing for justice. After all, no one wanted to leave a killer running loose. But Ennis had died on a private island. The only person who could insist upon a thorough investigation was the one who clearly did not want one.

"There's nothing to pursue," Fellows chimed in, "and no money available to hire a private detective. Last I heard the going rate was ten dollars a day plus expenses. The county can't afford an outlay like that."

"Speaking of money," Diana interrupted, "Mr. Somener paid for this—" her gesture indicated the refreshments— "but who bore the expenses of the funeral?"

She had reason to be curious, Ben thought. Ennis had been buried in a proper coffin, not a plain pine box, and in a regular plot rather than a pauper's grave.

"Miss Dunbar took care of everything," Fellows said. "Told me it was Ennis's money, from back pay and what she found in his effects."

Diana was no longer listening. "Mr. Somener is looking at his pocket watch," she said in an agitated voice. "I think he's about to leave."

"As we should," Oscar Fellows announced. Setting aside his plate, the contents untouched, he started for the door. Fields followed in his wake.

Reluctant as he was to give his friend bad news, Ben knew he could not put it off any longer. He had to warn Graham about Serena.

"Distract Miss Dunbar," he whispered to Diana.

A question about where she purchased her divided skirts was sufficient to divert Serena's attention away from Graham while Ben took the other man aside.

"Any luck finding Palmer?" Graham asked.

"No, but in the process several questions have arisen about Miss Dunbar. What do you know about her training as an archaeologist?"

Half of Graham's attention remained on the woman in question as he answered. "Aunt Min encouraged her interest in history. Serena used to visit her in Boston, as well as on Keep Island. In fact, Min was so fond of Serena that she left her a legacy."

Ben's eyes narrowed. "Money?"

"The contents of a certain trunk. I'm not sure what was inside."

"And after Min's death?" Ten years ago, Serena would have been only fifteen or sixteen. Still, some girls taught school at that age. Others were already married. "Did Serena attend college? How did she come to be an archaeologist?"

"She studied at Harvard. They were all there at the same time—Serena, Carstairs, and Ennis."

Not according to retired Harvard professor Lucien Winthrop, Ben thought. "Is it possible Serena once had a romantic relationship with Frank Ennis?" He'd decided before this conversation began that he might as well be blunt. Subtlety had never worked well with Graham, and he'd be right on the spot to deal with it if his old friend lost control of his temper.

The lines around Graham's mouth went taut. His lips compressed into a hard, thin line. His eyes blazed blue fire. Ben half expected to see steam coming out of Graham's ears.

"Defend the lady's honor later, Graham," he warned in a low, soothing voice. "For now, just answer the question."

"Two or three years ago, Ennis asked her to marry him," Graham said through gritted teeth. "She declined the offer."

"So they were never—?" Ben was about to say "intimate" but Graham didn't let him finish the question.

"She did not marry him," he snapped. "She's never been married. That's what she told me and I believe her. Ennis was just trying to make trouble with his lies."

Graham's words more than his virulent tone had Ben backing up a step. Ennis had claimed Serena was his wife? That shed an entirely new light on things. It also gave Serena another good reason to want the man dead.

"Graham, listen to me. Someone murdered Frank Ennis. He was poisoned and later drowned. Serena Dunbar has not been truthful about her educational background. An archaeologist from Harvard, someone who was there until just this last year, says she was a student only briefly. He's never even heard of Ennis or Carstairs. Furthermore, I believe there is a connection between Serena's arrival on Keep Island and the rumors that brought Justus Palmer to Maine to investigate criminal activity. What if—?"

Graham's short bark of laughter cut him off. "That's absurd. Do you hear yourself? You might as well accuse *me* of murder. That would make as much sense." He leaned in, ramming a finger into Ben's chest to emphasize each question he asked. "Is that what you think? That because I want to marry Serena myself, I killed her husband to clear the way?"

"Graham, I never said—"

"You didn't have to. It's clear you believe Serena had something to do with Ennis's death." The heat in his expression had been replaced by an icy glare.

"What else am I to think when you have just managed to

cover up a crime? With Ennis dead and buried, it suits you to forget all about the *way* he died." They were nose to nose, speaking
in hoarse, hostile whispers.

"I'd like to forget! I don't know how he died, but I certainly
didn't kill him and neither did Serena. Damnation, Ben, it was
an accident! Now I intend to get on with my life. And I intend to
share that life with Serena Dunbar."

"For God's sake, Graham, use a little common sense. At least
ask a few questions. Don't take everything she says on faith just
because you're in love with her."

"I know as much about Serena as I need to." He started to
walk away.

Ben caught his arm. "Graham—"

Turning, Graham broke the hold. The venomous look on his
face persuaded Ben not to touch him again.

"I've asked her to marry me and she's accepted," Graham
hissed.

Stunned, Ben stared at him, unable to think of a single thing
to say.

"The ceremony will take place on Islesborough two days from
now. I meant to ask you to be my groomsman, but perhaps it
would be best if we simply borrow a couple of strangers to stand
up with us." With that, Graham stalked off towards his intended
bride.

Diana and Serena had quickly exhausted the subject of women's
fashions, one that held little real interest for either of them. Serena's gray flannel suit was as plain as could be and Diana's traveling outfit of dark blue cashmere was not much fancier. For each,
the main concession to the solemnity of the occasion had been
the addition of gray illusion veiling to a hat.

"Let us dispense with formality," Serena suggested. "It serves
no useful purpose. I would be happy to have you call me by my
first name."

At Diana's doubtful look, Serena's smile faded. A hint of asperity came into her voice. "We may as well be at ease with each other. I expect we'll be seeing a great deal of each other in the future."

"You expect us to become friends?"

"Is that such a preposterous idea? We are both professional women, trying to succeed in careers dominated by men. I suspect we have a great deal in common."

"Perhaps." Decidedly wary, Diana struggled to discern the purpose behind this unexpected olive branch. Had Serena heard they were investigating her credentials? Was she trying to charm Diana out of continuing? Too little, too late if she was.

Diana glanced towards Ben. She had been keeping an eye on him while listening with half an ear to Serena's discourse. Graham Somener did not look happy. She saw him break away from Ben and head for Serena, but Ben caught up with him and said something that appeared to gave him pause. They stayed where they were, once again openly, if quietly, quarreling.

Since Serena's back was to the two men, she remained blissfully unaware of their conflict. "I am sure you are as devoted to writing articles for your newspaper as I am to discovering the secrets of the past."

"You intend to continue excavating, then?"

"Of course. In fact, I expect we can manage a half-day's work at the site tomorrow. We will be short-handed without Frank, but Paul is a dedicated archaeologist and I believe George Amity can be trained to do the simpler tasks."

"Does Mr. Carstairs call you by your first name, too?" Diana tried not to sound disapproving. Heaven knew she'd "dispensed with formality" often enough herself. Her life had too often been lived on the fringes of society ever to be a stickler for propriety.

"We have known each other for many years and, like me, he believes in the equality of the sexes. Does that shock you?"

"I am not easily shocked, but in my experience, it is often the gentlemen who object to excessive informality. Unless they are bent upon seduction, that is."

"Not Paul," Serena said with a laugh. "He had a twin sister with advanced ideas. She was a suffragist *and* an advocate of free love. I've always thought I would have liked her very much, but I never had the opportunity to meet her. She died at nineteen, a couple of years before Paul and I met."

"I hope she did not suffer a terrible fate for those beliefs, as some women have—locked up in an insane asylum, or imprisoned for demonstrating for women's rights."

"I do not believe so, although Paul has never said how she died. It grieves him too much to speak of her, I think. He only confided what I've told you on a rare occasion when he'd had too much to drink."

"Died in childbirth, no doubt," said Mrs. Monroe, who had abandoned her post by the window to join them and had been unabashedly eavesdropping on their conversation for several minutes. "Or from consumption. It's usually one or the other that takes women at such a young age."

Before Diana could respond, Graham Somener appeared at Serena's elbow. Diana started to speak, then saw his face. It was contorted with rage. As she had once before, when he'd been armed with a fencing foil, Diana quailed. This was a man who could kill when he was in a temper. She was certain of it.

"Come, Serena. We are leaving." Somener growled the words. Ignoring Diana, he ushered the other two women towards the door, bellowing at Paul Carstairs to "shake a leg." A moment later, all four of them were gone. Diana and Ben were alone in the hotel's private dining parlor.

Diana cleared her throat and glanced warily at Ben. "I take it he did not heed your warning about Serena?"

Ben looked shaken, his gaze still fixed on the doorway through which Somener had gone. "He's already asked her to marry him. The wedding is Saturday."

Diana's eyes widened. No wonder Ben looked so distressed. In a flurry of skirts she rushed to his side and placed both hands on his coat sleeve. She waited until he looked down at her to speak.

"We will find a way to stop him, Ben. We must. He cannot marry Serena Dunbar."

"Frank Ennis claimed he and Serena were married. She denied it."

"Well, of course she would. She could hardly marry your friend Graham if she already had a husband." This was an unexpected development, but Diana had no difficulty incorporating it into her theory about Serena.

"She could have said they were divorced. Instead she denied *ever* being married."

"Ennis's claim threatened her plans," Diana concluded.

"Especially if part of the plan was to marry Graham."

"And now that Ennis is dead, he's no longer a problem."

Ben's eyes were alive with fear. "If she killed Frank Ennis, what's to stop her murdering Graham after they're wed? With him dead, she'd gain complete control of his fortune."

It was an appalling thought, but it made sense. Releasing her grip on Ben's arm, Diana started towards the door. "We must go after them, convince him not to marry her. We cannot—"

"Wait. Talking to Graham won't do any good. Not right now. But there may be another way."

They stepped out of the hotel into a cold mist. The rain had stopped, but Ellsworth's maple- and elm-lined streets dripped moisture. By the time Ben had taken them to the county courthouse, even at the brisk pace he set, the brim of Diana's hat was sodden and drooping.

She removed it and gave it a shake while Ben requested a copy of *Maine Court Officer*. She had no idea what he was up to, but she followed him when a clerk showed him to a small stuffy room that was obviously used to store old records. The dust lay so thick on some of them that Diana at once burrowed into her bag for a handkerchief. The first sneeze followed only seconds after she located it.

By the time she stopped sneezing, Ben was thumbing rapidly through the pages of a thick, leather-bound book. "This is a handbook for officials. Everyone from coroners to justices of the peace. It contains all the laws of the state, including the revised statutes and public acts. If there is a legal way to stop a wedding, it will be recorded here."

"Do you know when and where the ceremony is to be?" Diana asked.

"Islesborough. Before a justice of the peace, I imagine. Graham's not much of a churchgoer."

Another sneeze manifested itself violently, followed by a second smaller explosion. Holding the handkerchief to her nose, eyes streaming, she mumbled, "Why Islesborough?"

"Closest town. See here." He tapped a page. "Someone who doesn't live *in* an incorporated town has to file marriage intentions with the town clerk of the nearest one."

"And at least five days ahead of time." Diana already knew that part. They had filed their own marriage intentions as soon as they'd returned to Bangor from New York.

A grim smile overspread Ben's face. "Ah, this will do. We can file what's called a 'caution' with the town clerk."

Diana leaned closer to read the entry over his shoulder. "This seems to be an effort to prevent bigamy. You can claim there is an impediment to the marriage if either the bride or the groom has a spouse already."

"That's the usual reason, yes, but surely the fact that the bride is a criminal is an 'impediment' as well."

"I am sure it would be . . . if we had proof of it to offer. If we did, we could also stop the wedding by having the sheriff arrest Serena."

Ben slammed the law book closed, sending up another cloud of dust. Diana hastily backed away, the handkerchief over her nose and mouth.

"If we're right about Serena Dunbar," Ben muttered, "Graham's very life is at stake. I will not let him make a mistake of this magnitude, not without trying to stop him. And I won't quibble at stretching the truth, if that is what is required."

As Diana followed Ben back outside the courthouse, her mind was awhirl. If they were right about Serena, and if Graham Somener married her, at best there would be a scandalous divorce. At worst, he might become her next victim. Ben was correct. They had to do something . . . anything . . . to prevent his oldest friend from making a terrible mistake.

She was not surprised when Ben announced that they would not be returning to Bangor by train the next morning, as they'd originally planned. Instead, they'd be catching the steamer to Islesborough.

80C3

Friday morning, the twenty-second day of June, dawned clear and calm. It was not ideal sailing weather, since there was not much breeze, but that did not affect the ferry Ben and Diana boarded in Ellsworth at 5:00 A.M. It set them ashore at Bar Harbor in time to catch the steamer *Cimbria*, departing at seven. They would reach Islesborough at half past twelve.

Diana yawned hugely as the deep-toned bell in the pilot house rang to signal their departure. They'd gotten little sleep the night before, although that was only partly due to their early departure time. Ben was not surprised when she dozed off sitting beside him in the saloon on the main deck.

She slept soundly, only occasionally disturbed by the sound of a horn, or a bell from a buoy or a lighthouse, or another boat. It did not seem to take her long to grow accustomed to and ignore the steady ka-chung of the engine, the swish of the wake, and the way the glass in the portholes rattled.

Ben, on the other hand, was unable to rest. What he was about to do to his oldest friend preyed on his mind, and yet he could not come up with any better solution. Serena Dunbar was undoubtedly a liar and a confidence woman and very probably a cold-blooded killer. He could not permit Graham, who had already suffered greatly because someone he'd trusted had betrayed him, to go through with the wedding. Bad enough what learning the truth now would do to undermine his friend's hard-won sanity. Finding out *after* he'd married her that she only loved his fortune was likely to push him past endurance . . . with potentially deadly and tragic results.

Diana woke when she smelled coffee. A meal was served en route, and afterward they went out on deck. Ben hoped the scenery would soothe his troubled conscience. After all, what he intended was a kind of betrayal, too, for all that he was acting to protect his friend.

By the time they'd steamed through Eggemoggin Reach and rounded Little Deer Isle into Penobscot Bay, he had convinced himself that he had no choice in the matter. It was surgery, he decided. Painful, yes, but with the result that the patient lived a long and healthy life afterward.

"A pity we don't have a stateroom," Diana murmured, shifting restlessly. "I could do with some real sleep."

"It's too short a trip."

"Long enough."

"A stroll will perk you up."

By the time they had explored every nook and cranny of the *Cimbria,* Diana's spirits seemed much improved. Returning to the rail, Ben pointed out some of the islands he knew by name—Beach and Butter, Pickering, and The Porcupines. The *Cimbria* passed close enough to one he didn't recognize to make out groves of spruces and gray-trunked beeches on the wooded shore. On another, they could see pastures and gently rolling grassy slopes. A third sported evergreens, oaks, beeches, maples, and yellow and white birches that grew right down to the edge of the rocks on the shore. Some looked welcoming, offering safe anchorage, while others did not appear to have any harbor at all and were surrounded by nasty looking ledges.

"That's Islesborough," Ben said after awhile, pointing towards a long, sinuous stretch of land. The breeze rifled his hair and beard and set the feather that decorated Diana's hat to dancing.

"I thought it was the mainland."

"An easy mistake. Islesborough is some thirteen miles long." He indicated a second, much smaller island a few miles to the east. "And there is Keep Island."

From the steamer, the promontory was clearly visible but the buildings beyond were not. Ben did not see any sign of the expedition tents, either.

"Do you suppose Serena will give up all pretense of excavating, now that she thinks she's going to marry Graham?"

"It did not sound that way," Diana replied. "She planned to get right back to work today, as soon as they arrived on the island."

"What's wrong?" Ben asked, seeing Diana's frown.

"A momentary doubt." She gave a dismissive wave with one silk-gloved hand.

"Tell me."

"It's just that the few times Serena has deigned to talk to me about archaeology, she's seemed genuinely enthusiastic about her excavation."

"A performance designed to take in the unwary."

"Yes, I'm sure you're right. Most confidence women are excellent actresses, even the ones who have never trod the boards. That she sounded sincere is just more evidence of her cleverness."

The boat steamed on, passing between Islesborough and Keep Island. There was nothing to see on the western side of the latter, which was all tall, bare, glassy cliffs with sea gull nests at the crests of the precipices and scudding clouds above.

"There are still a great many things that puzzle me," Diana admitted as they listened to the birds' raucous cries. The sound reached them clearly across the water. "A confidence game is an unlikely source for the rumors of criminal activity on Keep Island. Serena must be engaged in something more than that, but what?"

"She'd make a fetching pirate queen," Ben suggested.

Diana punched his arm. "Don't be sarcastic. The excavation would make an excellent cover for a smuggling operation, don't you think?"

"Smuggling seems most likely," he agreed as the *Cimbria* approached the steamship dock in Ryder's Cove.

"Smuggling what?"

"Liquor, without a doubt. Maine may be a dry state by law, but that has never stopped a man from getting a drink if he wanted one."

"Or if *she* did. And Serena is certainly no advocate of the temperance movement. The night of Frank Ennis's death she drank a great deal of wine at supper. Later, after she retired to her room, she topped that off with a considerable amount of brandy."

More damning evidence against the woman, Ben thought, although he'd never noticed her overindulging at any other time. "I wonder what prompted the binge—grief for Ennis? Remorse over killing him? Fear of arrest?"

"More likely," Diana said in a grim voice, "she was celebrating the successful elimination of someone who'd threatened to ruin one of her evil plans."

ഇറമ

A hotel with a dining room was located within sight of Islesborough's steamship dock. It was more boarding house than luxurious hostelry, but the proprietor was a loquacious sort and happy to answer Ben's questions while Ben and Diana consumed a midday meal of thick fish chowder and fresh-baked biscuits slathered in butter.

"Town clerk is Lincoln Gilkey," he told them. "You'll find him at his farm, about five miles down the road."

"Where can we hire a horse and buggy?" Ben asked.

"Right next door, Dr. Northcote."

"And the next steamer to the mainland?"

"That'd be the *Electra*. She makes the round trip from Belfast to Castine three times a day, with stops here at Islesborough each way. You won't be staying over, then?"

"That depends upon how much we can accomplish in the next few hours. The horse and buggy?"

The proprietor handled the financial end of the transaction, then led them into an attached barn. Right next door, as he'd said.

"Clat, harness Bernice!" he bellowed.

An amiable-looking little man with a slight limp popped out of a horse stall. He made quick work of his task, although it was clear he was a bit simple. "Anything else I can do for you, guv'ner?" he asked, tipping his disreputable-looking cap.

"Clat, is it?" Ben asked.

"Short for Clarence." He bobbed his head as if to confirm this bit of information.

"Well, Clat-short-for-Clarence, where might I find the local justice of the peace? I should have thought to ask about him before mine host returned to the hotel," he added for Diana's benefit.

"You want Sprague?" Clat stuck one finger under the edge of his cap and scratched.

"If he performs marriages, yes."

Obligingly, Clat gave them directions to the house of one Joseph A. Sprague.

"He's closer than Mr. Gilkey," Diana observed.

"We'll stop on our way back. No doubt talking to the town

clerk will be sufficient, but it occurred to me that the J.P. should be warned, as well."

They set off at a slow and steady pace. "You seem to know your way around the island," Diana remarked.

"Graham and I used to row over here when we were boys. There are several places on Islesborough that are prime hunting grounds for Indian artifacts. The Penobscot and Tarrantine tribes still visit here every year to pick berries, dig clams, split ash, and collect sweet grass. They make containers of various sizes out of the ash and weave the sweet grass into baskets to sell to tourists."

"Weren't there any Indian artifacts on Keep Island?"

"Not that we ever found."

"More proof, as if we needed it, that Serena's excavation is a fraud. If there weren't even Indians on Keep Island, how could she expect to find traces of her mythical European settlers?"

"Perhaps the curse kept them away," Ben suggested with a grin.

She did not return his smile. She'd forgotten all about that curse. "Do you have any idea how that story got started? People keep mentioning it, but like Mr. Palmer's 'criminal activities,' the details are vague. Do you suppose Graham concocted it himself to keep people away?"

"You'll have to ask Mrs. Monroe," Ben said. "According to Serena, she's the one who first mentioned it."

Diana was still contemplating the best way to learn more about the mysterious curse when they reached Lincoln Gilkey's house.

Islesborough's town clerk was a taciturn gentleman in his sixties who greeted Ben's attempt to file a "caution" with extreme skepticism. "What proof do you have of bigamy?" he demanded.

"None," Ben admitted, "but we have the most serious doubts about Miss Serena Dunbar's honesty. That she's a confidence woman is almost certain. She's undoubtedly a fortune hunter, as well. There's also the matter of the drowning death of one of her partners. As a physician, I can tell you that it was no accident."

"Jurisdiction over that death lies in another county," Gilkey interrupted. "It's none of my concern."

"Murder is everybody's business."

"Calm down, Northcote. You've said your piece."

With a visible effort, Ben kept his voice level. "In fact, I have not. As I understand it, the point in filing a caution is to postpone a marriage until irregularities can be investigated. That's called for here. To prove any of the charges I've made, as well as to determine whether or not Miss Dunbar is already married, requires time."

"I've known Graham Somener for years. He's as sharp as they come. Not likely he'd be fooled by a bit of muslin."

"I know him well, too," Ben argued, "and any man can fall prey to a woman's wiles."

"There is a detective out of Boston who may be able to shed some light on the situation," Diana interjected. "He's been investigating reports of criminal activities in the area."

Gilkey's derisive snort conveyed what he thought of interference from anyone from away. "I met Miss Dunbar when she and Somener came across to file their marriage intentions. She seemed a proper young lady to me."

"All I'm asking is that you not issue the license until this matter is settled."

"I make no promises," Gilkey said, and cut off further protests by showing them the door.

"Pigheaded old man," Diana grumbled as Ben assisted her into the buggy.

"Let's hope we can convince the justice of the peace. If Gilkey goes ahead and issues the license, it will only be good here on Islesborough. They'll still need the J.P. to marry them."

"You're certain they wouldn't prevail upon a preacher?"

"Highly unlikely. The only churches on the island are Baptist. Graham doesn't practice any religion, but he was raised Catholic."

At the Sprague house they had better luck. Joseph Sprague was appalled by what Ben told him. When he heard that another man claimed to be married to Serena Dunbar, he began to sputter indignantly. "I want nothing to do with bigamy, Dr. Northcote. Nothing at all."

Ben, Diana noted, had neglected to mention to either Mr. Gilkey or Mr. Sprague that the man who'd said he was Serena's husband was now deceased.

"I've already filed a caution with Mr. Gilkey," Ben told Sprague.

"That's that, then. If they don't have the license, I can't marry them."

"I'm afraid Mr. Gilkey expressed some doubts about our contentions. We have no solid proof, you see, so it's possible he will—"

"Stubbornly insist upon believing Miss Dunbar?" Sprague's grimace suggested that he knew his fellow islander very well. "Rest easy, Dr. Northcote. No matter what Gilkey does, I will refuse to conduct the ceremony."

Ben's step was lighter, his bearing less tense when they left the justice of the peace's house. It was a pity, Diana thought, that they had to rush back to Bangor. It was very beautiful on Islesborough—green and peaceful. Although she knew they were not on the mainland, Diana did not have the uncomfortable sense of being cut off from civilization that she'd experienced while on Keep Island.

When they were once more in the buggy, Diana glanced at the sky. "We have a little time yet before the *Electra* leaves. Is there enough for you to show me the place where you used to dig for artifacts?"

She saw that her request had pleased Ben and looked forward even more eagerly to the detour, but before they had gone very far, she caught sight of a familiar figure. A sudden foreboding had her grabbing Ben's arm and pointing.

"That's Paul Carstairs," she hissed. "What on earth is *he* doing on Islesborough?" She was certain Serena had said she planned to get as much work done at the excavation site as possible this afternoon. Surely that would require the presence of her remaining assistant . . . unless she *had* changed her mind in consideration of her coming nuptials.

Ben brought Bernice to a halt. In silence, they watched Carstairs walk rapidly away from the building he had just exited. There was something furtive about his movements. A moment later, he had passed out of sight around a curve in the narrow, winding dirt road.

Ben's brow furrowed as he stared after Serena Dunbar's assistant. "Perhaps he came to Islesborough for supplies." He didn't sound convinced.

Still beset by an uneasy feeling about Carstairs's presence on the larger island, Diana wondered if she had been careless in overlooking the fact that Serena's so-called assistants would also be her accomplices. "I think," she said to Ben, "that it would be a good idea to ask a few questions."

CHAPTER NINE

෨෧

The establishment Paul Carstairs had been visiting was Pyram Hatch's netmaking business. The entire Hatch family—husband, wife, young son, and three daughters of assorted ages—produced more varieties of net than Diana had dreamed existed.

Mrs. Hatch pointed with pride to a crab net. "Constructed of #12 thread twine, that is. Fourteen inches long with one and three-quarters mesh and a selvedged edge."

At a loss how to respond, Diana merely nodded. She and Ben had agreed to pretend she was interested in writing a story about Islesborough for the *Independent Intelligencer*. He'd taken Mr. Hatch aside and left her to interview the missus, who required no encouragement to talk Diana's ear off. Between comments about the virtues of each of three kinds of nets for lobster pots and descriptions of casting nets, pickle nets for ladling pickles out of barrels, and hammock netting, Mrs. Hatch related a capsule history of the island.

"A great many of us are descended from the first settlers. That's why you'll still find so many Gilkeys, Trims, and Pendletons about. I was born a Pendleton myself. So was Lincoln Gilkey's mother. Hear you stopped by to talk to him earlier."

"News travels fast."

"People know that buggy you're driving. And the horse." She waited, hoping for an explanation. Diana did not oblige her, lest whatever she said be repeated island-wide within the hour.

"What are these?" she asked instead, fingering a stack of what looked like black silk doilies.

"We make those for use in dentists' offices. We also make tennis nets, fly nets for horses, and ear-tip nets to cover and decorate horses' ears. Made of fine bleached cotton, they are. And these here are minnow nets, made of linen thread. They come in twenty inches or twelve."

"Did Mr. Carstairs require some particular sort of net?" Diana asked.

"Know him, do you? Nice fella. As a matter of fact, he stopped by to place a special order. Don't know what he means to use it for. Some archaeological thing, I'm guessing."

"You're aware, then, that there is an excavation on Keep Island?"

"Lord, yes. Would be some strange if anyone on Islesborough didn't know." She chuckled. "If it weren't for being on the other side of the county line that runs right down the middle of Penobscot Bay, Keep Island would be part of our town, it lies that close. Used to belong to an Islesborough man, too. My pa knew him well. Delmar Pingree was his name. Cantankerous old cuss, or so Pa used to say."

"I suppose it wouldn't be surprising, then, if one of the islanders stopped when he was out in his boat to take a look at the excavation?"

But Mrs. Hatch shook her head. "No time to lollygag when there's lobster or fish to bring in. Got a good many master mariners on the island, too, and they're even busier."

"Tourists then? I understand the island has many visitors in the summer."

"As to what they'd do, I couldn't say. Might go and gawk, I

suppose."

"And how would they do that?" Diana fingered the rough texture of a net hanging from the rafters. "Are there boats available to rent?"

"Some. Why is it you're asking, missus?"

"There was a small rowboat anchored off the south end of Keep Island the day of the diving accident. A dory?" She was certain that Mrs. Hatch knew all about Frank Ennis's death. "I was wondering where it came from."

"Rowed Nova Scotia style, was she?"

"I beg your pardon?"

"That's standing up and rowing forward."

"I'm afraid I didn't notice."

"Never mind. I expect it was young Billy Showalter's boat. Born in a tar-bottom dory, that Billy was. He'll rent her out, or row a tourist. Is he in trouble for taking that old man from the mainland out? Fella wanted a look at the . . . what did he call it? Oh, yes—site."

"Billy's not in any trouble. But this old man—do you recall his name?"

"Don't think he gave it. I'd have heard if he did. All I know is that he's white-haired and he walks with a limp. Has a cane. Seen him here on Islesborough once or twice before, but he's stand-offish. Never stops to chat."

Lucien Winthrop? Diana was about to ask more questions when Ben called to her.

"We need to leave. Now." The urgency in his voice was goad enough to get her moving. She took only time enough to press a monetary token of her gratitude into Mrs. Hatch's hand before hurrying back to the waiting horse and buggy.

"What's wrong?"

Ben untied Bernice's reins from the hitching post and vaulted into the driver's seat. "Carstairs isn't headed back to Keep Island. Hatch says he plans to go to Belfast on the *Electra*. This may be our best chance to question him about Serena. If we can get on board before he does, we can keep out of his sight."

"But if you want to confront him—"

"I want to find out where he's headed first."

Diana regretted losing the opportunity to question young Billy Showalter about the passenger he'd taken out in his dory, but she saw the logic of Ben's plan. Winthrop might have lied about knowing there was an excavation on Keep Island, but Carstairs had to be involved in Serena's scheme up to his eyebrows. If they cornered him, made him think they knew more than they really did, he might confirm their suspicions. If they were very persuasive, he might even present them with the proof they needed to stop Serena once and for all.

They secreted themselves on the little steamer without much difficulty. She was sixty-four feet in length, carried two lifeboats atop the pilot house, and had an enclosed saloon below. There was room enough—just—to avoid being seen while still keeping an eye on their quarry.

It helped that Carstairs spent the entire crossing at the rail, watching as the *Electra* drew ever closer to Belfast. When they docked, he obligingly set off without looking back. He left the steamship wharf at the foot of Miller Street on foot and made his way steadily uphill . . . directly to Lucien Winthrop's house. Winthrop himself opened the door and did not seem surprised to find Paul Carstairs on his front porch.

"He lied to us," Ben said. "Winthrop knows Carstairs."

"And he knew about the excavation." She repeated Mrs. Hatch's description of the man in the dory.

"You realize what this means?"

"It means Winthrop knows Carstairs. It doesn't mean Serena has suddenly become a paragon of virtue."

But Diana's conscience troubled her, as she knew Ben's must bother him. Based on the assumption that Winthrop was telling them the truth, they had concluded that the woman was guilty of far worse sins than lying about her training as an archaeologist. Without proof of her villainy, they'd taken extreme steps to thwart her wedding to Graham Somener.

Better safe than sorry, Diana told herself. But the possibility that they'd constructed a house of cards based on a tissue of lies left her feeling faintly ill. "We could go in. Confront them both together."

"No. I want to hear Carstairs's story. And I don't want him to realize we followed him here. We'll wait, see where he goes next, and then 'accidentally' bump into him."

"What if he's spending the night at Winthrop's house?"

"Doubtful. He has no luggage with him."

"Then he must plan to return to Keep Island today." She wondered how he'd gotten to Islesborough. If he already had a boat, why would he take the *Electra* to Belfast? She supposed he must have borrowed the tender.

Ben caught her arm, pulling her into cover behind a convenient hedge. Carstairs had reappeared on Winthrop's porch.

Twigs poked at Diana through the fabric of her shirtwaist, but she remained immobile until Carstairs had passed by. They let him get some distance ahead before they followed and did not approach him until he'd reached the center of town. There he was obliged to stop at a crosswalk to let a half-dozen young men on shiny new bicycles pass by. The steel wire spokes of the large main wheels reflected the blinding rays of the late-day sun directly into Diana's eyes.

"Mr. Carstairs," Ben called out in a jovial voice. "We did not expect to see you again so soon."

Carstairs gave a guilty start. "Dr. Northcote. Mrs. Spaulding." He tipped his hat. "This is a surprise."

"Members of the Belfast Bicycle Club, I presume," Ben said, indicating the riders. "They are quite famous around the state."

Taking her cue from Ben, Diana pretended this was a chance encounter and attempted to engage Carstairs in small talk. "I'll never understand how they keep their balance on those awkward-looking machines." The back wheels were disproportionately small and the seats, mounted directly over the larger front wheel, were little more than perches.

"I imagine they take their share of headers," Carstairs replied, forced into polite conversation.

When the last cyclist had gone past, Carstairs stepped off the curb. Diana seized his right arm, obliging him to escort her safely across the street.

"I've heard that on good road with rubber tires, a bicycle can outrun a horse." She tightened her grip as they reached the opposite sidewalk.

Ben closed in on Carstairs's left. Trapping him between them, they moved in unison towards the nearby Windsor Hotel. "This is where we're staying, Carstairs," he said, stopping in front of the entrance. "You?"

"I . . . uh, no."

"Headed back to Keep Island, then?"

"Yes. Yes, of course."

He looked so flustered that Diana took pity on him. "What is it that brought you to Belfast, Mr. Carstairs?"

"Oh, that. Well, I have an . . . er . . . acquaintance here . . . ."

"That would be Professor Winthrop?" Diana asked. She ignored Ben's scowl. They would get nowhere by beating around the bush.

Carstairs's eyes widened. "Now how in tarnation did you know that?"

She sent him a brilliant smile. "Very simple, Mr. Carstairs. Professor Winthrop is an archaeologist. You're an archaeologist. It seemed a safe guess." Except that *Winthrop* had claimed Carstairs was not. He'd said he'd never even heard of Paul Carstairs.

"Oh, I see," Carstairs said. "Yes. Well, the professor heard I was working in the area and sent word he'd like to see me, so I thought the least I could do was oblige. He was one of my teachers, after all." Carstairs was talking too fast, and a thin film of sweat had broken out on his forehead.

"At Harvard?" Ben asked.

"Yes. Yes, that's right."

"And Miss Dunbar was a student there, too, was she not?"

"Well, yes. That is, not at Harvard, precisely. She was a private student at the Peabody Museum. Now that's part of Harvard, but separate, too, if you take my meaning." He fumbled for his handkerchief and mopped his brow.

"Did Professor Winthrop know Miss Dunbar?" Diana asked. He'd *said* he'd never met her in person, only heard about the "ruckus" she'd caused.

A wash of red swept up Paul Carstairs's face. "Oh, they know each other, all right."

"Really?" Diana fluttered her eyelashes at him. "Do I sense a story there?"

Carstairs's color deepened. "It's not my place to say, Mrs. Spaulding. If you want the details of their . . . dispute, you'll have to ask Miss Dunbar. Or Professor Winthrop."

Ben clapped the other man on the shoulder in a companionable way, but he left his hand there, forcing the issue. "Why don't you come inside, Carstairs. You look as if you're about to pass out."

Between them, Ben and Diana all but hauled him into the hotel lobby and sat him down next to a potted plant. It gave the illusion of privacy.

"We have concerns about this excavation of Miss Dunbar's, Carstairs, the more so since Frank Ennis's death. Is Miss Dunbar a legitimate archaeologist or not?"

"She's had some training. Almost a year at the Peabody." He fiddled nervously with his collar, then blurted out the truth: "She's a crackpot. Always has been. Her theories are bogus."

"Is that why she had to leave the Peabody, Mr. Carstairs?"

His voice dropped so low as to be almost inaudible. "She

claimed she had proof of a pre-Columbian European settlement somewhere in New England, but she wouldn't produce it."

"She didn't mention Keep Island?"

"Not back then." Looking even more miserable, Carstairs added, "Professor Winthrop accused her of trying to perpetrate a hoax. She left in disgrace."

"Is that what you think? That she made the whole thing up?"

"I think she's deluded herself into believing she'll find something, but no one else thinks she'll make any discoveries on Keep Island. There's nothing there and never was."

"Then why are you working for her?"

"I needed a job." Carstairs sagged in his chair, his face as mournful as a bloodhound's. "No one else would hire me after my accident. They don't trust me to pull my own weight. And before you ask, that's why I agreed to meet with Professor Winthrop today, too. I've asked him to help me find other work. He was a top man in his field before he retired."

"I thought you said he asked you to meet him?" Diana cut in.

Carstairs nodded. "That's right. Gave me my chance."

"Why did he want to see you?"

The question made Carstairs edgy again. "He had questions about the excavation," he mumbled. "Wanted to know about the dive. How Ennis died. What's being done to find his killer." Carstairs raked distraught fingers through his hair, leaving it standing on end. "I've got to go. Got to find someone to take me back to Keep Island before dark."

"How did you get here?" Diana asked as he stumbled awkwardly to his feet.

"Mrs. Monroe was on her way to Islesborough to visit a sick friend, so I went that far with her in Mr. Somener's boat. Then I caught the *Electra* to Belfast. I really have to go!"

Neither Diana nor Ben tried to stop him, but he was almost running by the time he reached the hotel door. "Why do you suppose he was so nervous?"

"It's his natural disposition." Ben's tone was dry. "The Moxie Nerve Food doesn't seem to be helping."

"What sort of injuries did he sustain on his last expedition?"

"Broken bones. Infection. It took him a long time to recover. You can still see the effects. Then he was poisoned. Add in Ennis's death, and I'm not surprised he's jumpy."

"He knows someone murdered Ennis."

"Seems to. Do you want to talk to Professor Winthrop now?"

Diana frowned. "I don't think so. There's a more reliable way to find out which one of them is lying. I will send another telegram to the director of the Peabody Museum. This time I will be more specific about what I want to know and why."

The Western Union Telegraph Company was situated on the corner of Main and High, quite near the hotel. The same operator they'd spoken to on their last visit to Belfast obligingly dispatched Diana's somewhat lengthy and therefore very expensive message.

"I trust you've received no more threats, Mrs. Spaulding."

"None, thank goodness. Have you remembered any more about the person you saw?"

"As I told you before, it was just a shadow. A silhouette. Then I found the message to you and the money to pay to send it."

"And you've no sense of whether it was a man or a woman?"

The operator's face scrunched up with the effort to remember. "A man, I think, though I could not swear to it. The shape was bulky."

Diana described Lucien Winthrop, then Paul Carstairs, but neither description sparked any recognition. "I don't suppose the man might have been wearing a greatcoat with two small capes attached?" She threw out the question as an afterthought, not because she really thought that the mysterious stranger would turn out to be Justus Palmer.

"A tweed greatcoat?"

"Why, yes. Never tell me he—"

"Oh, no, that wasn't the man who sent the telegram, but I did see someone wearing a coat like that here in Belfast just a few days ago. Most unusual, I thought, for the season, although it was a damp evening. Still, I don't believe he was wearing it because he felt cold. He did not wear a hat, you see." A faint tinge of pink colored the telegraph operator's cheeks. "I couldn't help but notice that he had very dark hair and an interesting physiognomy."

Unfortunately, she could not recall the precise date when she'd seen the Boston detective. Diana wasn't sure why that was important, or even *if* it was, but Palmer's presence in Belfast did strike her as peculiar.

ാരു

They caught the 8:00 A.M. train the next morning, Saturday, which had them in Bangor, after a change of trains at Burnham Junction, at 11:49. At the house, a stack of letters awaited them. In among several acceptances to their wedding invitations was a letter from the Peabody Museum. It was not a reply to Diana's most recent telegram. There had not been time to answer that by mail.

Her face drained of color as she read the missive. Without comment, she handed the single sheet of embossed stationary to Ben. He scanned the page in growing consternation, feeling as if he'd been slammed into a wall by the time he was through. The letter had been signed by Frederick Putnam, director of the Peabody Museum, and was his account of the events in 1885 that had led to Serena's departure . . . and to Winthrop's.

"She wasn't lying," Diana said in a shaky voice. "Winthrop was. He stole one of her discoveries and claimed it as his own. Oh, Ben! What have we done?"

The previous evening, they'd discussed what they'd learned from Carstairs and decided that even if Serena had studied archaeology, as Carstairs claimed, she had still left the profession under a cloud. Winthrop might have lied about knowing her and Carstairs personally—out of a desire to disassociate himself from their ilk, perhaps?—but he had apparently told the truth about her departure from the Peabody. In essence, they'd concluded, nothing had changed. There had been no reason to try to stop what they had set in motion by talking to Lincoln Gilkey and Joseph Sprague.

Sick at heart, Ben mentally rearranged the pieces of the puzzle. He'd gotten it backwards, and because he'd stubbornly clung to the wrong theory, it was now too late to right the wrong he'd done Graham. There was no way to send a telegram to either Keep Island or Islesborough. The closest Western Union office was in Belfast, and by the time a telegram sent there was conveyed by boat, it would arrive too late to do any good.

Ben sank down into the nearest chair, his head in his hands. If he'd been right about Serena, Graham might eventually have forgiven him for interfering. Little hope of that now! "She told me she had rivals," he said in a wooden voice. "And that there was one archaeologist in particular who'd like to see her fail."

Diana's brows knit together in concern for him. "You acted with good intentions."

"I suspected Serena because I didn't want to believe Graham could be a murderer. I still don't think he is, but I should have considered other possibilities."

"It made sense that Serena should be a confidence woman." Ben heard the stubborn note in Diana's voice. "That was my theory, not yours. And it may still be valid. All we now know for certain is that she did not lie about spending time as a serious student of archaeology at the Peabody and that she was taken advantage of by an unscrupulous professor. She's still advancing a crackpot theory. Remember what Carstairs said."

"We know more than that." Ben's hands clenched on the crumpled letter. "We know Winthrop deliberately misled us. We know he was responsible for ruining Serena's chance to complete her formal training. He made false accusations against her."

He held up a hand to stop her protest that they didn't know for certain that the accusations were false. Putnam's letter revealed Winthrop's guilt but did not clear Serena. In all likelihood, he did not believe there was anything to be found on Keep Island either, but that was neither here nor there.

"Most important," Ben concluded, "we know that our interference prevented my oldest friend from marrying the woman he loves."

"Serena is—"

"I should never have meddled." He'd allowed his concern for Graham the former patient to blind him to the needs of Graham the man.

Tears brimmed in Diana's eyes. "You did what you thought best, Ben. And you cannot be sure that it wasn't. We have to continue searching until we find out what's really afoot on Keep Island, until we discover who really did kill Frank Ennis."

"That could be difficult if we're kept off Keep Island at gunpoint." Graham wasn't likely to let Ben back onto his property, let alone into his life.

Maggie Northcote's screech cut off any reply Diana might have made. "Ah hah! I thought I heard someone out here in the hall!"

Elmira was right behind her. "What were you two thinking of to stay away so long? Did you mean to leave me alone to entertain that dreadful old man? Fine kettle of fish that would have been."

"Oh, Lord!" Diana moaned. "I completely forgot. This is the day my grandfather and Aunt Janette are scheduled to arrive."

"It is the day they have already arrived," Maggie corrected her, "on the morning train. They've been here for ages. Now come along. I need your advice on my menu."

Diana obediently followed her, but Ben did not. It was cowardly, he knew, but he did not feel capable of dealing with family just now, his or hers. "I've got to check my surgery," he mumbled, and before anyone could stop him, he was back outside and in the doctor's buggy he'd left under the porte cochere.

He wallowed in guilt all the way to his office. What he had done to Graham was unforgivable.

There were no patients waiting. His surgery had a stale and dusty smell. That very emptiness put an abrupt end to Ben's brooding. The decision he'd been agonizing over for months was suddenly not at all difficult to make. He might have made some mistakes of late, but he was not about to make another one. It was time to shut down his practice. He would sell it to another doctor and move on.

Both his training and his inclination had long urged him to focus on the area where he could do most good. Because of Aaron's precarious mental state, he'd made himself an expert in the care and treatment of the insane. The likelihood that he'd failed to diagnose Graham Somener correctly only fueled his determination to do better. He would learn from the best, study until he was certain his patients had the best care available, the best hope of a cure.

At his desk, he began to make notes. This transition would have to be orderly. More than that, he had to marshal his arguments before he told Diana what he intended to do. He'd need her support if he was to succeed.

The hours sped by. Ben was just collecting the pages he'd covered with his bold scrawl and stretching stiff muscles when there was a rapping at the back door. Captain Amos Cobb stood there, a folded piece of paper in his hand.

"Mr. Somener wanted you to have this," he said. "Sent me on special, all the way upriver from Bucksport to deliver it."

Ben was almost afraid to read the message. Lincoln Gilkey had said he'd known Graham a long time. It only made sense that whether he'd refused to issue the marriage license or not, he'd told Graham about Ben and Diana's visit. Ben expected a scathing condemnation.

Instead the paper was an invitation to visit Mr. and Mrs. Graham Somener "at home" on Keep Island. "I've decided you meant well with your warning," Graham had written. "All is forgiven. How can I hold a grudge when I am now a happily married man? We were wed on Islesborough earlier today by John Pendleton Farrow, J.P."

Under Captain Amos Cobb's incredulous gaze, Ben began to laugh. There were *two* justices of the peace on Islesborough. The possibility had never even occurred to him. And Clat—poor, simple, short-for-Clarence-Clat—hadn't seen any reason to volunteer more than the one name when Ben had asked him who performed marriages.

❧❦❧

To Diana's relief, everyone seemed to be behaving themselves. At least no one was at daggers drawn. Without being asked, Ed Leeves, Diana's recently acquired stepfather, had undertaken the Herculean task of reining in his bride's tendency to bait Maggie and snipe at the Torrences.

He'd also befriended her grandfather. She was pleased to see Isaac Torrence so chipper, especially after such a long journey by train. His shoulders might be stooped, his hands gnarled and latticed with thick blue veins, but he was plainly enjoying himself, even laughing at a slightly risque remark made by the flaxen-haired, black-eyed gambler who'd married his former daughter-in-law.

After supper, which Ben inexplicably missed, Torrence disappeared into the library, still chatting amiably with Leeves. Aside from the fact that the latter owned gambling dens, parlor houses, and saloons—the kind where men drank, not the genteel parlors found on steamers—and wore two inch heels on his boots to make him taller, he was a perfectly presentable gentleman. And, as Diana had somewhat belatedly remembered, he'd originally come from the same area of New York State as her relatives. His sister still lived there. No doubt he and her grandfather could find any number of benign topics of conversation. She hoped so. If she had her way, Isaac Torrence would never learn that his daughter-in-law had ended up owning a Denver parlor house, or why. Nor would he ever find out what a thoroughgoing villain his own son had been.

In many ways, Diana's grandfather was still a stranger, but short as their acquaintance was, she knew he had a genuine affection for her. She was his only son's only child. She was, as he had told her many times, more precious to him than gold.

Diana's aunt seemed equally fond of her. As Maggie and Elmira drifted off towards the parlor, Aunt Janette drew Diana aside. "Good news," she announced. "I found those papers I told you about."

For a moment Diana could not remember what papers she meant. Then she recalled that on the third visit she'd paid to her grandfather's house, just before returning to Maine, Aunt Janette had promised to look for a family history one of their relatives had compiled. Diana had been—and still was—interested in the subject. Only a matter of weeks ago, she'd believed she had no living kin at all, save for her mother, and no hope of ever learning anything more about her ancestry than the few stories her father had told her when she was a child.

"I'd forgotten how interesting our family history is." Her angular face alight, Aunt Janette led the way upstairs to the guest room Maggie had selected for her. It was right next door to the one Diana had formerly occupied.

"You mentioned that your father told you we were descended from a famous female herbalist," Aunt Janette said, when they were settled in a pair of chairs upholstered with a pattern of elaborate rococo scrolls and sprawling flowers. "That isn't quite the case."

Diana felt a twinge of disappointment. "Never tell me she wasn't real?"

"Oh, she existed. And she did write a book about herbs. But she wasn't our ancestor. We are descended from her stepdaughter, Rosamond. Or perhaps Rosamond was her adopted daughter. The records are a bit unclear on that point. At any rate, this Rosamond was her heir."

"Do the papers you've found say any more about the herbalist herself?" Diana asked. "I have been toying with the idea of writing a book about forgotten women of the past. Ordinary women, for the most part, though I suppose those who led truly uneventful lives will not have been remembered at all. Have you noticed that when men write history books, they give short shrift to the role women played in our past? Surely there must have been a few females who made significant contributions to history."

"Undoubtedly," Aunt Janette agreed. She had opened a case and taken out a sheaf of yellowed paper.

Warming to her topic, Diana leaned forward in the chair. "It is a pity we are not really descended from the herbalist, but that doesn't mean I can't tell her story. If I can find sufficient information about her, that is."

"If you are short of facts, why not invent them?" Aunt Janette asked. "Write a novel rather than a biography."

Diana winced. Ben's mother had already made that suggestion. "I am more comfortable dealing with what is real, although I must admit that until recently I did not pay much attention to history." The hint of a personal connection to past events was what had piqued her interest. That curiosity, which had first flared to life when she'd met Aunt Janette, was now rekindled.

"I think," she said cautiously, "that this is what I have been looking for." This project—unlike the idea of interviewing the rich and famous—*felt* right.

"I'll be happy to help," Aunt Janette offered. "When there did not seem likely to be any more Torrences after Father and I departed this world, collecting stories about our ancestors seemed a foolish waste of time. But now that you are here to carry on the heritage . . . well, I talked with the town historian before I left home and he was most helpful. Did you know that the country's oldest and most prestigious genealogical organization is right here in New England? In Boston. The New England Historic Genealogical Society library has a huge collection of manuscripts and books. That's where I'd start the search for our Rosamond's stepmother."

"Memories and family legends are as important as dry facts. Perhaps more so." Diana extracted her little cloth-covered notebook from the deep pocket of her skirt and appropriated the pencil with which Aunt Janette had been sketching a rough family "tree" onto the back of one of the yellowed pages. "In the meantime, tell me everything you know about this ancestress of ours and the herbalist who raised her."

CHAPTER TEN

 ℬℭ

Ben returned home late to find Diana in his bed. He had no complaints, except that his fiancée was restless—not quite awake, but tossing and turning. When a floorboard creaked as he trod on it, she sat up with a little cry of alarm.

He leaned across the bed and kissed her, then whisked her embroidered white lawn wrapper off a chair and searched for her brocade slippers. "Come along. Too much has happened today. Neither one of us will sleep well until we've had a bit of physical activity. I prescribe a brisk walk in the garden."

"That isn't your usual remedy."

"I can tell you're not in the mood for lovemaking." *Yet.* "Besides, I have a few things to tell you. For one thing, Graham and Serena are married."

He gave her a quick summary of events as she fastened her buttons and slid her feet into the delicate little slippers. Then they crept like naughty children along the hallway, down the stairs, and out into the night.

A full moon shone down on them from a cloudless sky, making it unnecessary to carry any other form of illumination. The night air was clear and warm but without any hint of dampness.

Ideal, Ben thought, for stargazing . . . and for courting.

He took Diana's arm and set off along the gravel path that cir-
cled the herb garden, moving between the raised beds of basil and
chervil, dill and fennel, nep and valerian. "Walking is excellent
for calming the nerves," he said softly, "but there is something to
be said for pausing to steal a kiss."

"We could stay right here and . . . kiss . . . for quite some
time."

Ben had no objection. He held her close and stroked one hand
over soft curves, lost in the moment until something moved in
the shadows.

Ben caught sight of it only out of the corner of one eye. When
he looked directly at the spot, he saw nothing untoward. Imagination?

He indulged himself with another kiss, but the sense of someone watching them did not abate. Annoyed, Ben slung one arm
around Diana's shoulders and continued walking.

A light breeze had sprung up since they'd come outside. He
tried to tell himself that was the cause of the shrubbery stirring.
Nothing more.

Then he saw it again. Movement where there should have been
none. Ben squinted at the shadows.

"What is it?" Diana asked in a worried whisper.

"I could have sworn—" He shook his head. "Probably a cat,
or some other nocturnal creature hunting for prey."

A slight rustling sound was their only warning before a gentleman in a double-caped tweed greatcoat stepped out of the bushes
and onto the path directly in front of them. Diana bit back a
gasp, and Ben had to work hard not to yelp.

"Good evening," the stranger said in a deep, resonant voice.

"You!"

"Who is this, Diana?" Ben asked, although certain he already
knew the fellow's identity.

"Justus Palmer." She confirmed Ben's assumption.

Once he stopped bristling at the other man's intrusion into what should have been an intensely private moment, he found nothing alarming or objectionable about the detective. Palmer was shorter than he was, with a stocky build and ordinary features. His steady gaze, however, especially when combined with his failure to speak after his first greeting, soon proved unnerving.

"How did you get through the gate?" Ben let his irritation show. "It should have been locked at this hour."

"Locks rarely pose a problem for me." Palmer's voice was smooth and soothing, intended to mollify.

Ben shook off the compulsion to apologize for his rudeness. "Perhaps you should consider waiting for an invitation, Mr. Palmer."

"But I have that already," the other man replied, "the one dear Magda issued. A charming woman."

"She goes by Maggie." Irrationally irritated by Palmer's presumption, Ben could not prevent annoyance from seeping into his words. He snapped them out, cutting as a whiplash, and took a threatening step towards the other man.

"Not always."

"Gentlemen, please." Diana placed herself between them, one hand on each man's chest, and literally pushed them apart. "Gracious! This is like trying to shove aside two blocks of granite!"

Ben had not realized he'd leaned in, or that his gaze had locked with Palmer's. He had the disorienting sensation that he'd lost a few minutes of time. His voice descended to a low rumble, the next thing to a growl. "What do you want, Palmer?"

"Why, Dr. Northcote, it was my understanding that you and Mrs. Spaulding had been looking for me."

The wave of dislike that washed over Ben was so intense he had difficulty speaking. He fought the urge to remove the smirk from Palmer's face with a roundhouse punch. It took several deep breaths and a shake of the head before he could clear his mind.

This was absurd. He didn't usually have so much difficulty re-pressing inappropriate emotions. How ironic it would be if he had to treat himself, as well as Aaron and Graham, for the inabil-ity to prevent outbursts of temper.

Diana, who did not appear at all bothered by Palmer's pres-ence, regarded Ben with a puzzled look. When he failed to answer the detective's questions, she did it for him.

"In the beginning, we wanted to ask you who your client was and why he was spreading false rumors about Keep Island. We know you talked to the sheriff of Hancock County and that you turned down the chance to meet Mr. Somener yourself. We know that you were in Belfast, though not why. Did you go there from Ellsworth? Is that why we found no trace of you in Bangor?"

"Have you considered taking up detective work, Mrs. Spauld-ing?"

"There is no need for sarcasm, Palmer," Ben snarled.

"But I am sincere! And as it happens, I am free now, as I was not before, to answer your questions. The case is closed. I found no evidence of smuggling or any other criminal activity on Keep Island."

"We thought perhaps Miss Dunbar . . . or Mr. Ennis . . . ." Diana's voice trailed off.

"No, Mrs. Spaulding. The claims were entirely false. No one had heard the story before I talked to them. In fact, you might even say that I *started* the rumor with my questions."

"There was murder done on Keep Island." Ben hoped his blunt statement would rattle Palmer and was disappointed when it did not.

"We thought it might be connected to the matter you were hired to investigate," Diana added.

"When I heard about the murder," Palmer said, "I returned to Boston and made inquiries into the career of the murdered man. It did not take me long to connect him to my employer or to conclude that the man who hired me might have had reason to cause trouble on Keep Island."

"You're saying your own client lied to you?" Ben wasn't sure he believed any of what Palmer was telling them, but it made an interesting tale. He leaned against a decorative archway, arms folded across his chest, prepared to hear the rest of the fellow's story.

"A situation, sadly, not unheard of in my profession, although I am usually better at sensing deceit. I pride myself, in the usual way of things, on being able to spot problem cases early on and avoid them."

"But . . . who hired you?" Diana asked. "And why?"

"Can't you guess?"

"You were in Belfast as well as Ellsworth and Bangor," Ben said slowly. "Lucien Winthrop?"

"Very good, Doctor." He made Ben a mocking bow.

Winthrop had hired Palmer, Ben thought. One small mystery solved. But what did that imply?

"When we talked to Winthrop," Diana said, "he lied to us, too, pretending among other things that he didn't already know about the excavation on Keep Island. He also claimed he was not acquainted with Miss Dunbar's assistant, Paul Carstairs, but he sent for Carstairs some days after the murder and promised to help him find other employment."

"Winthrop also lied about knowing Miss Dunbar," Ben said. "When her crew was ill, she spoke to me of professional rivals, one in particular. She meant Lucien Winthrop." In a few concise sentences, he filled Palmer in on the contents of Diana's letter from the Peabody Museum.

"A pity Professor Putnam couldn't tell you who killed Mr. Ennis, or what Winthrop is up to now."

"You cannot be suggesting that *Winthrop* killed Frank Ellis," Diana protested from her perch on the low stone wall dividing the herb garden from a flowerbed. "Why should he? *How* could he? He is an old man who cannot walk without the aid of a cane."

"Will you be seeing your employer again?" Ben eased away from the archway, suddenly restless.

"That is extremely unlikely. When I informed him that there were no irregular activities on Keep Island he paid me enough to cover my fee and expenses and provide a considerable bonus besides."

"Why a bonus?" Diana asked.

"To keep me from investigating further, I expect."

"And so you dropped the case?" Ben's contempt for the other man crept into the question. It seemed to him that Palmer might have done more, and sooner, to clarify matters.

Palmer shrugged. "I had other clients who required my attention."

"And yet you are here, in the middle of the night."

"In your mother's garden," Palmer said agreeably. "A fine and private place to pick monkshood, henbane, tansy, and foxglove." He indicated each plant in turn as he named it. "Do you realize that there is poison enough here to do away with every archaeologist in New England?"

Diana's eyes widened at his words. She started to speak but, after a wary glance at Ben, changed her mind.

"Did you discover anything to indicate that Professor Winthrop might have gone so far as to kill Frank Ennis?" Ben asked, "or that he might have hired someone else to murder him?"

"I have no proof."

"But you must have suspicions." Diana was on her feet, hands fluttering in agitation.

Palmer's considering gaze lingered on her a bit too long for Ben's comfort. Then the detective caught and held Diana's eyes with a hard stare. "It would be wise of you to go to Keep Island, Mrs. Spaulding. Apprise Miss Dunbar of the situation. Warn her that Winthrop is up to something. Warn her, Mrs. Spaulding. Will you do that?"

Diana blinked slowly. "Of course. I will do as you say, Mr.

Palmer." Meekly—too meekly—she thanked him for his help and bade him a polite good night.

Ben watched Palmer stride off until his departing figure was swallowed up by the shadows of a hedgerow. What had just happened?

Diana, her face reflecting the same bemusement Ben felt, started to speak, then fell silent.

"Did he just hypnotize you?"

"I . . . I don't know. The last few minutes are a trifle . . . blurred."

Hypnosis was a subject about which Ben knew very little . . . except that a truly skilled practitioner could sometimes cure patients of their fears by planting suggestions in their minds while they were in a trance.

"I do want to warn Serena," Diana whispered, "but is that my own idea . . . or his?" Her voice rose to a panic pitch on the last two words.

Ben wrapped his arm around her shoulders and gave her a reassuring squeeze. When he felt a shudder run through her, he decided it was past time they went inside.

"Hypnosis is just a stage trick," Diana said after a moment's walking. She sounded as if she was trying to convince herself it was true. "Success requires only a powerful personality, and sometimes a conspirator planted in the audience."

"I bow to your greater knowledge of theatrical performances, but there may also be practical, scientific uses for the ability. I've heard that some dentists use the technique to keep their patients from feeling pain." Of their own volition, his fingers reached up to massage his jaw.

"Nonsense. If hypnosis were possible, that would mean Justus Palmer could make you or me or anyone else he chose, do anything he wanted us to, even if it went against our natures. The man simply has a charismatic nature, as you do yourself."

The more she talked, the steadier she became. Ben decided

not to disabuse her of her conviction. "Do you want to return to Keep Island?"

"*Someone* should warn Serena that an old enemy has surfaced nearby."

Ben glanced from side to side as they strode along the walkway at a rapid clip. Palmer had vanished with as much stealth as he'd appeared. Or had he? Might he still be lurking somewhere, watching and listening?

Annoyed with himself for allowing the other man to get under his skin, Ben was nevertheless resolved to find out more about the private detective. Why, he wondered, did *Palmer* want them to go to Keep Island? That talking to Graham and Serena fell in well with Ben's own inclination was neither here nor there. He was suspicious of the detective's motives.

Back in their room, Diana did not at once return to bed. Her expression troubled, she waited for Ben to take a clean nightshirt out of a drawer, then blurted out news that stunned him: "Palmer was here Tuesday night. Maggie told me about it on Wednesday morning, but I didn't believe her."

Ben froze in the act of placing his pocket watch on the dresser. "Here?"

"They met in the garden. She . . . she said he bit her on the neck."

Surprised into a laugh, Ben felt himself relax. "Let me get this straight—you don't believe in hypnosis but you do believe in vampires?"

℘◌℘

Since Graham Somener did not know about Ben and Diana's visit to Islesborough, he welcomed them with open arms. Unfortunately, and against Diana's advice, Ben immediately confessed everything they'd tried to do.

"You damned—"

Ben caught Somener's raised fist before it could land.

"You've got some nerve showing your face here after spreading lies about my wife!"

"Now, Graham—"

Diana started to step between them. After all, a similar effort had worked to stop a fight with Palmer. "Ben had the best of intentions. He—"

Somener knocked her outstretched hand aside with a stinging blow. "Be quiet. Both of you. I do not want to hear another word. How you dare to show your faces here when you believe—"

Ben grabbed his old friend by the shoulders and shook him. "I'll atone for my mistakes later, Graham. Right now we have more information you need to hear. Justus Palmer was hired by Professor Lucien Winthrop. Winthrop is the source of the rumors about criminal activities on Keep Island."

"Professor . . . who? I've never heard of the man."

"Serena has."

"Where is Serena?" Diana interrupted.

"In the library." But when Diana turned in that direction, Graham Somener bellowed at her. "Leave her be!" He started after her, fists raised. "I want you off my island. Both of you. Now!"

Ben moved to block his way. "You'll have to throw us off bodily, starting with me."

"With pleasure." The gleam of anticipation in Somener's eyes was reflected in Ben's as they raised their fists in the classic bare-knuckle boxing pose.

Horrified, Diana tried again to intervene.

"Stay back," Ben ordered.

"You're going to fight?" She could not stem the alarm in her voice. The last time Ben had resorted to fisticuffs, he had not come out of the match unscathed.

"Just a friendly little bout." Neither Ben's grin nor his tone of voice were convincing. "Don't worry about us, Diana. Go and find Serena."

Without warning, Somener attacked. Ben deflected the fist with one arm, gave a whoop of exhilaration, and tried to strike his opponent in return. Blows fell fast and hard after that, but none of them seemed to inflict much damage. Diana stared at them in disbelief. They actually seemed to *enjoy* throwing punches at each other.

At first blood, spurting copiously from Graham Somener's nose, Diana beat a hasty retreat. She couldn't tell any more if they were truly angry with each other or not but she had no desire to watch them work out their differences with their fists.

She found Serena just where Graham had said she'd be, so engrossed in reading that she did not even look up when Diana entered the room.

"Good day to you, Serena." She wondered if the other woman would rescind the invitation to use her first name when she learned what Ben and Diana had tried to do.

"Diana! I did not expect to see you so soon." Serena rose hastily from an overstuffed chair to cross the room and tuck the old book she'd been perusing into a drawer in Graham Somener's big partner's desk.

"I've come to apologize," Diana said, "and to ask questions. Let me start with this: did you know that Lucien Winthrop lives in Belfast?"

The flicker of surprise in Serena's eyes answered before she spoke. Moving with a stiffness that denoted wariness, she faced Diana. "Winthrop is here? In Maine?"

"And has been for some time. He knows you're here, too."

Softly but colorfully, Serena cursed. Diana let the tirade wind down before she attempted to ask any more questions. It was plain enough how Serena felt about the professor.

"If we are to accomplish anything," Diana said when the other woman seemed to have calmed down enough to listen, "we must be honest with each other. Let me say first that Ben and I made a mistake, but you are yourself to blame, at least in part."

"What are you talking about?" Serena gestured towards a chair and settled into its mate herself, sprawling in an unladylike manner that nevertheless struck Diana as looking extremely comfortable, especially as Serena was once again dressed in her men's clothing.

Wondering if the other woman would attempt to punch her in the face when she'd finished, Diana plunged into her own confession, ending with the misguided attempt to stop Serena's wedding. By then Serena's face was set hard as stone and she was sitting bolt upright.

"You thought I was a confidence woman?" she asked through gritted teeth.

"Or a fortune hunter." She'd left out the speculation that involved smuggling and piracy. "Consider what we saw, Serena. You were excessively secretive about what you were doing here, you lied at the inquest—" She held a hand up to stop the other woman's protest. "At the least you changed your story. And that one night when you drank to excess you were muttering about ruined plans. You were obviously overwrought about something. Add in the condemnation of a known authority on matters archaeological and what else could we think but that you were up to no good?"

"I drank too much and lied at the inquest for the same reason—I was worried about Graham." Too restless to remain seated, she leapt from the chair and began to prowl the confines of the library.

"You're telling me you thought Graham killed Frank Ennis?"

"I thought it was possible. It wasn't until after everyone left that we were able to talk things through. He's not a murderer and neither am I, but we came to two decisions that night. The first was to discourage the investigation into Frank's death. Graham had enough bad publicity to last him a lifetime over that business with the building collapse. The second decision was to wed. We went the very next day to Islesborough to file our marriage intentions."

"Not to Belfast?"

"No. In fact, I've never been to Belfast. I've always traveled here by way of Bucksport on the *Miss Min*."

"Someone sent a telegram to me from Belfast on that same Monday afternoon. It warned me to stop meddling."

"I didn't send it. Nor did Graham." She flung herself into the chair behind the desk and plucked up a penknife to fiddle with.

"What about Paul Carstairs?"

"What about him?"

"Is he here on the island?"

She nodded. "As far as I know, he hasn't left since we first set up camp, except to go to Ellsworth for Frank's funeral."

"In that you are wrong. He made at least one trip to Belfast, by way of Islesborough, on Friday. I wonder now if he was also there on that Monday. Since you and Graham were on Islesborough, you wouldn't know if he stayed here or not."

"Why would Paul threaten you?"

"A good question. I might be able to answer it better if you'd tell me first about your relationship with Professor Winthrop."

"He was my mentor at the Peabody Museum." Her restless movements stilled. "You say he now lives in Belfast?"

"Yes."

She looked up and met Diana's eyes. "I didn't know. I swear it."

"Carstairs told us that Winthrop sent for him. Was he also one of Winthrop's pupils?"

"Yes. We all were. Paul and Frank and I. At first I thought it a great honor to work with him. He is quite famous in his field."

Diana's eyebrows lifted at the bitterness in Serena's voice.

"That was before I realized that he was a charlatan and a thief!" With a sudden, violent gesture, she drove the penknife into the blotter.

Diana left the safety of her chair to stand on the opposite side of the big desk. "I thought he was the one who accused *you* of deceit?"

"Oh, he did . . . once he realized I was on to him. He is unscrupulous, Diana. Over and over again he encouraged promising students to share their research with him, then appropriated their discoveries as his own. I was lucky. I had developed a theory on another subject, one much less important than the matter of settlers on Keep Island. When Winthrop stole that first idea, I realized I had to keep secret the details of any new discoveries."

Serena sprang out of the chair and once more began to pace. There was no doubting her sincerity. If it had been the professor who'd been murdered, Diana would have looked no further for the killer.

"It infuriated Winthrop to realize I was on the trail of something big. Once I'd convinced him he would never have enough information to claim the discovery as his own, he set out to ruin me. He was very thorough. He convinced everyone that my theories on the subject of early European settlers were absurd. Then he made it seem as if I had set out to trick them. No one would believe me when I accused *him* of underhanded tactics. If it had not been for two old friends, I would not even have been able to field a professional crew for this expedition."

"Ah, yes. Old friends. I'm afraid that was another point that made you seem suspicious. Mr. Ennis apparently claimed that you and he had been married."

"Never married!" Serena's eyes snapped with renewed fury.

"What, then?"

Quickly regaining control of herself, she shrugged. "We'd *talked* about marriage, but that was before Winthrop's accusation that I had deliberately perpetrated a fraud. His lies resulted in a polite request that I leave the Peabody. Frank had his own career to think about. He stayed on at Harvard."

"And yet he agreed to help you this summer."

"As a personal favor. Unfortunately, it turned out that he expected personal favors in return."

"And Carstairs? Why did he join you?" Serena's circling had begun to make Diana dizzy. She seated herself and stopped trying to watch the other woman pace.

"Paul was very ill earlier this year. He said that spending his summer on an island off the coast of Maine was just what he needed to recover his strength." She frowned. "It's also possible no one else would hire him. Raw good health is a necessity for an archaeologist."

"When Ben and I talked to Professor Winthrop, he claimed he had never met you and had never heard of Ennis or Carstairs."

"Well, those are outright lies. I was a private student at the Peabody Museum. Paul and Frank were graduate students. Winthrop is an assistant there."

"Was. Professor Putnam *did* believe you, Serena. In time, he found evidence enough against Winthrop to force him into retirement."

"But not enough, apparently, to ruin his reputation or restore mine!"

Diana understood her bitterness, but there were other things that still puzzled her. "Faced with expulsion, you failed to provide proof of your theory. Do you *have* any?"

Serena hesitated, but Diana's quiet determination seemed to sway her. "It was complicated. I wasn't well acquainted with Graham then, but I knew what he had gone through after the building collapse. I could not in good conscience reveal the location of this island without talking to him first, and he was holed up here, seeing no one."

"Your research wasn't enough?"

"Not when the great Lucien Winthrop took a stand against me!" She led Diana to the corner of Graham's library she'd staked out as her own. "This is what I had. First, a rare copy of a book published in 1558." Extracting it from a shelf, she offered it to Diana. "I taught myself Italian in order to be able to read it."

The worn leather had the smell of great age, and Diana handled the little volume with exquisite care. The title page would have been a challenge to interpret even if it weren't in a foreign language. Diana found the top line, *DEI COMMENTARII DEL*, easy enough to make out, but after that the letters became increasingly difficult to comprehend.

"This," Serena explained, reaching for another volume, "is the 1873 translation of that book by Richard Henry Major, published as *The Voyages of the Venetian Brothers Nicolò and Antonio Zeno, to the Northern Seas, in the XIVth century, comprising the latest known accounts of the lost colony of Greenland; and of the Northmen in America before Columbus.*"

"How is this connected to the ship you are looking for?"

"These voyages led to an attempt at colonization, or so I believe." She extracted yet a third volume, *History of the Voyages and Discoveries Made in the North*. "John Reinhold Forster wrote this in 1784. In it he identifies the northern 'Prince' referred to in the Zeno narrative as Henry Sinclair, a Scot holding the Norwegian title of Jarl of Orkney. I believe my early settlers were Scottish."

"If that is so, why has no one ever heard of them before?"

"At the end of the fourteenth century, there was war between England and Scotland. Many records were destroyed, many lives lost. Among those killed in battle was that same Henry Sinclair. If he did explore these regions and afterward send settlers here, they'd soon have been forgotten after his death. No other ships would have followed that first one to these shores. And, when no shipment of timber was forthcoming from the New World, those left behind in Scotland would have assumed that the first ship was lost at sea."

"Perhaps it was."

"Or perhaps it reached this very bay, this very cove, this very island. The passengers aboard survived, cut off from any contract with home."

"Why are you so convinced you'll find something here, Serena?

Why on *this* island, when there are so many along the coast?"

"I have my reasons."

Diana was about to challenge this evasive answer when she caught sight of another volume farther along the shelf, one that seemed familiar to her. Pulling it out, she recognized the same 1835 issue of the *Journal of the Royal Geographical Society of London* that she'd seen on Winthrop's desk.

"That contains an attack on the information contained in Master Zeno's book," Serena said. "Captain C.C. Zahrtmann's 'Remarks on the Voyages to the Northern Hemisphere, ascribed to the Zeni of Venice' claims the entire tale was a fabrication. Of course, he is wrong."

For Diana, the fact that there had been a copy of this publication at Lucien Winthrop's house was proof positive that Winthrop took more than a passing interest in Serena's excavation. "Winthrop was here that day, you know," she told Serena. "He was the man in the dory with the binoculars."

"Did he also poison my men and kill Frank?"

"I don't know. He appears to be a petty, vengeful little man, and I saw for myself what a misanthrope he is, but a murderer?" Diana shook her head, undecided.

Serena reshelved the book with more force than was strictly necessary. "He does not want me to succeed. If I do, it will prove I was right all along."

"Let's say he was responsible. What purpose did Frank Ennis's death serve?"

"It stopped work."

"Only temporarily."

Serena left the shelves, wandering the room with apparent aimlessness. She paused by the window to look out at the expanse of lawn stretching away towards the promontory. It was a perfect summer's day, fair and a bit cooler than it had been of late, with a light breeze to stir the leaves and the long blades of grass.

As Diana stared at the scene over the other woman's shoulder,

MacDougall came into view. He was hard at work in spite of it being the Sabbath, pushing one of those newfangled lawnmowers. For a few minutes the two women watched him walk back and forth, back and forth, across the greensward, letting the blades do the work of a dozen men with scythes.

"There is one reason why Winthrop might have killed Frank," Serena said at last. "What if he still hopes to claim my discoveries for himself? It was only after he failed to appropriate my research that he started his vicious campaign to discredit me. Before that, he seemed to accept the logic of my theory. Perhaps he expected me to be blamed for Frank's death. Winthrop might have believed that if I were arrested, tried, and imprisoned, he could persuade Graham to let him take over the excavation."

Graham Somener sported a black eye and a swollen nose. Ben had a cut on his cheek and severely bruised knuckles. Both men were smiling when Diana and Serena joined them before the midday meal. Punching each other seemed an odd way to make peace, but if the bout had cleared the air, Diana was glad of it.

"I doubt I'd have been so forgiving if someone had tried to stop my wedding," she murmured. "I do apologize, Serena."

"I have, it appears, more serious things to worry about than misunderstood motives." She looked Diana up and down. "But I won't say it wouldn't have felt good to slap you very hard across the face."

Startled, Diana blinked at her, relaxing only after the other woman burst into laughter.

"You should see your expression! Did you really think I'd do it?"

"You are . . . unconventional," Diana ventured.

"Only if you never met Min Somener."

"Did she have something to do with your decision to study archaeology?" Diana asked.

Serena hesitated. "Min pursued history in a more refined way.

She loved nothing better than to read about the past. I like to get my hands dirty."

"Do many women pursue careers in archaeology?"

"Quite a few. And a number of these women have made names for themselves in the field . . . in spite of what Professor Winthrop may have told you." A faint smile made Serena's lips twitch with amusement. "Men, as you may have guessed, dominate the profession, and most of them think only men should interest themselves in archaeological matters."

Diana made a sympathetic sound. "I have some familiarity with that attitude, Serena. Oh, there are plenty of other females who are journalists, but only a few actually venture into a newsroom every day or go out after stories. Unlike their male counterparts, most women send in pieces written at home."

"You understand, then."

"At least a little. And I know I envy you your working costume."

Serena laughed. "The trousers, you mean? Both my clothing and my methods were inspired by a very great woman named Jane Magre Dieulafoy. For most of the last decade and all of this one, she has excavated with her husband in Egypt and Persia. In the early years she discovered there were advantages to traveling dressed as a man. When she returned to Paris in 1880, she continued to wear trousers and does so to this day."

"And her methods?"

"She advocates doing a survey before digging, followed by a probe of debris under the earth to extract a sample. She keeps an excavation journal to record every object and structure found. For each find, each extraction, she writes down the relative and absolute position, makes a drawing of the object in situ, and assigns a find number. Only then is it transported from the site and stored. She takes photographs, too."

That all sounded logical to Diana, but she gathered from the way Serena spoke that not all archaeologists were so careful.

"Where did she receive formal training?"

"Neither she nor her husband were trained as archaeologists. They used common sense and a love of history as their guides. Indeed, it is difficult for a man or a woman to obtain a degree in archaeology as so few institutions offer one. Of those that do, many are still closed to women students. Even the most prestigious institutions in this country prefer to accept women only as 'informal private students' rather than admit them to a regular program of study."

"Fascinating as this is, ladies," Graham interrupted, "Mr. Carstairs will be joining us at any moment. Is he to be trusted or not?"

"He's an old friend," Serena said.

"And a former student of Lucien Winthrop's," Diana reminded her.

"Paul paid a courtesy visit at Winthrop's request. Isn't that what you told me he said?"

"He was extremely nervous all the time we were talking to him."

"You probably frightened him. He's the shy and retiring sort. He always has been."

"Don't be too trusting, Serena," Diana warned her. "*Someone* killed Frank Ennis, and that it might have been Paul Carstairs, acting on Lucien Winthrop's orders, makes as much sense as any other theory we've come up with."

Mrs. Monroe rang the chime to announce that dinner was served at the same moment Carstairs rushed in from the hallway. "Sorry I'm late," he apologized. "I lost track of time down at the site." He skidded to a stop when he caught sight of Ben and Diana. "Dr. Northcote. Mrs. Spaulding. I didn't expect to see you here."

"Come along, Paul," Serena said in a brisk voice. "We can talk and eat at the same time."

As soon as they were settled at the dining room table and Mrs.

Monroe had begun to serve, Serena repeated her suggestion that Lucien Winthrop had been trying to shut down the excavation on Keep Island.

Carstairs said nothing, but his eyes went as big as the proverbial saucers.

"That theory still leaves a great many unanswered questions." Ben speared a slice of ham from the meat platter.

"What concerns me," Graham said, "is that Serena may be in danger. If Winthrop was trying to drive her away from the site so that he could excavate here himself, then what is to stop him from killing her, and Carstairs, and Amity to further that same plan?"

"What would be the point?" Diana passed a plate of freshly baked dinner rolls, taking one for herself. "He'd only call attention to the fact that Ennis's death was a murder, and he'd lose Serena as a scapegoat."

"Why are you so certain Professor Winthrop killed Frank?" Carstairs asked in a tentative voice. "How did he do it?"

"He must have slipped unnoticed onto Keep Island—Diana was able to, if you recall—and poisoned the provisions. When that didn't work, he returned and damaged Frank's air hose."

"All unseen? An old man like that?" Ben looked skeptical.

"Don't let that cane he carries fool you," Serena said. "Lucien Winthrop is a trained archaeologist. He's accustomed to traveling over rough terrain. I doubt anything on this island would present much difficulty."

"She's right about that," Carstairs put in without looking up from his food. "He's sure-footed as a mountain goat."

"But why kill?" Ben asked. "Yes, I understand that he hoped Serena would be blamed, and he'd be able to take over the excavation, but there must be non-violent ways to cause problems for her and achieve the same end. Is it possible he also had a personal grudge against Frank Ennis?"

"If he blames me for his forced retirement, then it makes perfect sense to me that he would become obsessed with claiming my discoveries as his own." Serena's glower put thunderclouds to shame. "He'd do anything to achieve that end. Make no mistake, Lucien Winthrop is a thoroughgoing villain."

The crash of a dropped serving dish made everyone jump. Mrs. Monroe stood, face ashen, staring at Serena in shock. At her feet, an unsightly heap of mashed potatoes lay congealing amid shards of a broken bowl.

"Mrs. Monroe, what is the meaning of this?"

Ben held up a hand to silence Graham. "Mrs. Monroe? Are you ill?"

She blinked at him, and tears leaked out of the corners of her eyes. "Oh, Mr. Ben. I didn't know. Well, how could I? I didn't think there was any harm in it."

"Any harm in what?" he asked gently.

"That Professor Winthrop. He asked me to do him a favor, to collect any mail going off island and turn it over to him. He promised he'd send it on, said he just wanted to read it first. Said he needed to know what was going on here. Said it was important, and that Miss Min would have wanted him to know."

"Aunt Min?" Graham looked flabbergasted. "What does she have to do with this?"

Prudence Monroe flushed and twisted her hands together. "I've been here a long time, Mr. Graham. You know that."

"Yes, Mrs. Monroe. Of course I do. Now what the devil has my aunt to do with Lucien Winthrop?"

"They were . . . very good friends."

Lovers? Diana saw the astonishment on every face, but when she thought about it, the idea was not so impossible. Graham's aunt and Lucien Winthrop would have been of an age, and Min Somener, from all reports, had been an independent soul. She'd had a town house in Boston, too. That she'd been an acquaintance, and more, of a professor at Harvard was not such a great leap.

With careful questioning, the whole story tumbled out. Several weeks earlier Mrs. Monroe, a native of Islesborough, had been visiting friends there on her day off when she'd run into Lucien Winthrop. She'd met him before, when he'd visited Min on Keep Island, and knew that her old mistress had trusted him. When he'd confided that Min had shared secrets about the island with him, then hinted that Serena was not to be trusted, Mrs. Monroe had reluctantly agreed to his request that she intercept communications from Keep Island to the outside world. In the event, there had only been three letters, including Ben's.

"And the others?" Graham's voice was icy but Diana could sense the fiery explosion building just beneath that surface calm.

"One from you to Miss Beatrice Law," Mrs. Monroe said.

Graham's expression darkened. "A note of condolence to my former partner's sister. He died several months ago but I only recently found out about it."

"And a letter from Miss Dunbar to some foundation in New York City."

"A request for funding." Serena sounded bitter. "No wonder I never heard anything from them. That's what he wanted, all right. To stop me from moving forward."

"Why did you need more funding?" Graham's uncertain temper flared, shifting with unsettling swiftness to focus on his new wife. "I told you I'd provide everything you needed."

"I didn't want to be beholden to you. Not after it became clear that we . . . that you and I . . . oh, botheration, Graham! I didn't want to take advantage of your feelings for me."

Diana chewed thoughtfully on a hot, buttered roll. It seemed more and more likely that Winthrop had killed Frank Ennis, but how could they prove it?

Abruptly, Serena turned on Mrs. Monroe. "How much did Min tell Lucien Winthrop about this island's history?"

How much did Min know? Diana wondered, and wondered, too, what more Serena was holding back. If Min Somener was the reason Serena had developed an interest in history, was Min also a link to those early European colonists? Had Min uncovered their story before either Serena Dunbar or Lucien Winthrop had a clue to their existence? Just what had been in that trunk Min had willed to Serena?

Mrs. Monroe ignored Serena's demand for information, busying herself cleaning up the mess on the floor.

"Mrs. Somener asked you a question." Graham's stern voice commanded obedience.

"I couldn't say." Mrs. Monroe held herself stiffly and glared at her employer.

"Did Winthrop question you about Keep Island's past?" Diana asked.

The housekeeper made a derisive noise. "Wanted to know about legends and such. Lot of nonsense, that is. All that business about the island being cursed."

"Legends," Ben mused. "It all comes back to legends. This is the ancient land of Norombega, where there was once said to be a white tribe."

This was news to Diana. She did not think that detail had been mentioned during the conversation between Ben and Lucien Winthrop. Then again, she'd missed most of it when she'd slipped away to explore the professor's library.

"Are you saying that the source of that legend might have been the presence of early European settlers?" she asked. The idea still seemed far fetched.

"Why not? In a generation or two, if they didn't just die out, they'd have been absorbed into the native population, but the story of a white tribe would have survived." Ben's enthusiasm proved contagious.

"Along with a legend about a curse on the island," Graham mused. "Perhaps that had its origin in the shipwreck. Bad luck for somebody."

"The story could just as easily have stemmed from sickness

among the settlers . . . or *because* of them," Serena put in. "Any historian will tell you that Europeans brought deadly diseases to these shores. Measles wiped out entire tribes after colonies were established in what is now Massachusetts. If a great many people died on this island, what more natural than for those who witnessed their deaths to decide the place was cursed?"

Mrs. Monroe snorted. "Tale I heard says something was buried here long ago. Something dangerous. Lethal. That's why everyone had to stay away."

"A body," Ben suggested, "ravaged by a disease others feared to catch."

"How do you know that it was something that was buried, Mrs. Monroe?" Diana asked.

The housekeeper shrugged. "I expect my grandfather told me. He had lots of stories, and he told them over and over again when I was a child."

CHAPTER ELEVEN

❧☙

Ben and Diana strolled to the top of the promontory to watch the sunset. As the brilliant yellows and pinks faded into purple over the distant Camden Hills, just visible across the width of Islesborough, Ben felt more content than he had in days. Graham had come around, after releasing considerable aggression with his fists, and forgiven him for trying to stop the wedding. He'd even agreed that he might have done the same thing had their positions been reversed. Ben's fears about his old friend's mental state had been assuaged.

Only one problem remained, the question of who *had* tampered with Frank Ennis's air hose. Was Lucien Winthrop the cause of all the trouble on Keep Island? And if he was, had he hired someone to do his dirty work? Ben was keeping an eye on Paul Carstairs, but it occurred to him that Justus Palmer was also a likely suspect.

"I heard from my friend in Boston," he told Diana, "the one I asked to visit Palmer's office. With everything else that's been going on, I forgot to mention that his telegram was delivered to my office shortly after Captain Cobb showed up there. It seems that Palmer's office is rarely open. The neighbors say it appears to be a legitimate business but Palmer keeps odd hours and works alone. Often the lights burn all night, and he frequently meets clients long after respectable folk are in their beds."

"Perhaps he is a vampire, after all," Diana suggested with a grin.

"I very much doubt it, but he could be a killer. What if he did more than look into rumors for Winthrop?"

"Ben," she said, placing one hand on his forearm and waiting until he looked at her to speak. "I know you don't like thinking about it, but perhaps Palmer's helpfulness the other night had more to do with Maggie than with Winthrop."

"He's years younger than she is!" Repulsed by the picture in his mind's eye—Justus Palmer embracing Maggie Northcote in the herb garden—Ben clenched his teeth.

"I know their association seems slightly scandalous, but—"

"I don't want to discuss it, Diana!"

"I understand. When my mother toddles off to bed with her new husband in the middle of the afternoon, I don't like to think about *that*, either."

"Hardly the same—" He broke off. It had every appearance of being exactly the same, and he did *not* want to dwell on the details. "Can we go back to talking about murder?"

Diana sighed. "For two people who wished to avoid ever coming in contact with crime again, we have not done very well."

"There is no real need to involve ourselves further. We've warned Graham and Serena. Besides, she is probably right. It was a ploy to have her blamed for Ennis's death. It failed. End of story."

"Except that Ennis's killer goes unpunished."

That went against the grain, but Ben didn't know what they could do about it. They had theories, but no hard facts. Nothing, certainly, that would hold up in a court of law.

"It seems a poor reason for murder," Diana said after a while. "Stealing another archaeologist's work."

"I've known of cases where men killed for far less."

"Is it a sort of madness that makes someone take a life?"

"Sometimes it is." Ben realized he'd never have a better opportunity to reveal the one secret he was still keeping from his fiancée. He took her in his arms and kissed her lightly on the forehead. "Diana, I am thinking of giving up my practice."

She shifted in his embrace, trying to see his face. If his announcement distressed her, she gave no sign. Her expression was calm. Her eyes conveyed curiosity and interest. "What will you do instead?"

"I've been offered a position at the Maine Insane Hospital in Augusta."

"You are already a trustee there."

"There's more I can do. As trustee, my only obligation is attendance at the quarterly meetings, when we tour the facility to inspect the wards and audit the accounts. Maine's madhouse is as well run as any I've seen. Even when it was established back in 1840 it was a model for its kind, with separate wings for men and women and a dispensary, kitchen, laundry, engine building, and chapel. New rooms for the help, an elevator, and bath rooms have been added since, and there is a new building planned. Unfortunately, that is because the wards are already overcrowded. There are 578 patients, Diana, and but three physicians to tend to them. Dr. Mary Lowell has only just been added to assist Dr. Sanborn and Dr. Hill."

"A woman? Well, I approve of that."

He chuckled. "Her gender is not so surprising when you consider that there is also a woman on the current board of trustees. My point, however, is that the hospital desperately needs a fourth physician."

"You?"

"Why not?"

"The hospital is in Augusta. You'd spend hours on the train every day to travel back and forth, unless you mean to relocate."

"I believe that will only be a temporary inconvenience. Bangor's state senator is a member of the legislative committee on insane hospitals. He plans to propose that a second facility be built in Bangor, to serve the northern part of the state."

"That will take time." She sat on the rock so well placed for that purpose, folded her hands in her lap, and smiled up at him. "Perhaps you could set up a clinic for patients in the Bangor area—those whose families are unable to care for them at home. Later, when funding is approved for a state facility, those patients can be transferred to the new hospital."

Ben stared at her, struck speechless at the ease with which she'd come up with a perfect solution to his dilemma.

"You'll need a staff, of course," Diana continued.

"And guards. I am not so foolish as to assume there is no danger involved in working with the insane. But I do believe some of them can be cured." In fact, he had been thinking that hypnosis might provide part of the answer.

"You've made great strides with Aaron."

"I am not as certain of that as you are." Ben winced as he recalled his brother's most recent outburst and his complete failure to diagnose Graham correctly. Still, there had been a time, not so very long ago, when he'd feared he would have no choice but to lock Aaron away. That had prompted him to learn everything he could about mental disorders and their treatment. He'd soon discovered that doctors who were ignorant of both cause and cure, often put their patients through needless suffering. He could do better than that.

Ben and Diana talked for another hour there on the promontory overlooking Penobscot Bay. He sketched out his hopes and dreams while she listened. When he at last wound down, she gifted him with a gentle smile and her confidence.

"You will make it happen, Ben. I have faith in you."

஠௸

Paul Carstairs did not report to work on Monday morning. He did not seem to be anywhere on the island, and Graham's sailboat was also missing.

The reason seemed obvious to Diana. Carstairs had realized they suspected he was in cahoots with Lucien Winthrop and had taken off for parts unknown.

"Why leave now?" Ben asked. "Ennis's death was ruled an accident. The county attorney won't be easily persuaded to reopen it."

"I don't care why he left," Graham said. "I'm just glad he's gone. He won't be allowed back. We know to watch out for both him and Winthrop now." He sent a fond glance towards his wife, who was carefully sifting through a shovelful of dirt George Amity had dug up for her. "I'll keep MacDougall and Landrigan on watch. I'll hire more men for guard duty from Islesborough. And more men to work on the excavation, too. Serena will have everything she wants. She'll find what she's looking for."

Ben nodded and repeated the party line: "Winthrop's plot to take over her expedition has failed. He must realize by now that there's no possibility he'll ever be allowed to excavate on Keep Island."

Diana wasn't so sure. "What if he decides he wants revenge? We've thwarted his plans."

But Ben shook his head. "I spent quite some time talking to the man. He's petty and misanthropic, quite capable of stealing someone else's ideas, and capable, too, of holding a grudge, but my impression was that he's sly rather than violent. The most logical conclusion is that he hired Carstairs to cause trouble, and Carstairs went too far."

"You don't think Winthrop intended Frank Ennis to die?"

"He may have assumed the damage Carstairs did to the hose would be discovered when Ennis checked his equipment."

"Then that means Carstairs *let* Ennis die." Diana found the idea deeply disturbing.

"*If* he was as involved in this as we think," Ben pointed out. "This remains pure speculation, and—" he shot an apologetic glance at Graham—"I've speculated incorrectly before. It's equally possible that Winthrop acted alone."

"I want to examine Carstairs's possessions," Diana said.

As Graham had no objection, the three of them left Serena to her digging and went back to the house. Carstairs had moved into a room on the third floor after the incident with the morphine.

Mrs. Monroe gave a little shriek of surprise when Ben opened the door. "Goodness but you startled me, Mr. Ben! I was just tidying up in here."

In spite of the feather duster she held in one hand it was clear she had been doing more than that. The drawers in the bureau were open, their contents in disarray, and a number of Paul Carstairs's possessions—clothes, papers, and toiletries—lay jumbled together in a heap atop the unmade bed.

"Find anything interesting?" Diana asked.

Sarcasm did not sit well with Mrs. Monroe. Scowling, the older woman clapped both hands to her hips and glared at all three of her accusers. "I've got a right to know what's going on around here."

"Some, yes, Mrs. Monroe. But other things need not concern you." Graham fixed her with one of his formidable scowls. "Why were you searching Carstairs's belongings?"

"Because he took off, that's why. Plain as the nose on your face," she added in an irritable mutter.

"He seems to have left behind everything he owned," Ben remarked.

"That's consistent with fleeing in panic," Diana said.

"You may go now, Mrs. Monroe." Graham's tone was as autocratic as Diana had ever heard.

The housekeeper's resentment-filled glare would have given most men pause, but Graham didn't see it. He was too busy inspecting the clutter on the bed.

"Maybe he just got tired of taking orders," Mrs. Monroe grumbled. "Years of service, and what do I get: 'You may go now, Mrs. Monroe.'" With an angry swish of skirt and apron, she stormed out of the room.

"Aren't you afraid she'll quit?" Diana asked. Good help was hard to find.

Graham shook his head. "She'll burn the roast tonight, then forget all about it."

"She's right, you know," Ben said, as he examined the contents of the drawers Mrs. Monroe had already rifled. "She should be told what's going on. If she'd been involved earlier, we'd have known about Winthrop much sooner."

"I know how to handle Mrs. Monroe. Her family and mine go way back." Graham bent down to peer beneath the bed. "Huh! Moxie. A case of it." He tugged it out and removed the top to reveal rows of the familiar bottles, each one protected by its distinctive paper wrapping.

"There were two cases of that in his tent." Diana frowned, remembering something else. "Frank Ennis told me that Carstairs convinced him to try a bottle. He said he didn't like it very much. In fact, he thought at first that it was the Moxie that made him sick. What if it did? What if Carstairs put morphine in the Moxie?"

"Did Amity drink some too?" Graham asked.

Ben nodded. "I asked all three of them to list everything they'd consumed for two days before they fell ill. There were undoubtedly smaller doses in other foods first, but Moxie would have hidden the taste of the final, larger dose."

"Wait," Diana objected. "There is one thing that makes no sense. Carstairs was poisoned, too. He almost died. Why would he have taken such a risk?"

"It would be an extraordinarily dangerous thing to do," Ben agreed, "unless he believed he had built up a tolerance for the drug. That's entirely possible. He took a bad fall on his last job. Broke some bones. Infection set in. He'd have been given something for the pain."

"It was on an expedition to Casa Grande," Graham confirmed. "Serena told me about it when Carstairs first came here. She felt sorry for him."

"If he was treated with morphine, he might already have had a supply of the drug when Winthrop hired him to disrupt the excavation." Ben shook his head at Carstairs's foolishness. "If we're right, it was a horrendous risk to take. All three of them could easily have ended up dead."

A distant whistle put an end to the discussion. The *Miss Min* had docked and, in accordance with the message Landrigan had been charged to deliver to Captain Cobb as soon as he arrived, she would not depart until Ben and Diana were aboard.

"That's it, then. All we can do for now." Ben offered his arm to Diana. "*Our* wedding is Saturday, Graham. Will you and Serena be there?"

"We will."

"So will Horatio Foxe," Diana reminded them.

"Ah, yes, the newspaper editor who thinks he's discovered something sensational about me. I'll talk to him. I'm certain we can come to terms."

Diana opened her mouth to protest that Foxe could not be bribed, then shut it again. It was up to Graham how he dealt with the press.

They left Keep Island aboard the *Miss Min,* Captain Cobb under orders to steam straight to Bucksport so that Ben and Diana would arrive there in time to catch the afternoon train back to Bangor.

She should feel relieved, Diana told herself. Their part in the trouble on Keep Island was over. But throughout the trip, her mind kept circling around the loose ends that remained. She didn't realize she'd sighed aloud until Ben asked her what the matter was.

"It's petty of me, but now that Graham has so clearly taken control of the situation, I feel a trifle left out."

"It isn't as if there aren't still some minor mysteries to be solved."

"True. The rumors that the island is cursed, for example. Where did they come from? And I still don't understand why—"

"On the other hand, there are only five days left until our wedding," Ben reminded her. "Shouldn't you be concentrating on that?"

"You're right. I cannot in good conscience spend any more time thinking about anything else. There are dozens of last-minute details to see to. The rest of my family and other guests will be arriving. Mother will need muzzling."

"And you must pack for a wedding journey that I now think will take us away from home for several months."

"Months?" That news caught her off guard. The last she'd heard, he planned on a week at the Poland Spring House. "Where are we going?"

"Abroad, if you agree. Now that my professional life is about to take a new course, there are several doctors I would like to consult with, in England and on the Continent."

Delighted and distracted by the prospect of foreign travel, Diana did not let unsolved mysteries impinge on her thoughts again until well after they were back home in Bangor.

80Q3

Ben let himself into his office late Monday evening with a sigh of relief. His home had turned into a madhouse, and he knew whereof he spoke!

He wandered through the rooms that had meant so much to him only a few years ago. Even the familiar smell of carbolic had started to fade. A fine film of dust covered the bell jar that protected his microscope.

He'd done good work here, been of service to the community, but there were plenty of other doctors to take care of Bangor's sick and injured. There were others qualified to be city coroner, too.

He found some cartons in a store room and began to gather what he would take with him. Most of the equipment could stay with the practice when he sold it, just as it had come to him when he'd bought it.

Busy with sorting and packing, Ben had no idea how much time had passed when a knock pulled him away from his task. Justus Palmer stood on the back stoop.

"Come in," Ben invited, opening the door. "I've been wanting to speak to you."

"And I you," Palmer said.

A few minutes later they were settled in Ben's office, Ben at his roll-top desk and Palmer in the patient's chair. Ben had offered brandy. Palmer had refused.

"First and foremost," Palmer began, "my intentions towards your mother are honorable. I enjoy her company and her conversation. And she, I think, finds me equally entertaining."

Ben said nothing. He didn't approve, but he'd been raised to believe that a woman had the right to make up her own mind.

"I also owe you an apology. The first time I met Mrs. Spaulding, I encouraged her to follow you to Keep Island. By telling her she should not go there, of course. I planned to question her upon her return. In the event, that proved unnecessary. I learned all I needed to from Sheriff Fields."

"Why not go to the island yourself?"

"You already know the answer. I cannot tolerate traveling by boat, not even across the smallest body of water." He shrugged. "It is a weakness I abhor, but there is nothing I can do about it. It is my nature."

"Why tell me this now?"

"Because I have a feeling we will be seeing a great deal of each other in future." He smiled, and Ben knew the other man sensed his discomfort.

"If that's all you came to say—"

"It is not. I cannot afford to spend any more time on this Keep Island business. Other cases require my attention. But one or two further bits of information have come my way. You may make of them what you will."

Ben leaned back in his chair and steepled his fingers on his chest. "Such as?"

"Professor Winthrop is no longer in Belfast. No one knows where he's gone."

Proof of the man's guilt? After a brief debate with himself, Ben told Palmer that Carstairs was missing, too, and summarized what they had concluded about his connection to Winthrop.

"I know nothing more about him," Palmer admitted, "but I did discover that Winthrop was once great friends with Graham Somener's aunt. He was distraught when she died."

"Winthrop was in love with Min Somener?" There was another couple Ben had difficulty imagining together!

"I don't know about love, but he apparently expected to be mentioned in her will. He complained to several of his cronies at Harvard that she reneged on a promise to bequeath him all her papers and books."

"The legacy she ended up leaving to Serena Dunbar, perhaps?"

"That seems likely, although Winthrop does not seem to have known about Miss Dunbar until well after she turned up as a student at the Peabody."

"As I understand it, she didn't tell anyone there about her connection to the Someners and Keep Island."

"A secretive lot, these archaeologists. I am glad to be done with them." Palmer stood, prepared to take his leave, but Ben called him back.

"What can you tell me about hypnosis?"

Palmer's eyebrows slightly lifted. "Why would you think I know anything about the subject?"

"It's obvious you have some command of the art." More than a little, Ben suspected. "I am interested in the process."

For some reason, even though he still was not sure he liked or trusted Justus Palmer, Ben felt comfortable telling the other man his plans. When he'd summarized what he hoped to do, he explained that he thought it might be useful to him to master the techniques of hypnosis.

"You are laboring under a misapprehension," Palmer said slowly. "I possess nothing more than a certain facility with the power of suggestion, and that works well only with weak-willed individuals. Sheriff Fields remembered part, if not all of the visit I paid to him, when I had hoped to erase his memory of it entirely. Lucien Winthrop proved completely immune to any influence. And dear Magda has a distressingly accurate recollection of every moment we have spent together."

The reminder that Palmer had been meeting Maggie North- cote in the garden in the middle of the night and, apparently, nibbling on her neck, had Ben's stomach twisting into knots. His muscles went taut, and his hands curled into fists. Enjoyed her *conversation*, did he?

"Mr. Palmer," Ben said in a low rumble, "may I suggest that in future you visit Mrs. Northcote at a more seemly hour than midnight, and in company?"

Palmer's steel-gray eyes caught and held Ben's gaze. "Are you inviting me to pay a social call, Dr. Northcote? Perhaps you will even invite me to attend your upcoming nuptials? Is that what you mean to say, Dr. Northcote?"

Momentarily caught by the rhythm and timbre of Palmer's voice, Ben nodded. Then he shook his head with a violence that made the other man laugh.

Only with weak-willed individuals, indeed!

"Who the hell are you, Palmer?"

"Just an old friend of Magda's, Dr. Northcote. A very old friend."

§∞Q?

With Ben spending the day in town on Tuesday, arranging details of their wedding journey and meeting with the young doctor interested in buying his practice, Diana found that she could not, after all, withdraw completely from her investigation of events on Keep Island. Curiosity, if nothing else, prompted her to pursue one minor point, in between last-minute wedding preparations and organizing her wardrobe for the trip abroad. With her aunt's able assistance, she sent a query to the New England Historic Genealogical Society.

"Here it is," Aunt Janette cried, waving the telegram in triumph. "The reply to your wire."

"Mr. Pingree's heirs?" Delmar Pingree, according to Mrs. Hatch of Islesborough, was the name of the man who'd sold Keep Island to the Someners, the man whose heirs, or so Maggie Northcote had once told her, Jedediah Somener had cheated out of their rightful inheritance. The Pingrees, Diana thought, were the most likely source of the story that the island was cursed.

"Heir," Aunt Janette corrected, consulting the telegram. "An only child named Susan. She married a gentleman called Perley Brown and had just one child herself, her daughter Prudence."

"Gracious!"

"You know who she is?"

"I believe I do. A Mrs. Prudence *Monroe* is Graham Somener's housekeeper, and if I am not mistaken, her mother's given name *was* Susan."

"Yes, that's the one." Aunt Janette surrendered the slip of yellow paper. "Prudence Brown married Amariah Monroe—such names these islanders have!—and he died a year later."

"Gracious," Diana said again, for it had belatedly occurred to her that Mrs. Monroe had been in an even better position than Paul Carstairs to do Winthrop's dirty work. They already knew she had been in contact with the professor. Perhaps the association had not been as innocent as she'd claimed.

Shaken, Diana remembered the look Mrs. Monroe had given Graham in Paul Carstairs's bedroom. There had been a great deal of pent up resentment in that glare. Were there even deeper emotions hiding just below the surface? What if Mrs. Monroe believed that Jedediah Somener had cheated her grandfather—the same one, presumably, who'd told her tales about the island? If she wanted revenge, then it made sense that she might join forces with Lucien Winthrop.

Of their own volition, Diana's hands covered her mouth to hold in a little cry of dismay. Mrs. Monroe could easily have poisoned Serena's crew, which would explain why Carstairs had not been spared. Had he really fled, Diana wondered, or had Mrs. Monroe done away with him to protect herself? A knock on the head with a marble rolling pin perhaps? The housekeeper's presence in Carstairs's room might not have been so innocent, either. They'd assumed she'd been searching his possessions, but what if she'd gone there to take them away, to support the assumption that Carstairs had fled?

Maggie Northcote in full voice brought Diana back to her senses with a start. "Hellooooo!" she called from the first floor. "Company!" She stretched out each syllable, sounding entirely too cheerful.

"Now what?" Diana muttered, but she did not dare ignore the summons. Leaving her aunt behind with the accumulation of papers and telegrams, she sailed forth from the bedroom where they had been working.

The answer to her question stood in the foyer below, resplendent in a brand new four-button cutaway suit that looked exactly like every other one he owned. His sand-colored hair was slightly mussed from the hat he'd just removed, and he was already fumbling in his breast pocket for a cigar.

"Diana, my dear!" Horatio Foxe greeted her. "You're looking splendid."

"What are you doing here?"

"You invited me to your wedding. Don't you remember?" He grinned at her, showing a mouth full of straight but tobacco-stained teeth.

He was a small, wiry man with glittering hazel eyes. The first time Diana had met him, he'd put her in mind of a leprechaun, and he was just as tricky to deal with as one of those mythical little men. She knew better than to think he had only one reason for anything he did. "And?"

"And I have information on your oh-so-interesting Mr. Somener."

"Do tell?" Maggie hovered, eyes bright and curious. She'd met Foxe several months earlier and had proclaimed him "fascinating" on that occasion.

Diana sighed. "You may as well tell us both. Whatever it is, I assure you it will not convince either of us to think less of Graham Somener."

"Come into the parlor," Maggie invited. "Make yourself comfortable. And yes, you may smoke that cigar. I adore the smell of a good cigar. I have been considering taking up the habit myself."

Foxe lost no time lighting his cheroot, but he was more leisurely about revealing the information he'd brought. He blew a circle of smoke towards the ceiling and settled himself comfortably in a chair before he finally began to speak. "What I found actually relates to Somener's partner, Vernon Law."

"He's dead." Graham's letter of condolence to Law's sister had been one of the pieces of mail Mrs. Monroe had turned over to Lucien Winthrop.

"Thunderation, Diana! Don't interrupt. Yes, he's dead, but do you know how?"

She had to admit that she did not.

"Graham Somener's partner didn't just die. He was murdered."

"What? Why would someone murder him?"

"Because, my dear, he was responsible for that building collapse five years ago, not Graham Somener. Vernon Law also absconded with the profits of their company. Because Somener refused to cast blame, people assumed he was equally guilty. Press coverage at the time blamed them both. Law vanished for awhile, then turned up in Arizona. He lived quietly in a remote area, so remote that he'd been dead several days before he was found. That was six months ago. The local authorities found no clues and have no suspects in the case."

"How was he killed?"

"Shot in the head."

"Poor man," Diana murmured.

"Some might say he got what he deserved, but that's neither here nor there. Seems to me his murder opens up the possibility of a connection to recent events on Keep Island."

"And just what do you know about them?" Diana had been careful to tell him very little in the telegram she'd sent.

"More than you might think. I've got connections. I've seen a transcript of the coroner's inquest."

Diana didn't ask whom he'd had to bribe. She didn't want to know. She was quite certain, however, that his source had not been a certain local newspaper editor.

"Are you telling us you think someone is seeking vengeance on both men because of the deaths in the building collapse?" All but dancing in delight, Maggie looked from Foxe to Diana and back again. "How wonderfully bloodthirsty!"

Foxe blew a smoke ring with a self-satisfied air. "Sensational story, no question about it. Out of all those who lost their lives, it seems that one had a friend or relative who believes in an eye for an eye."

"Vernon Law could just as easily have been shot during a robbery," Diana reminded him. "Or he might have double-crossed someone else, someone out there in the Wild West where everyone carries a gun. Someone less forgiving than Graham Somener."

"All true," Foxe agreed. "But add in the dead man on Keep Island and my theory becomes much more plausible. It defies coincidence to think that Graham Somener would be connected to *two* murdered men in less than a year."

"It has been five years since the building collapse," Diana pointed out. "Why would anyone wait so long for revenge?"

"Five years?" He snapped his fingers. "An instant. Besides, it would have taken time to track down Law and Somener. Both moved to remote areas of the country."

"No. It doesn't make sense. The attacks here were against the archaeologists, not Graham Somener."

"He might be the real target," Foxe insisted, "and what happened to the others just a ploy to muddy the waters before killing him. Tell me what has been happening here—the things that did not come out in the inquest."

Diana obliged, since he'd doubtless be able to find out on his own, but she gave him the abbreviated version of events.

"I admit this Professor Winthrop seems a likely villain," Foxe conceded when she'd finished. "I never have trusted academics. And that fellow Carstairs is suspicious, too. But of all the choices, I like the housekeeper best." He grinned around his second cigar. "Makes a better story if she did it. Talk about revenge served cold! The plot could well span three generations. I can see the headlines now: 'Lethal Legacy Destroys Island Paradise.'"

"Lethal Legend." Diana corrected him before she could stop herself, then grimaced. She was not going to play this game. Winthrop was the logical mastermind, with Carstairs and Mrs. Monroe as his pawns.

"It sounds as if Somener has taken steps to protect his wife," Foxe mused, "but he doesn't expect to be the object of a murder-ous attack himself. If I'm right, he's in danger. Tell you what. I'll go to Keep Island and warn him."

A most unladylike snort escaped Diana at this transparent excuse to get close to the story. "He won't let you near the place."

"He will if you come with me."

"She can't go running off again," Maggie protested. "Not with her wedding only four days away."

But she could, Diana thought. And she probably should. Although she was almost certain that Lucien Winthrop was the one responsible for Ennis's death, aided and abetted by either Prudence Monroe or Paul Carstairs, it would be reckless to take chances. If Mrs. Monroe really was out to punish Graham for stealing her inheritance, or if some unknown relative of the victims of the building collapse *had* killed Vernon Law, then Horatio Foxe was right. *Graham* was the one in danger. And as long as Winthrop and Carstairs were missing, they would be blamed for any new violence. If the real killer was someone else, he or she would get away with *another* murder.

৪৩৫

Early the next morning, Diana and Ben caught the train to Bucksport, boarded the *Miss Min*, and once more made the journey to Keep Island. Graham and Serena were surprised to see them, but listened without comment to the details of Vernon Law's death and Horatio Foxe's theory. Foxe himself had been left behind in Bangor. Maggie Northcote had been put in charge of keeping him there and had promised to manage it even if she had to tie him up and stuff him in a closet.

"Do you know where we can find a list of the victims of the building collapse?" Ben asked.

"I have one," Graham admitted. "In the library."

They all trouped along after him and consulted the list he produced, but it yielded no familiar surnames. Diana had never heard of any of the victims or their next of kin.

"There are only two women's names," Diana commented. "Miss Judith Briggs and Mrs. Edith C. Alleyn. What kind of building was it? I don't believe anyone has said." She'd assumed, for some reason, that it had been residential.

"It housed several businesses. Miss Briggs was a secretary at an insurance company. Mrs. Alleyn was consulting her lawyer at the time of the collapse." A tormented expression on his face, Graham let the list fall on the desk. "Your friend Foxe is just trying to resurrect old scandals. I have this list because I made reparations. I know money can't replace lost lives, but I did what I could. I tried to make up for what happened. God knows, I tried. I can't imagine that anyone would still want to punish me after all this time. Law's murder can't be more than a terrible coincidence."

Perhaps, Diana thought, Foxe was wrong. That did not mean, however, that Graham and Serena were safe. "There is another possibility," she announced. "I have uncovered something that suggests Prudence Monroe may have been more involved in Winthrop's schemes than we supposed. Did you know she's the only descendent of the man who sold this island to your grandfather?"

"What of it? That's no secret."

Although surprised that he knew, Diana soldiered on. It was foolish not to explore every possibility. "Does she have a reason to resent you and your family? To think the island was, er, stolen from the Pingrees?"

Graham's glower returned with a vengeance. "My grandfather paid a fortune for this land. It's neither his fault nor mine that Delmar Pingree squandered it all before he died."

"So the story of a gambling loss was only a rumor? How did Mrs. Monroe end up working for you?"

"Aunt Min hired her after Mrs. Monroe was widowed. They were both quite happy with the arrangement."

"Speaking of Mrs. Monroe," Serena interrupted with a too-bright smile that immediately put Diana on her guard, "I'll just check on how dinner is progressing, and let her know there will be two more at table."

Diana was right at her heels as she entered the kitchen. Mrs. Monroe gave them a black look, but she did not reach for her heavy marble rolling pin or any of the other potential weapons at her disposal.

Diana kept a wary eye on the knife rack as Serena marched up to the older woman and shook an accusing finger at her. "You never told me your family once owned this island."

"You never asked."

"What more haven't you shared?"

"Can't think of anything that'd be your business, *Mrs.* Somener. Unlike some, I'm more interested in the present than the past."

"You were with Min for years. I'd think some of her enthusiasm for history would have rubbed off."

"I always liked the story about the curse." Smiling secretively, Mrs. Monroe put a sprig of parsley atop the pork roast she'd just taken out of the oven.

"Did your grandfather invent it?"

"Not likely. He was downright superstitious about this place. Wouldn't set foot on Keep Island for love or money."

Diana believed her, but even more surprising was the way Serena visibly relaxed as soon as Mrs. Monroe denied any interest in the island's past. It was almost as if she'd been afraid that Mrs. Monroe knew something Serena wanted kept secret.

After puzzling over her observation for a moment, Diana ventured a question: "What did you think Delmar Pingree knew about the island, Serena?"

"What could he know?" The flash of fear in her eyes was so quick Diana almost missed it.

"Were you afraid, perhaps, that someone other than Min was aware of Keep Island's connection to those early Scottish settlers?"

Serena's shoulders tensed, and she bobbled the dinner roll she'd just filched from a pan keeping warm on the back of the stove. It would have fallen to the floor if Mrs. Monroe hadn't snatched it out of the air.

"Min made a couple of trips to Scotland," the housekeeper volunteered.

"Hmmm." Diana mused aloud. "I wonder. What did Min Somener tell you, Serena? What did she give you? You were willed the contents of a trunk. What did it contain? What did Lucien Winthrop think was going to be his? What was worth killing Frank Ennis to obtain?"

"I didn't—"

"Oh, for goodness sake! I know *you* didn't kill Ennis. I meant Winthrop. What is he after? Why does he believe you're likely to find it on *this* island?"

Serena gave a convulsive shudder and hugged herself, as if she were freezing. "There's a coin."

For a moment, the silence in the kitchen was absolute. Even Mrs. Monroe stopped rattling pans to listen.

"Min found a coin," Serena elaborated. "That's what she left me, along with her diaries. She took it to Scotland and showed it to scholars there. They dated it to the end of the fourteenth century. Just the right date to have come here with settlers who arrived in 1401."

CHAPTER TWELVE

ဢၣ

Following the midday meal, after Ben and Graham went off to meet with the two new guards Graham had hired, Serena produced a thin and much worn metal disc from her pocket.

"That's the coin?" Diana regarded the object with skepticism. It was so smooth that she could barely make out the design.

"A silver groat, issued no later than 1399. Apparently, the experts can tell from the letter punches used to make the dies. And there is a mint signature. It's English. That crowned head is supposed to be King Richard II. But coins from England were frequently found on the Scottish side of the border, so that doesn't mean anything."

Neither did finding the coin on Keep Island, Diana thought. It could have been lost here at any time before Min Somener found it. Perhaps it had been some coin collector's lucky piece, and that coin collector had been visiting Jedediah Somener. As proof of Serena's colony, it seemed slim indeed. "Did Winthrop know about this?"

"I'm not certain. Min must have told him something, enough to convince him he'd been cheated when he found out that he wasn't in her will. I didn't know about that until you told me," she added.

"Where, exactly, did Min Somener find the coin?"

"In the area where I am excavating, of course."

"No luck finding more?"

"Not yet, and I should get back. I left George Amity working alone. He's willing enough, but he's had no training. I do not like to leave him there unsupervised."

It occurred to Diana that no one had questioned George Amity about Paul Carstairs. The oversight was understandable. Amity kept to himself and didn't say much. He was easy to overlook.

While Serena inspected the work her remaining crew member had done, Diana nodded to that cheerful little man. "Excavation going well?" she asked.

"Well enough. This archaeology stuff is some interestin' once you get started. I like pokin' around, lookin' for things." He rubbed his knobby knuckles to ease the swelling in the joints, perfectly willing to answer her questions.

Sadly, Amity had no new information to offer. He didn't know Professor Winthrop. He hadn't seen anyone tampering with the food, the Moxie bottles, or the diving suit. And he'd played cards with Paul Carstairs but had not been privy to the other man's confidences.

"Don't talk much," was his laconic assessment of Carstairs.

"Do you know if he left the island the day Mr. Somener and Miss Dunbar went to Islesborough for their marriage licence?"

"Might have done. He made himself scarce soon as they was gone."

"What about the day before their wedding? After everyone returned from the funeral?"

"I can tell you that," Serena cut in. "He wasn't feeling well enough to work. He went straight to bed when we got back."

"In fact," Diana corrected her, "he went to Islesborough to buy a net."

"Whatever for?"

"You didn't order one?"

"I can't think of any use we'd have at the excavation for a net."

Another mystery, Diana thought. There were entirely too many of them! She'd have to ask Mrs. Monroe about that trip to Islesborough, since Carstairs had said he'd tagged along with her when she'd taken the sailboat and gone to visit a sick friend. She was about to return to the house and do so when Serena caught her arm in a vise-like grip. She was staring at something out on the waters of Penobscot Bay.

"That's Graham's sailboat! The one Paul stole."

"Where?" Diana caught only a glimpse of a boat passing out of sight beyond the point. She did not get a good look at it. "Was Carstairs aboard? Was Winthrop?"

"Two men. I couldn't tell who they were, but I'm sure it was Graham's boat. I've seen it often enough."

"Is there anywhere to land on that side of the island?" Diana had a vague recollection of seeing it from the deck of the steamer from Bar Harbor to Islesborough. In her memory the shoreline did not look inviting.

"It's mostly swamp backed up against more cliffs."

"Is anyone guarding that part of the shoreline?"

"I doubt it. It would be all but impossible to get to the house from that direction. There's no path."

Diana's gaze skimmed across the high ground. The point of land jutted out into Penobscot Bay to form one side of the little cove. Just now the tide was high. The mouth of the cave Ben had shown her on the day of the dive was no longer visible. "Did you know there was a cave up there?" she asked Serena.

"No. Where?"

Diana pointed. "Ben and Graham played there as boys. It seems to me that if someone could climb that far, then they'd be able to reach the top of the ridge without much difficulty. It looks like it would be a scramble, but—"

Alarm flared in Serena's eyes. "They could come over the ridge at low tide and reach the excavation site."

A chill ran through Diana. "If they can get this far, they can also go up the path to the promontory and gain access to the house. If I were you, I'd be much more worried about that!"

Ben had planned to be on board the *Miss Min* with Diana when the little steamer left Keep Island following her second daily stop. Graham had already agreed to alter Captain Cobb's schedule once more, so that they'd reach Bucksport in time to catch the train back to Bangor. Everything changed when Diana and Serena came running up to the house with word that Lucien Winthrop and Paul Carstairs might have landed on the island.

The search for the intruders began at once and continued throughout the day. They located Graham's sailboat easily enough, spotting it from the cliff top where it had been abandoned in the swamp. But of the men who'd come ashore, there was no sign.

They split up to search, each party armed. Ben, accompanied by MacDougall and his rifle, carried a pistol in his coat pocket, an old Army sidearm issued during the Civil War. Awkward and heavy as it was, Ben doubted it would be of much use, but it was better than nothing. He reached for it when he heard the crunch of boots on gravel. Someone was coming towards them along the path.

Signaling MacDougall to keep still, Ben pressed himself flat against a boulder. It jutted out far enough to conceal him. Quietly drawing in a breath, he steadied himself. To judge by the slow, uneven steps, it was Winthrop approaching, but old man or not, it would not do to underestimate him. If nothing else, he'd be armed with the cane he used as a walking stick.

It looked as if Serena had been right about Winthrop's ability to move over rough terrain. To elude them this long, the fellow had to be half mountain goat. But he was slowing down now. Only to be expected. He'd been roaming Keep Island for more than five hours.

To Ben's surprise, it was not Winthrop but Paul Carstairs who stepped out into the fading light, his thin frame picked out by the last rays of the sun as that golden orb disappeared behind the promontory above. Carstairs movements were awkward, as if he'd used up his last reserves of strength. He might well have done so. Carstairs had almost died of morphine poisoning only a fortnight ago, and that on top of a serious injury less than a year earlier.

Ben stepped out of concealment, pistol held steady in both hands. "Stop right there," he ordered.

Carstairs gave a start, his eyes going wide. "What the—"

"Where's Winthrop?"

"I—I don't know."

"You brought him here?"

"Well, yes, but—"

"Then we need to keep searching. MacDougall, tie Mr. Carstairs's hands behind his back. Then go find Mr. Somener and tell him I'm taking our prisoner to the house to question him."

"You're making a mistake. Winthrop did it all. Everything."

"Then why are you here?"

"He insisted I bring him. He . . . did me a favor. I . . . I didn't know how to refuse."

"You brought a man you know is a murderer back to the scene of the crime?"

"No! That is, he didn't mean to kill anyone. I don't think he did. And he's not trying to hurt anyone now. He just wants the treasure."

And then he fainted.

"MacDougall!" Ben bellowed.

Between the two of them, they got Carstairs's limp form back to the house. Ben did a cursory examination while he was still unconscious, decided there was nothing seriously wrong with him, and made sure he was roped securely to a chair before he shoved a bottle of smelling salts under his nose. By then, Graham had arrived. Diana, who had remained indoors with Serena and Mrs. Monroe during the search, had already joined Ben in the library.

"Alright, Carstairs," Ben said, when the prisoner came around. "What's this treasure you say Winthrop is after?"

Although he still looked dazed and sick, Carstairs seemed willing to cooperate. "That's what he called it. I swear it. He doesn't care about archaeological discoveries anymore. He thinks there's something of great value buried on this island, and he wants to find it so he can live comfortably in retirement for the rest of his life."

"And does he know precisely where this treasure is?" Graham's temper was barely leashed. He was almost as protective of his island, Ben thought, as he was of his wife.

"He has to find the map first. That'll tell him. Min Somener's map. She was supposed to leave her papers to him when she died, but she willed them to Serena instead. That's what he's after. He thinks one of those papers is a map that will lead him to the treasure. To great riches."

"He's incoherent," Graham said in disgust. "Babbling."

"And he's mistaken," Diana said. "Or rather, Winthrop is. Serena has some diaries and an old coin, but no treasure map."

"Where *is* Serena?" Ben asked. "I'd have thought she'd want to be here." Even Mrs. Monroe had poked her head in when they'd first showed up with the unconscious Paul Carstairs.

"She had a headache and went to lie down. Shall I fetch her?"

"No, let her rest." From the look Graham gave Carstairs, Ben suspected he did not want his new wife to witness what he might do to the miscreant. The guess was confirmed when Graham seized Carstairs by the throat and gave him a vicious shake. "Who did you plan to kill this time?"

"I never killed anyone," Carstairs gasped after Graham loosened his grip enough to allow him to answer.

"You had to have been the one who interfered with Frank Ennis's equipment," Ben said. "How much did Winthrop pay you to disrupt the excavation?"

"Are you mad? I didn't even know Professor Winthrop was in the area until last week—the same day I saw you in Belfast."

"Then you did it on your own?"

"No! No, that's not what I meant."

"Was the morphine in the Moxie?" Diana asked.

The startled look in Carstairs's eyes could have been because the suggestion was so unexpected . . . or because he was surprised Diana had figured it out.

"Look, you've got it all wrong." Suddenly Carstairs sounded much more lucid. "You didn't find morphine in my possessions, did you?"

Ben conceded the point. They had no proof he'd doctored the Moxie and poisoned himself and his colleagues, or that he'd tampered with the air hose. Neither did they have any proof that he had not. "How much did Winthrop pay you?"

"I wasn't working for him!"

"Why did you steal Graham's boat? Why did you leave?"

"I was afraid of just what's happened—that you'd suspect me. I went to Winthrop because he was the only one who could help me find another job. And the old buzzard came through. I leave for Mexico in a week to excavate some newly-discovered pre-Columbian ruins on the Yucatan Peninsula."

For a moment Ben almost believed him, but Graham wasn't buying his story. He seized Carstairs by the hair and jerked his head back. "The truth, this time."

"That is the truth!" Carstairs wasn't faking his fear. Sweat beaded his forehead. He rolled his eyes in Ben's direction in mute appeal.

"Let's say we believe you." Ben moved close enough to prevent Graham from taking any drastic action. "That doesn't explain your presence here, now, with Winthrop."

"I told you. I felt obliged to do him that one favor. I brought him over and I promised to wait and take him back, but he didn't return. I was looking for him when I ran into you."

"You've no idea where he is now?"

"None. Look, I know I shouldn't have brought him. And I should have come straight here to warn you once I had. I wasn't thinking. I . . . I'm sorry." There were tears in his eyes.

Disgusted, Graham released him. Carstairs sagged, bound though he was. In a barely audible voice he whispered, "Winthrop would have come here to the house, looking for the map. Are you sure Serena's only sleeping?"

Diana rapped lightly on the bedroom door, but there was no answer. Louder knocking also went unheeded, so she turned the knob. Serena was not there. She was nowhere in the house.

The sun had been down for two hours by the time they had new search parties organized. With only the full moon and the light of lanterns to guide them, no one was optimistic about finding Serena before morning.

Graham was frantic. "Why would he do this? If he was after Min Somener's map, why kidnap Serena?"

"Maybe she caught him searching for it," Diana suggested, "and he took her with him as a hostage."

"Why?" Ben asked. "Far easier to knock her out, or even kill her."

"We're missing something." Diana glanced at Carstairs, still trussed up like a Christmas goose. He'd stopped cooperating and had settled into a sullen silence after Graham had punched him in the face in an effort to convince him to provide more information.

The searchers went out in short forays, reporting back to the house in between. George Amity stayed behind, armed with a rifle, to guard Diana and Mrs. Monroe and the prisoner. Diana would have liked to have a gun herself, but there were not enough to go around. She had to be satisfied with tucking a sharp little penknife into her pocket. It would be useless against a more serious weapon, but she nonetheless found its presence on her person a comfort.

It was after one in the morning when Landrigan spotted the body caught on the pilings of the steamboat wharf. Diana wanted to go with the men, but Ben forbade it. "Stay here where it's safe," he ordered. "Keep all the doors and windows locked. If Winthrop has murdered Serena, he won't hesitate to kill again."

Resigned, Diana obeyed. Leaving Amity on guard in the hall-way, she returned to the library.

"You could let me go now," Carstairs said. "It ought to be pretty clear I had nothing to do with this."

"I think we'll just hold on to you for a bit longer. There's something about this whole affair that doesn't make sense."

In fact, there was quite a lot that seemed inexplicable. And there was one thing in particular that bothered her about Paul Carstairs. He kept glancing at the mantel clock. His eyes had darted in that direction at least a half dozen times in the short while she'd been in the room.

Diana prowled. She stopped at the shelf where Serena kept her books and was staring at it when she remembered something. The day she had left Ben and Graham to settle their differences with their fists, she'd found Serena reading in the library. She hadn't put that book away on a shelf. She'd tucked it into one of the drawers in Graham's desk.

A quick search revealed a leather-bound diary and a small metal box. Diana's hands shook slightly as she pulled both out of the drawer. The bookmark in the diary took her to the page on which Min described finding the coin. There was no sketch of the location, but it was clearly near where Serena had been digging. Next she pried open the box. The silver groat nestled safely in a bed of soft blue velvet. So much for the theory that Serena had surprised Winthrop in the act of stealing her inheritance from Min Somener.

Diana sent a suspicious glare in Carstairs's direction. "Is it Serena's body they've found or the professor's?"

"I imagine it's Winthrop's. The tide would have washed him up about there." Carstairs sounded so matter-of-fact that it took a moment for his words to sink in. When they did, shock held Diana both motionless and speechless . . . until he began to laugh.

"Why did you kill him?" Although her question was barely audible, Carstairs heard her.

"He was slowing me down. Damned old fool. As if Min Somener had anything worth stealing! I threw him off a cliff."

"Then Winthrop wasn't behind this. It was you all along." A stray connection came together. "You sent the telegram, the one telling me not to meddle."

"That was a wasted effort," Carstairs said in disgust.

"When you were in Belfast that day, did you meet with Winthrop?"

He sighed, as if in resignation. "You may as well know the whole story. I met him several times, starting weeks ago, before we came to Keep Island. He thought he was using me to get to the treasure. He was a fool! I was the one using him."

"I think he suspected that. Why else would he have hired Justus Palmer?"

"I'm beholden to you for that information, Mrs. Spaulding. I'd never have known about the detective if you hadn't told us he was on the case. The same day I sent that telegram to you, hoping to discourage you and Dr. Northcote from meddling further, I did pay a visit to Winthrop. I told him to call off Mr. Palmer." He gave a rueful chuckle. "If I'd known Winthrop was planning to meet with you the very next day, I'd have put a stop to that, too. Unfortunately, he didn't think the interview worth mentioning. He hadn't made the connection, you see. He knew Benjamin Northcote was Somener's oldest friend, and I told him Northcote had been on the island, but he didn't realize that D. Spaulding was Dr. Northcote's fiancée."

"Where's Serena?" Diana asked. Other explanations could

wait. The more Carstairs confessed to, the more certain Diana became that Serena was in danger.

"I'll tell you. Soon. Ask me another question first. I'm sure you must have dozens of them."

Diana knew he was toying with her, but she couldn't think of any way to force him to give her the one answer she really wanted. For the moment, she played along. "Whose idea was it for Winthrop to get Mrs. Monroe to intercept letters?"

"Mine. I wanted the island cut off. Somener thwarted my first plan by sailing to Belfast and sending a telegram to Dr. Northcote. We'd have recovered on our own. I didn't use that much morphine."

"Was it in the Moxie?"

"Why, yes, the last and largest dose. How clever of you to figure that out."

"But I'm not the first to come to that conclusion, am I? Ennis must have guessed. That's why he had to die."

"My, you *are* putting the pieces together." Carstairs grinned at her with what looked like approval. She found his attitude odious. He was basking in a sense of his own cleverness, the villain! "Frank was suspicious. I couldn't risk having him interfere with my plans, so I got rid of him. Pity. I liked Frank."

"What plans?" Obviously more than stopping the excavation, and nothing, she'd warrant, to do with Min Somener and some imagined treasure. "Why poison yourself and the others? You could all have died."

"Exactly. And for that reason I would not be suspected when someone *did* die later." Carstairs glanced at the clock again, and Diana felt a pulse of fear. He was stalling for a reason. That couldn't be good. She had the uneasy feeling Carstairs wasn't talking about Frank Ennis when he spoke of someone dying "later."

"Where's Serena?"

"Safe. For the moment."

"What do you want?"

"Untie me and I'll tell you."

"Not a chance."

"Time's running out for Serena."

"What do you have against her?"

"Not a thing. Graham Somener is the one I want to see suffer. The loss of his beloved new bride is a very just punishment for what he took from me."

Diana stared at him. Finally, her sluggish brain produced the tidbit of information she needed to put the rest of the pieces of the puzzle together. "You had a twin sister who died," she said slowly. "Her name was Edith Carstairs Alleyn. She was in the building when it collapsed. The building constructed by the firm of Somener and Law. And since she was a married woman, your name wouldn't have been listed as next of kin."

She could tell by the expression on Carstairs's face that she'd got it right.

"There's more. You were at Casa Grande early this year. That's in Arizona, I believe. Did you go there to excavate, or to kill Vernon Law?"

"If my hands were free I would applaud you, Mrs. Spaulding. I did kill Vernon Law, and soon, very soon, my revenge will be complete."

She followed his gaze to the clock.

"How can you justify hurting Serena? She has been your friend for years." Just like Frank Ennis.

A sly expression came over Carstairs's face. "I'll strike a bargain with you, Mrs. Spaulding. If you untie me, I'll tell you where Serena is. You might still be able to reach her in time. If you hurry."

It was just past two o'clock in the morning. What—?

And then she had it. High tide that afternoon had occurred shortly after two. It would be coming in again now, covering the entrance to Ben's "pirate cave," drowning anyone who might be inside.

Diana felt her face blanch. The cave had been searched early in the hunt for Winthrop and Carstairs, but Carstairs knew this island well. He'd have been able to dispose of Winthrop, then creep into the house to steal away with Serena when she went upstairs to rest, all without being seen. He'd taken her to the cave after the searchers had gone elsewhere. He'd probably just left her there and been heading back to the sailboat when Ben had caught him.

"You've guessed, haven't you?" Carstairs's voice was low and taunting. Evil. "It won't do you any good. You can't possibly fetch the men back from the wharf in time to rescue her."

"Then I guess it is up to me."

"You'll never succeed on your own. Untie me and I'll help you." He glanced at the clock again. "High water is at 2:43 A.M."

If she released him, he'd be more likely to knock her on the head and take off than he would be to help her rescue Serena. Diana left him without a backward glance, stopping only long enough to warn Amity to keep an eye on the prisoner and to collect a lantern from the kitchen. With its light and that of the full moon to guide her, she raced through the gardens and across the meadow to the promontory.

Descending the narrow trail, she was in an agony of suspense, convinced that at any moment she would lose her footing and fall to her death. It was no solace being unable to see the jagged rocks below. Her imagination conjured them up as great stone spikes waiting to impale her.

Every turn in the twisting path was a new challenge. It did not help that she was perspiring heavily in the damp night air. Her bare hands—she'd been in too great a hurry to don gloves—kept slipping off what few handholds she found.

Eons later, she arrived safely at the bottom.

She tried to run across the rock and pebble strewn beach, but the way was too treacherous. Stumbling and sliding, praying all the while that she could locate that other path, the one leading to the cave, she lurched onward until she reached the place where she thought the trail began.

At first she feared she would not be able to find her way without Ben's help. Crashing waves drowned out her little sounds of distress as she flashed the lantern this way and that, seeking any sign of a route to the cave. The spot had been shielded by a boulder. She remembered that much. But there were so many rocks, and they all seemed huge.

And then she saw it—a faint ribbon picked out by moonlight. Unable to guess how much time she had left, Diana flung herself onto the narrow path.

Only a few yards along, she splashed through a pool of salt water. The puddle was deep enough to soak through her boots and dampen the hem of her skirt. She stepped into another and another as she raced along, for although the path wound upwards, it also extended farther out towards the bay. The higher she went, the shallower the encroaching water became, but that would not be the case for long. The tide was rising. She would not be able to retreat in this direction. She'd have to continue upwards towards the ridgeline above.

Diana was panting by the time she reached the entrance to the cave. Water lapped at the face of the cliff only a few inches below her feet. She almost dropped the lantern in her rush to get inside. She was trembling uncontrollably. How fast did the tide come in? How long would it take to flood the interior of the cave?

"Serena?" Her voice came out as a hoarse croak. She called again more loudly.

No one answered. Had she been wrong? Straightening, since the interior of the sea cave was both higher and wider than its mouth, Diana held her lantern aloft. The fissure extended deep into the cliff and disappeared around a curve.

Moving as rapidly as she could, Diana followed one bend, then another, grateful there were no side passages to confuse matters. And then she saw it—the faint glow of lamplight.

The illumination silhouetted a fall of rock, revealing a narrow secondary passage beyond. Diana wondered if that section of the cave had been accessible when Ben was a boy, but suspected it had not. Even to her inexperienced eyes, there seemed to be signs of recent excavation.

Certain that this was where she would find Serena, Diana hurried towards the opening. She had to turn sideways to slip through and was glad she was wearing a divided shirt *sans* bustle. It was still a tight squeeze. She stumbled as she popped out on the other side, almost knocking over the lantern that had been left burning on the cave floor.

A series of muffled grunts greeted her arrival. Diana gaped in astonishment. The interior of the cavern had widened out again. It extended upward to nearly double her height. At the far end a huge net had been attached to the rock formation that jutted out from the roof of the cave. Inside this suspended prison, bound and gagged but very obviously alive, lay Serena Dunbar.

With a cry of mingled relief and distress, Diana put her lantern down next to the one Carstairs had left behind and pulled the penknife from her pocket. So this was what he had purchased from Pyram Hatch, netmaker! She thanked God when she saw that it was made of fine silk rather than heavy rope. Small as it was, her knife was sharp enough to slice through it.

Once she'd sufficiently enlarged an opening, Diana reached inside and cut the bonds that bound Serena's wrists. Carstairs had left her ankles free.

"We must hurry," she said as Serena pulled the gag from her mouth. "The tide is coming in."

To add to the urgency, one of the lanterns began to flicker, a sure indication that it was about to run out of fuel. But Serena— regaining her feet—did not follow Diana.

"There's something here." Seizing the lantern that still shone steady and bright, she crossed the cavern with long, determined strides. To Diana's horror, she was moving away from the entrance, stopping only when she reached a narrow ledge at shoulder level.

"Serena, there is no time for this!"

"Only a moment. I must get a closer look." Placing the lantern on the ledge, she began to dig with her bare hands at the section of the cave wall just above it. It was an awkward position from which to work. She had to reach above her head to get at the spot. "There's been an earthquake, I think. It opened up passages that were sealed off for decades, perhaps even centuries. Something manmade is here. An inscription, I think. I can't quite—"

"We haven't time for this, Serena!"

"I've almost uncovered it." Serena's excitement made her voice shrill, and she was bouncing as much as balancing on her toes. "It's a figure of some sort. My God, Diana! It may have been left by my settlers!"

"If it has been here that long, it can wait another day. We can't. Come on!"

Diana seized Serena's arm, hauling her bodily away from the ledge. She didn't bother collecting Serena's lantern. She had the other in her free hand. Her sense of imminent danger, and the prospect of certain death if they didn't get a move on, gave her the strength to drag the other woman towards the mouth of the cave.

"Carstairs said high tide is at 2:43 A.M. It's almost that now."

Finally perceiving the danger, Serena stopped struggling and began to cooperate.

As they turned the last corner, the mouth of the cave came in sight.

Diana stared at it in horror. It was lower than the point where they stood. The slope was so gradual that she hadn't realized on the way in that she'd been moving steadily upward.

"Oh, my God," Serena whispered.

Water filled the entrance halfway to the top. A veritable lake separated the high ground on which they stood from the only exit. There was no way to escape, even if they reached the mouth of the cave. On the other side of that opening, the path no longer existed.

"We're completely cut off," Diana whispered.

Serena's voice was equally hushed and fearful. "If we try to get out that way, we'll end up in Penobscot Bay."

"Can you swim?"

"It wouldn't matter if I could. Even an expert swimmer wouldn't survive. Anyone foolish enough to enter the water from here would be dashed against the cliffs by incoming waves."

"I have no desire to be battered to death," Diana said, "but neither do I relish the thought of drowning."

Serena looked back the way they'd come, her expression thoughtful. "The cavern I was imprisoned in is higher ground."

"You don't think it will flood?" Diana scarcely dared hope that they still had a chance of survival.

"I think Carstairs believed it would." Serena's smile was sour. "What I believe is that we will probably be quite cold and possibly very wet before the night is over. But I do not think we will drown."

With the ominous sound of crashing waves at their backs and the incoming tide lapping at their heels, they retreated. As they moved ever upward, Diana strove for optimism. She was not going to die in this cave. She had too much to live for.

"See there?" Serena pointed to the faint marks that indicated the water line.

Diana's stomach lurched when she saw how high they were.

"I'd have drowned in that net," Serena said, "but now we have a good chance of surviving. If we can climb up onto that little ledge, we will be above the level of the tide."

Diana eyed the perch. The lantern Serena had left there revealed a narrow strip barely wide enough for them to stand side by side, assuming they could hoist themselves up there in the first place. The ledge was even with Serena's shoulders and at eye level for Diana.

"We'll manage," Serena said cheerfully. "I'll boost you up, then cut off a section of the netting and hand it to you. See there, where that rock sticks out? Anchor the silk around that and toss the end down to me. I can use it to climb up beside you."

Grimly determined to live, Diana followed her orders. It was a scramble. She acquired numerous scrapes, bruises, broken fingernails, and tears in her clothing, but in the end they were both safely ensconced on the ledge before the incoming tide had climbed even halfway up the wall below. The net gave Diana something to hang onto, for which she was profoundly grateful. Her knees were so wobbly, she worried they might not keep her upright.

"Excellent!" Exhilarated by the success of her plan, Serena grinned happily.

Diana couldn't help but smile in return. They *were* going to survive. In just a few hours, the water would recede. They'd be cold and wet, but still alive.

A wave lapped at the wall inches below her toes and she shuddered. It was too close for comfort. "How long before the tide ebbs?"

"Long enough," Serena informed her in a cheerful voice, "to finish uncovering what is on this wall."

~ ❧ ~

The Hammond Street Congregational Church was a red brick edifice with a single square tower that contained both a clock and a bell. Its steeple was painted white, its spire light gray. On Saturday, June 30, 1888, with family and friends filling the two straight blocks of pews cushioned with crimson plush, Diana Torrence Spaulding married Benjamin Northcote.

The sun shone through tall windows, making the rosewood pulpit gleam. It glinted off the gold ring studded with Maine tourmalines that Ben placed on Diana's finger, sliding it easily into place in spite of her glove because she'd taken the precaution of splitting the seam on her ring finger.

She was determined that everything about this day should run smoothly.

When they turned to walk down the aisle as husband and wife, Diana's happiness knew no bounds. To be married to Ben was wonderful, a joy increased by sharing it with the assembled well-wishers. So many of them had traveled great distances to be with them on this special day. All her mother's family had come. Elmira, after a stern lecture from her daughter—and a few threats—had been persuaded to be civil to them. Elmira and Ed Leeves sat with Elmira's two brothers and with Isaac and Janette Torrence. Horatio Foxe was beside Maggie Northcote, resplendent in one of her more outrageous gowns. Justus Palmer had sent word that he was unable to attend the wedding but would arrive before the end of the reception. Maggie, or course, insisted that this was because he was a vampire and couldn't come out until after sunset.

Diana's theatrical friends were in the congregation, too, along with her former landlady. So were Serena and Graham. Serena's smile was almost as wide as Diana's. In fact, Diana didn't think the other woman had stopped grinning since they'd emerged from the cave.

What they'd uncovered on the rock face had turned out to be a primitive version of a memorial brass. Some sort of punch, Serena claimed, had been used to create it, and by drawing chalk lines between the indentations, one could clearly see the figure of a woman dressed in medieval garb.

Beneath the figure was an inscription in Latin. Translated it read: "Cursed be he who disturbs my bones."

The piece Diana had written for the *Independent Intelligencer*, her last as an employee of that newspaper, had carried the headline LETHAL LEGEND OF KEEP ISLAND EXPOSED. In fact the inscription was not all that unusual for the times. William Shakespeare had put something similar on his tomb. It was pure speculation that something had happened after the lady's death to make it seem that the curse had power. The details had been lost in the mists of time, but Diana was convinced that Serena and Ben had been right. The woman had died of some European illness unknown in America, and it had spread among the native peoples, creating the legend that Keep Island was cursed.

Whatever had happened, it was a long time ago. The island had not brought ill luck to Serena or to Diana. The only one who was not happy on her wedding day was Paul Carstairs. He was in jail awaiting trial for the murders of Vernon Law, Frank Ennis, and Lucien Winthrop.

When Diana and Ben left the church, they were transported in a hired brougham to the Northcote mansion for the reception. The next hours passed with incredible swiftness. Diana renewed old acquaintances and met new ones, and through it all gave thanks that there were no explosions between members of her family. For once, everyone genuinely seemed to get along. She doubted the truce would last, but she was grateful for the respite.

"Where are you going on your wedding journey?" Horatio Foxe asked, red-faced and jovial after a liberal sampling of a bowl of punch to which "medicinal" brandy had been added.

"To England first," Diana told him, "and then on to the Continent. Ben has research to do and so do I."

"You're really leaving me?"

"There is no shortage of journalists, and I have made my decision. I am going to write biographies of women, beginning with a distant family connection." She reached out to Ben as he came up beside her, squeezing his hand. "Wish me luck, Horatio. I am going in search of an ancestor named Rosamond and the Elizabethan gentlewoman who raised her."

A NOTE FROM THE AUTHOR

ဆာလ

Rosamond and the Elizabethan gentlewoman who raised her are, of course, Rosamond and Susanna Appleton from my sixteenth-century Face Down Mystery Series. This family connection, introduced in *Deadlier than the Pen*, seemed logical to me. My two sleuths have a great deal in common for all that they lived in very different centuries.

Many people were generous in helping me research this book. In particular I'd like to acknowledge Dana Cameron, archaeologist and mystery writer, Michele L. Brann of Reference Services at the Maine State Library, Linda Graf at the Islesboro Public Library, and Rowland (Bunny) Logan of the Islesboro Historical Society.

There is no real Keep Island, but all the other towns, cities, and islands are real. Similarly, the names of town, city, and county officials and local business people are taken from history wherever possible. If photographs or portraits were available, I've attempted to describe these individuals accurately. For those whose descriptions have not survived, I used a gentle application of poetic license. Any errors in presenting people or places on Islesborough (now spelled Islesboro), or in Bangor, Belfast, Bucksport, or Ellsworth, are mine.

The story of Henry Sinclair's discovery of America is speculative history. It *could* have happened. The books and authors mentioned in the text are real, as are their arguments about whether or not the expedition really took place. The theory that Sinclair later sent colonists to the New World and that they ended up shipwrecked on Keep Island is my own invention.

The phases of the moon and times of high tide are as accurate as I could make them, thanks to the 1888 *Farmer's Almanac*. I have also tried to adhere to extant steamboat and railroad timetables, but in order to avoid stranding my characters halfway to their destination for hours, even days, I made up the *Miss Min*.

More information about the Diana Spaulding Mysteries, including a bibliography of all my sources, can be found at www.kathylynnemerson.com.